THE
LAST
PRIESTESS

ELIZABETH BAXTER

VINCI
BOOKS

Vinci Books

vinci-books.com

Published by Vinci Books Ltd in 2026

1

A CIP catalogue record for this book is available from the British Library.
Paperback ISBN: 9781036708467

The EU GPSR authorised representative is Logos Europe, 9 rue Nicolas Poussion, 17000 La Rochelle, France
contact@logoseurope.eu

Printed and bound in Great Britain by Clays Ltd, Elcograf S.p.A.

By Elizabeth Baxter

The Songmaker

The Last Priestess
The King's Mage
The Traitor's Song

Chapter One

Maegwin de Romily woke with a headache on the morning of her execution.

As she roused from frightening dreams, she became aware of smells first: damp stone, rotting straw, an undercurrent of urine. Next came sounds: the slow drip of water, the skitter of rats, the hushed voices of the other prisoners. Then finally, sight. Dawn sunlight fell through the barred window so brightly it brought tears to her eyes and made her head pound like a drum, beating out the rhythm of her heart.

She levered herself into a sitting position and clasped her head as pain rampaged through her brain. Last night, after she had smashed her knee into his groin, the guard had punched her so hard she was surprised to find all her teeth still in place. But at least he'd left her alone after that. A headache and swollen jaw were a small price to avoid rape.

She leaned forward, pressing her forehead against the cold, damp stone of the cell floor, hoping for some relief.

"Sho-La, my mistress," she whispered. "Give me the strength to meet my death with honor. I am lost in the dark. Guide me." The words echoed off the walls and faded into silence. There was no answer.

Maegwin glanced at the window. Outside, in the town of Mallyn, life went on as normal. The townspeople would be getting dressed, emptying chamber pots, cooking breakfast and doing the simple things people did every morning. In a few hours Maegwin would be led to the gallows and hanged and nobody in Mallyn would care.

Maegwin shook her head, pushing the somber thoughts away. Instead, she brought to mind the morning prayers she'd been taught in the temple of Sho-La.

Blessed Mother, guide me.
Blessed Mother, heal me.
Blessed Mother, teach me.
Blessed Mother, I am yours.

"Pssst! Maegwin? You awake?"

She crawled to the door and slumped against the bars. "Good morning, Morran."

A bearded face appeared at the cell bars opposite. Deep lines framed eyes filled with worry. "Ah, lassie, you had me frightened last night. It would have been easier to let him have what he wanted. I thought he was going to kill you."

Maegwin smiled wryly. "Would it have mattered, Morran?"

The old man's face became stern. "Now, don't go talking like that. We aren't beaten yet! Something will turn up, you'll see. The Songmaker will save us."

Maegwin sighed. She was tired of hearing him prattle

on about this Songmaker of his. "How many times, old man? I'm not one of you."

"Well mayhap you should be. Where has loyalty to the king got you, eh? He's going to hang you whether you be a rebel or no."

Maegwin didn't reply. He wouldn't listen. For Morran there were two choices: you were either loyal to the king or loyal to the rebels. But Maegwin had never sworn loyalty to either and yet she'd been dragged into the conflict anyway.

Maegwin closed her eyes, remembering the day that had changed her life forever. Had it really only been a week ago? How could her life change so much in so short a time? She recalled the soft pressure as her sword blade slid between Lord Meryk Hounsey's ribs and punctured his fiercely beating heart. She tasted the spray of hot blood across her face and smelled the sweat that soaked his expensive clothes.

And heard the screaming of her sisters.

"Hoi, Morran!" someone shouted, jolting her from her thoughts. "Are you rambling on about your bloody Songmaker again? I was an idiot to listen to your lies! Damn you to the Darkness, old man. Your sweet words have brought me nothing but a noose!"

"Ah, you're a chicken-hearted bastard, Randle!" shouted Morran. "If not for you they wouldn't have caught the rest of us. You deserve to hang!"

"Really? And what would you have done if they had captured your wife and son? Kept your mouth shut and sacrificed them for your precious Songmaker I suppose?"

"Better that than betray the cause. You lost your faith, Randle. The Songmaker will save us, you'll see."

Randle laughed shrilly. "Fool! I doubt the Songmaker even knows your name! He certainly won't give two shits when you're dancing on the end of a rope!"

Morran retorted but Maegwin shut their voices out, shuffled over to the window, and lifted her face up to the sunlight. She had no desire to spend her last hours listening to them argue. Through the bars, she could see a blue sky dotted with tiny wisps of clouds. A beautiful summer's day.

A good day to die.

———

Rovann rode into the clearing and yanked the reins, pulling his horse to a halt in a spray of mud. The acrid odor of charred wood lingered on the air, strong enough to make his horse snort and stamp, unwilling to go closer.

Rovann studied the scene. A once-magnificent building lay in ruins in the center of the clearing. The walls and roof had collapsed, leaving a heap of rubble. Blackened beams stuck out from the pile like the fingers of a corpse.

The surrounding forest lay quiet and peaceful, giving no clues to what happened here. In an oak nearby a squirrel chirped angrily at Rovann's intrusion. A blackbird alighted on a holly branch, stared at Rovann with one beady eye, and then took off into the trees.

The saddle creaked as Rovann swung his leg over the horse's back and jumped to the ground. Drawing his short-sword, he padded silently toward the ruins. Crouching at the base of a wall, he placed his palm on the blackened stone and closed his eyes. Nothing. No resonance remained within the granite. The fire must be at least a week old.

Rovann straightened and re-sheathed his short-sword. There were no clues here. Lord Cedric Hounsey, on whose land the temple lay, claimed the blaze had been an accident. But Rovann suspected otherwise. Yet, without survivors to dispute the lord's story, there was little he could do about it.

Rovann kicked the ground in frustration, sending up a shower of ash that blew back at him, covering him in a fine gray cloak.

His horse, Glynn, snorted and gazed at his master with ears pricked forward. Rovann trotted back to his mount and noticed a piece of parchment pinned to the trunk of a large sycamore. He strode over and ripped it down. He scanned the crude black letters, his breath quickening. There was still a chance. But he had to get to Mallyn. And fast.

Swinging into the saddle, he kicked Glynn into motion, leaving behind the woods and coming down onto the paved Kingsroad. Glynn's hooves made a loud 'clip-clop' on the hard stones. The sun was just poking above the tree-line. Lazy streamers of mist rose from the fields. Farm workers dotted the road, pulling carts or carrying tools. They stared at Rovann with wide, fearful eyes, wary of strangers.

Rovann chewed his lip. If he didn't reach Mallyn by midday... Shaking his head, he choked the thought. He would not fail. Could not. He had a duty to his king, to his people. Rovann smiled crookedly. *Duty.* That word again. Istra always hated how he was torn in two.

Duty? she would say. *Must it come before everything? Before us?*

Ahead, the Kingsroad forked. Rovann cursed, pulled Glynn to a stop and threw his hands up in frustration. The roads were identical with no way-markers to aid the travel-weary stranger.

"What do you think, Glynn?" he asked his horse.

The chestnut gelding flicked his ears idly.

Rovann closed his eyes and slowed his breathing to a deep, steady rhythm. He felt the life around him: the thump of Glynn's heart, the rustle of rodents in the undergrowth, the movement of worms in the soil. Thousands of tiny life forces shimmered, connected by the all-encompassing tapestry of the Eorthe. Rovann pushed his senses further out and found it: a mass of iridescent life energy so strong it could only indicate a town full of people. It lay to the south-west, many miles distant.

He opened his eyes and sank forward, fatigue flooding his limbs. Pressing his head into Glynn's mane, he breathed in the musty smell of the horse and impressed the image of their destination on the beast's mind. Clinging on, he pressed Glynn into a gallop down the south-western road.

Blessed Mother, I hear you.
Blessed Mother, I see you.
Blessed Mother, I feel you.
Blessed Mother, I come to you.

The rattle of the lock jolted Maegwin from her prayers. The door creaked open and two guards entered. They were both scarred, hard men. Without a word, they yanked her to her feet. She didn't resist. They fixed a pair of iron mana-cles round her wrists and marched her out.

The other prisoners pressed up against the bars of their cells as she was led past. They stared with dull, emotionless eyes, knowing they would soon share her fate. Morran's eyes glittered with tears and his old face was full of sorrow.

Maegwin smiled at him. "I'll save you a seat in the after-life, old man."

Morran reached through the bars and squeezed her arm. "Be brave, lassie. Be brave."

The guards marched her from the cells, through the guardhouse, and to a small office. Inside, a bald man sat behind a desk, staring at her with pitiless eyes. Maegwin had met this man just once before, when she had first been brought to face the king's justice. Amin Shador, the governor of the Mallyn jail. She knew little of him, except what the other prisoners had said. The disgraced younger son of a lord, he'd been sent here as punishment for bedding his brother's wife. Maegwin knew she would get no mercy from him.

Sho-La, my light, my guide, my mistress, she thought. *I come to your halls.*

"Your name?" Shador demanded.

"You know my name."

"Indulge me."

Maegwin tipped her chin up. "Maegwin de Romily, priestess of Sho-La."

Shador inclined his head gravely. "Maegwin de Romily, you have been sentenced to hang for the murders of Lord Meryk Hounsey and three of his guardsmen. You will now go to your death. Do you understand?"

She nodded.

"Do you wish to see a priest?"

"No. Get on with it."

"As you wish."

Amin Shador stood and donned a long black cape. He led her from the room, the guards following close behind.

As she stepped outside, the midday sun sliced into Maegwin's eyes like broken glass. Everything was picked out in stark brilliance: the circular courtyard, the thick gates, the crowd staring at her, the wooden platform on the far side. A gallows grew out of this platform like a bald, ugly tree. A noose hung from it, slowly turning in the breeze.

Shador snapped at the guards, "Take her quickly to the scaffold. Let's get this done."

Shador strode purposefully forward and the guardsmen

propelled Maegwin after him. A path opened for them but the crowd pressed close on both sides. The threat of anger filled the air. Maegwin's eyes moved over the crowd, searching for a spark of compassion. She found none. The people of Mallyn glared at her with eyes full of violence. They saw only a murderer and traitor.

"Faithless whore!" a man hissed.

"The Fates will send you straight to the Darkness!" an old woman shouted.

The executioner, a massive man wearing sweat-stained leather and a crude wooden mask over the top half of his face, waited patiently beside the gallows with his arms folded. "And how is milady this morning? Ready to give us all a good show?"

She smiled at him. "I forgive you for taking my life. May Sho-La grant you mercy."

The grin on the man's face faltered. He grabbed Maegwin's elbow and forced her up onto a three-legged stool. The scaffold creaked as the executioner pulled the noose over Maegwin's head. The rope felt coarse and prickly where it lay against the skin of her neck. Soon she would drop and the noose would tighten, crushing her windpipe, choking the life from her...

A wave of fear clenched her stomach. Her heart pounded.

Sho-La, my mistress, she thought desperately. *Please give me courage!*

Shador unrolled a parchment and read in a monotone voice, "By order of the Lord Sheriff of Mallynshire, according to the laws of King William of Amaury, I hereby announce that Maegwin de Romily..."

Maegwin stopped listening. A family of crows landed noisily on the wall and hopped about, looking for something to scavenge. In the crowd, a child turned in his mother's arms and regarded Maegwin solemnly. Why had a child been brought to watch her die? Surely he was too young to be taught such hatred?

Maegwin turned her gaze skyward. The heavens were a clear, perfect blue. Yes, it was a good day to die.

"...to be hanged from the neck until she be dead. Fates have mercy on her soul."

With a crunch of splintering wood, the executioner kicked the stool out from under her. Maegwin fell. The noose snapped tight, pain exploding through her. Maegwin choked, desperately trying to suck in a breath. Blood pounded in her ears. Her eyes bulged in their sockets and she squeezed them shut. Her body bucked and jerked. As her muscles convulsed she felt her legs kicking. As her breath left her, the movement became slower, slower, slower.

Then stilled.

With a stab of frustration, Rovann saw that the entrance to the jail was closed. He bellowed at people to move as Glynn pounded down the cobbled street. Standing in his stirrups, he raised his hand, opened himself to the Realm of Air, and threw a blast of wind at the gates. They burst open with a groan.

Rovann rode through and pulled Glynn to a skidding halt, foam flying from the lathered horse's mouth. A crowd of townsfolk filled the courtyard, all staring at him. Surprise, fear and a little anger radiated from the onlookers but he had no time to spare for them. He scanned the scene, taking in the details. On the far side of the square stood the gallows, the body of a woman dangling from the noose.

Cursing, he drew his belt knife and flung it. The blade sliced through the rope and the woman fell to the floor with a dull thud.

Rovann nudged Glynn into the crowd, people scurrying out of their way in alarm. Guards moved through the throng toward him and on the platform a man shouted, "Stop him! Arrest that man!"

Rovann ignored them. As Glynn reached the platform, Rovann kicked his feet from the stirrups, vaulted onto the saddle and jumped from the horse's back to the platform. A masked man lumbered toward him, the executioner perhaps, but Rovann sent him staggering backward with a flick of his wrist.

Rovann knelt by the woman's side and rolled her onto her back. She had green eyes that stared sightlessly upward and a swollen tongue protruding from her mouth. Rovann sliced the noose from her neck and wiped sweaty strands of red-gold hair away to allow him to feel her pulse.

Frowning, he looked around until he spotted a small, bald man watching him with anger on his face. "Are you the governor? Fetch me a stretcher, man. This woman is still alive."

Maegwin was falling through a void. Wind whistled past her ears. Pressure pushed at her from all sides. Her stomach felt as though it was rising into her chest. She tried to scream but no sound escaped her crushed throat. Then suddenly everything went still and she floated in silence and darkness.

Am I dead? she thought. *Is this it?*

Surely not. In death, Sho-La waited to carry her followers to the glory of the One Light. Didn't she?

"Blessed Mother!" Maegwin cried. "Sho-La! Mistress!"

In the nothingness, something moved by Maegwin's side. A voice spoke by her ear. "Will you give in so easily?"

Maegwin jumped. "Who's there?"

"Will you abandon your revenge?"

"What do you mean? Who are you?"

"Your savior. I can give you what you truly desire. Vengeance."

Maegwin saw a shadow looming beside her. Fear squeezed her heart.

"What is this place? Where am I?"

"You are neither dead nor alive, Maegwin of Sho-La. This is the in-between. What is your choice?"

"My choice?"

"Life or death. It is always a choice. Will you live and take your vengeance? Or will you die and leave your tormentors unpunished?"

Maegwin felt something harden in her heart. "I would choose life and vengeance."

Laughter echoed in the darkness. "Excellent."

A tremor of fear trickled through Maegwin. What choice had she just made? "Who are you?"

"I am your redemption. Remember me."

Then she was rushing upward toward a bright light. The pressure around her neck eased and she felt the grainy texture of wood against her cheek. She opened her eyes and found herself staring at the angry faces of the crowd. On the wall, the family of crows were squabbling over a scrap. One of them won the battle and took off with its prize, its wing-beats sounding heavy and ponderous in the still air. In the crowd, the child was still watching Maegwin. Seeing her looking at him, he broke into a broad smile and pointed with one chubby hand.

Maegwin reached out and felt rough planks beneath her fingers. She was lying on the scaffold. She was alive. Her heart was still beating. Her lungs drew in great breaths of sweet, sweet air. Her nostrils inhaled the scent of wood and dirt.

Hands grasped her beneath the armpits and pulled her up. She tried to stand, feet scrabbling against the platform, but her legs kept folding beneath her. The hands lifted her onto a stretcher.

The crowd erupted into a chorus of angry shouting. Someone — Shador? — said, "Open the gates. Disperse the crowd and make sure nobody hangs around outside. I've seen riots start this way."

Everything went dim and from the silence, Maegwin guessed she had been taken back inside. She was lifted onto something soft. Cool hands probed her neck. After a moment, they retreated.

"Will she live?"

"I think so."

There was the chink of a kettle and the sound of pouring water. A hand lifted her head from the pillow.

"Maegwin? I need you to drink. It will help you."

A cup was set against her lips and a warm liquid dribbled into her mouth. She swallowed reflexively. The fluid tasted bitter and it scraped her throat raw, as though she was drinking molten metal. She gasped, slumping back onto the pillow.

"Give it a moment. It will pass."

Maegwin lay gasping as pain flared and tears squeezed from the corners of her eyes. After a moment, the agony eased and her sight cleared. She was lying on a couch in Amin Shador's study. The governor himself sat on the corner of the desk talking to a man Maegwin didn't recognize. The newcomer wore a long blue cloak and knee-high boots. He had wavy blond hair held back from his face by a leather band.

As if sensing her gaze, the stranger turned and knelt by Maegwin's side. "My name is Rovann de Lacey. I'm the king's messenger. Can you sit?"

Maegwin slowly pushed herself into a sitting position. Waves of dizziness raced through her head, making her grab the edge of the couch for support.

"Why?" she croaked at the man.

"Don't speak too much," Rovann said. "Your throat will take a while to heal."

Maegwin touched her neck where the noose had been. The skin felt hot and angry. What was happening to her? She had died on the gallows. Hadn't she?

Rovann placed a hand under Maegwin's chin and gently lifted her face, forcing her to look at him. His eyes were the palest blue she'd ever seen but clouded with something. Sorrow, perhaps.

Rovann handed her a mug and Maegwin recognized the sharp scent of the drink he'd given her earlier. "Finish this. It will dull the pain."

Maegwin stared at him. *Why?* she wanted to ask. *Why didn't you just let me hang?*

She took the cup and gulped down the liquid, baring her teeth at the stinging taste. Rovann nodded in satisfaction.

The governor pushed himself from the desk. "What do you intend, my lord?" His voice held a mixture of suspicion and respect.

Rovann stood. "I intend to escort Maegwin de Romily to Tyrlindon."

Tyrlindon? Maegwin thought. *The capital?* She grabbed

Rovann's arm and gasped a few times before croaking, "Why?"

"You may be useful to the king."

"Useful how?"

Rovann glanced at Shador then back to Maegwin. "I think you have information that will expose a traitor. If that proves to be the case, the king may look favorably on your sentence."

Maegwin snorted. "A deal?"

Rovann shrugged. "You might see it that way. If you come to Tyrlindon there is a chance you will live. If you stay here you will die."

Maegwin smiled wryly. This king's messenger did not mince his words. "What information do you think I have?"

"I won't discuss that here. What do you say? Will you come to Tyrlindon?"

The governor stepped forward. "I must protest! You want to take a convicted murderer out of my custody yet will not explain your reasons. I will not allow it!"

Rovann turned to the governor. "Do you want to take it up with the king?"

Maegwin could almost see the thoughts churning behind Shador's eyes. Considering Mallyn's recent change of allegiance, the governor must tread warily around this king's man.

At last, the governor said, "No, my lord."

"Good." Rovann reached into a saddlebag and pulled out a scroll bearing the king's seal. "This will tell you all you need to know."

Shador took the scroll, broke the wax seal with a loud 'click' and read it. He nodded. "She's all yours, my lord."

Rovann turned to Maegwin. "Well?"

Who is this man? Maegwin wondered. *Who is he that he can ride in here and issue orders to the king's officials?*

Maegwin's thoughts turned to old Morran. The rebel had regaled her with stories of how the king and his mages ruled the land with an iron hand. Of how they mercilessly crushed dissent and destroyed any who opposed them. In the temple of Sho-La Maegwin had kept out of such things. But now a king's man wanted her help. And yet, what choice did she have? If she didn't do as he wished he would send her back to the scaffold.

She sighed. "When do we leave?"

Chapter Two

"I urge you to reconsider," Shador said. The governor's bald head gleamed in the afternoon sunshine. "I can give you six of my best men to escort you to Tyrlindon. She is more dangerous than she seems."

Rovann glanced to where Maegwin waited on the other side of the courtyard. She stood by the horse the governor had provided, gently stroking the beast's nose. She had tied a purple scarf around her neck to hide the red weal left by the noose. Rovann was not surprised she wanted to hide it. The welt marked her like a brand.

Criminal, it would whisper to any who saw it. *Traitor. Untrustworthy*.

"I appreciate the offer, governor," Rovann replied, pulling on his riding gloves. "But I won't deprive you of your men. I'm sure Maegwin will give me no trouble. "

"You'll trust her word?" Shador snorted. "When you know what she did to Meryk Hounsey and his men?"

Rovann began checking Glynn's stirrups. "Trust has nothing to do with it. It's about necessity. I must travel quickly and secretly, neither of which would be possible if your men accompanied us."

"And if she should turn on you?"

Rovann let the stirrup fall, met the governor's eyes. "Then I'll deal with her. She won't escape the king's justice, governor."

Shador nodded, his eyes suddenly respectful. "Good speed to you then. Let's hope Maegwin de Romily finds justice in Tyrlindon."

"Let's hope that," Rovann agreed but suspected they were talking of different things. He clasped the governor's hand and swung into Glynn's saddle. Maegwin did the same, holding the reins loosely in one hand.

With a last nod to the governor, Rovann nudged his horse into motion, leading Maegwin out onto the streets of Mallyn. It was mid-afternoon and the town was busy. Rovann guided Glynn through the hollering crowds, heading downhill toward the main gate. Maegwin steered her horse with a touch here, a word there, keeping pace with Rovann.

At last, they reached the town gates. Rovann ground his teeth as a slow-moving wagon blocked their way. As soon as they were free of the crowds of hawkers, pickpockets, whores and beggars that hung around outside the town walls, Rovann kicked Glynn into a canter and he and Maegwin moved down onto the Kingsroad.

They rode steadily northeast, each wrapped in their own thoughts. Maegwin remained silent and he was glad of it. He was in no mood for conversation. Impatience chewed on Rovann's nerves. They needed to reach Tyrlindon before Lord Cedric Hounsey discovered Maegwin's release but Rovann didn't fancy their chances. No doubt the old warlord had spies within Mallyn, and would soon learn what had transpired today. The grizzled warrior's response would be swift. And brutal.

As they rode, the Kingsroad became busy. People trudged along the winding road in silent, wary groups. Some pulled small handcarts with the accumulation of their lives tossed inside. Eventually, when the trickle of travelers had become so thick Rovann found himself having to pick his way carefully through the crowd, he reined in and hailed the nearest one.

"What news? Why do so many walk the Kingsroad? It's not market day in Mallyn tomorrow."

The man he addressed, middle-aged with a shock of white hair, put his arms around his two daughters and held them close. "It's the Songmaker! He's called a mage storm on Angard. He means to destroy the town! If you have any wit, you'll flee, and go no nearer that cursed place!"

Rovann looked at the sky. No clouds marred its blue surface. "I can't see any storm gathering."

The man shook his head, his bushy eyebrows pulling into a frown. "Not yet maybe, but it's coming, you mark my words. You'll see the closer you come to Angard. The Song-maker is taking his revenge! I said if Mallynshire declared for the king we would bring the Songmaker's wrath down on us! And where are the king's men? Where are the soldiers when we need them?" He clutched his daughters and hurried away.

Maegwin guided her horse closer to Rovann. "What does he mean? What's a mage storm?"

Rovann didn't reply. Clucking to Glynn, he nudged the horse into a walk.

"Wait!" Maegwin said, following close behind. "Answer my question! What did that man mean by 'mage storm'?"

Rovann frowned at her. "It's not your concern."

"Not my concern?" she cried, her eyes flashing dangerously. "That man said Angard is under attack. I have a right to know what I'm walking into. This is my life!"

"Your life," Rovann snapped, "belongs to the king. Or had you forgotten that?"

Before she could reply, Rovann kicked Glynn into a trot, pushing past Maegwin and hurrying down the road. After a moment, he heard her following.

Dusk was descending when Rovann spotted a timber-built inn up ahead. It sat at a crossroads where the Kingsroad split, one branch leading north toward Angard and Tyrlindon, the other east to Silverport and Mandrake. Rovann pulled Glynn to a halt and stared at the inn. Light spilled from the windows and the sound of a lute came from inside. He was tempted to take a room, if only to hear the gossip about what was happening up in Angard, but decided against it. There might be Hounsey men staying there.

Reluctantly, he took the northern road.

Night fell, filling the land with inky shadows. The stars appeared: the Scythe, the Princess, the Swan. Rovann watched the shadowy countryside pass by on either side. Mallynshire, a landscape of cultivated fields, irrigation ditches and homesteads, was a testament to King William's achievements. In his father's time, this land had been untamed wilderness, a fenland that resisted all attempts to settle it. But King William had built great dykes to drain the fens, and offered any family who wanted to live here a parcel of land, a plow, two cows and the promise that they would be beholden to no lord save the king.

A white owl alighted on a branch nearby. The bird watched Rovann with eyes the size of saucers. *Why do you walk my domain?* it seemed to say. *This is my realm.* Rovann met its unblinking gaze until it took off in silent flight.

The road began to climb steadily. At the top of the rise, the silhouette of a small wood blotted out the stars.

Maegwin spoke for the first time in hours. "Perhaps we should camp there for tonight. There will be more shelter than amongst the fields."

Rovann nodded his agreement and they dismounted and led their horses into a small clearing within the fringe of woodland. Whilst Maegwin saw to the horses, Rovann spread out the bedrolls and started a fire. They ate a meager supper of dried meat and travel bread. Neither spoke.

Maegwin stood. "I'm going to have a look around, if you have no objections?" She stared at him, her eyes full of defiance. *Try and stop me*, the look said.

"As you wish."

She nodded once and walked off into the night.

Rovann didn't bother watching her go. Perhaps she would try to run. Let her. She wouldn't get far. And besides, right now Rovann felt the overwhelming urge to be alone.

Maegwin walked twenty paces into the wood and halted behind the wide trunk of an oak. Laying her palms against the gnarled bark, she turned back to watch Rovann. His brooding face was painted orange by the flickering flames of the campfire. He held a piece of wood in one hand, whittling it with a knife as he stared into the fire.

Maegwin was surprised that he'd let her leave camp. She was a criminal and he her jailer. Did he expect her to run? Was this some sort of test?

Maegwin pressed her lips into a line. It didn't matter

what he thought. She was a priestess of Sho-La and her word was her bond.

The thick carpet of last year's leaves muffled the sound of her footsteps as she turned and padded into the woods. It was time for evening prayers and she wished to be alone. The smell of mold, wet vegetation and earth reached her nostrils. Creatures rustled in the undergrowth. Frogs croaked somewhere nearby. The shadows beneath the trees seemed to brush Maegwin's skin like soft, grasping fingers.

Maegwin.

She stopped, cocking her head at the faint voice.

Maegwin.

The call came again, a whisper on the breeze. She stumbled toward the sound, pushing through the trees. She realized suddenly that the frogs had stopped their croaking and no creatures rustled in the undergrowth. The wood was eerily silent.

She staggered up a short rise, slipped, scrambled up, shoved aside the branches of a willow tree, and found herself looking down at a still pool. Its surface was as smooth as glass. She glanced at the sky and a shiver tiptoed down Maegwin's back. How could she not have realized? It was the dark of the moon. A night of power. She knelt on the pool's mossy bank.

She closed her eyes. A presence tickled her senses, raising the tiny hairs along her arms. Something powerful was close by. She opened her eyes and saw a face in the depths of the pool, regarding her with cool appraisal.

"Sho-La," Maegwin breathed.

The goddess's face was ageless. She had alabaster skin and long hair the color of a raven's wing. Her eyes were black holes that opened into nothingness, voids that led down, down, into the in-between.

Maegwin gasped in sudden recognition. Her heart thudded with fear. She had seen this face before, at midday, as she dangled from a rope and fell into darkness.

Will you abandon your vengeance?

Maegwin hadn't recognized Her then. She did now. This was the Dark Goddess, the aspect of Sho-La that reveled in despair and terror.

"What has been done to you, my child?" the Dark Goddess whispered.

Maegwin opened her mouth to speak but fear stole her words. Worship of the Dark Goddess was outlawed in the order of Sho-La. The shadowy rites of her followers had no place in the worship of the Blessed Mother.

But Maegwin's faith in the Blessed Mother had only brought her pain.

"My sisters are dead, mistress," Maegwin croaked. "I've failed you."

"No," the goddess snapped. "You only fail when you abandon vengeance. I demand restitution. A life for a life."

Memories flashed before Maegwin's eyes: the grinning faces of Lord Meryk Hounsey's soldiers, the hiss and crackle of flames, the terrible stench of seared flesh and burning hair. But most of all, she heard her sisters screaming. Endlessly screaming.

Maegwin had taken four lives that day. But it was not enough. Could never be enough. *A life for a life*, she thought. *I will avenge you all.*

"Good," said the Dark Goddess. "You begin to understand. Serve me, and we will have vengeance."

It was the dark of the moon. On this night the veil between the Realms thinned, and the powers of the Outer Darkness came closer to the world. A night of power. A night of beginnings. And of endings. All her life, Maegwin had followed the teachings of Sho-La. Through Her light, Maegwin was able to forgive those who hurt her. But now she couldn't. She felt like a dry, empty husk.

This was the dark of the moon and the Dark Goddess ruled here. Those who entered her service left sentiment behind.

Maegwin bowed her head so low her forehead touched the surface of the water. Its cold seeped into her skin.

"I will serve you, my mistress."

The fire popped. Rovann glanced up at the sudden whoosh of sparks, then back to the piece of wood he held. His hands moved automatically, cutting and shaping, sending slivers flying off in all directions. He had no idea what the carving would become. He never did. The wood would find its own shape in the end.

A sudden gust of wind eddied through the clearing, scattering leaves and swirling his hair around his head. It seemed as if a door had opened and quickly closed. A soft hand pressed against his cheek, flooding him with warmth. Rovann put down the carving and looked up.

A tall figure stood by his side. She could have passed for human, except for the wings that spread from her shoulders. Symbols burned in the air around her, sigils of the gate she'd opened.

The angel brushed an iridescent hand along his jaw line. Rovann leaned into the touch and for a moment felt the peace of the Realm of Aethyr, the Realm closest to the One Light. Only for a moment. She withdrew her hand and the darkness of the wood crashed back in.

23

"Why do you torment yourself?" she asked in a voice like the ringing of bells.

Rovann glanced at the carving lying at his feet and realized it resembled a woman. "I have much to pay for."

The angel shook her head. "Do you claim control over the will of others? Not even the Lords of the One Light claim that. Istra chose her own path. You have so many burdens already. Would you add the weight of her death?"

Rovann looked into the angel's eyes and saw the compassion written there. He shook his head. "How can I do otherwise? I swore an oath to stand beside her my whole life. But I didn't. How can you say the guilt isn't mine?"

The angel shifted and a light breeze rustled Rovann's hair. The sigils pulsed with silver smoke, showing the strain of holding the gateway open. "You have a life to live. She is beyond you now."

A faint hope stirred in Rovann's chest. "Is she in the Realm of Aethyr? Have you seen her?"

The angel shook her head.

"Then I'm right, aren't I? She's been thrown into the Outer Darkness for what she did."

"You don't know that," the angel replied. "Perhaps Istra has already passed into the One Light."

Rovann's eyes strayed to his whittling knife. Its blade was sharp enough to open his veins. Would that allow him to see Istra again?

The angel placed a hand over his. "You must not have such thoughts. It is not your time. You must choose life. You have a duty to your Realm and your king."

Rovann glanced at her sharply. "You know of my quest?"

"Your quest is more important than you realize. Something is gathering within the Realm of Earth. Even the

Sluargh, trapped in Chaos, feel it. They have been probing the borders of the Realms, searching for a way through. The veil grows thin. If it tears, the powers of Chaos will rampage through the Realms of the living. The angels cannot act here within Earth, so it falls to you to discover this threat." The angel's form began to fade as the Realm of Aethyr pulled her back.

"How? What can I do?" Rovann asked, "I'm only one man."

As her form dissolved, her voice carried on the breeze. "Not anymore. Now you are two."

The sigils flared once, and she was gone.

The night seemed murkier than before. Despite the lingering summer heat, a chill settled into Rovann's bones. Thick shadows congealed under the trees. Was Chaos gathering there, just beyond the veil, ready to punch a hole into this reality? Rovann's eyes strayed to the half-finished carving. Did Istra's soul wait on the other side of the veil as well?

The bushes rustled and Maegwin strode into camp. Stepping carefully around the fire, she sat down cross-legged on her blankets and stared into the flames. Rovann picked up the carving and began whittling once more.

"Can't you sleep?" Maegwin's voice was so soft he barely heard her.

Now you are two. Did the angels mean for Maegwin to serve them?

He shrugged. "What have you been doing?"

She stared at him suspiciously. "What's it to you?"

Rovann sighed. "Are you always so friendly?"

"I didn't realize my social skills were on trial." She closed her eyes, drew a deep breath, and opened them again. "Sorry." Her voice was far from apologetic.

Rovann grunted. Tucking his carving into a pocket, he

reached for the ale skin and took a swig. He held it out for Maegwin who grasped it with a nod of thanks.

"Will we reach Angard tomorrow?" she asked.

"By the afternoon if the roads are clear. I hope the town is still standing when we get there."

She raised an eyebrow. "I knew it. You believed that man on the road. You think the Songmaker has called a storm on the town! And here's me thinking old Morran's stories were all horseshit."

A log rolled out of the fire with a flurry of sparks. Maegwin picked up a stick and pushed it back in, patting at the grass. In this dry summer heat, a stray spark could set the forest ablaze.

Rovann thought for a long time before he answered. "We have precedent," he said at last. "Nine months ago the Songmaker called a blizzard down onto Sheshna, up in the Angrial Pass. Hundreds died. The attack on Sheshna blocked the trading routes into Chern. For nine months, there has been no trade along the eastern border. Now he plans an attack here, in the heart of Amaury. He is growing bold."

"And I am being dragged into a war I did not choose."

"I could return you to Mallyn if you'd prefer," Rovann snapped.

Her eyes flashed with anger. "Why did you take me from the gallows? What information do you think I have?"

"I won't discuss that here. We might be overheard."

"What? We are in the middle of nowhere! Who would hear us out here?"

"There are some who could listen from the other end of Amaury."

Maegwin folded her arms across her chest. "You mean

mages. Who are you? What sort of man would escort a convicted criminal to Tyrlindon unaided?"

Rovann poked at the fire and did not answer.

Maegwin wasn't satisfied. "And tomorrow you wish to go to Angard, to confront a mage powerful enough to call a storm. A man who hopes to best such a mage must have greater power still, don't you think?"

There was a strange edge to Maegwin's voice, making Rovann glance at her sharply. She stared back at him, the firelight casting eerie reflections in her eyes. What did she want from him? He didn't owe her any explanations.

"Get some rest," he muttered. "We move on at first light." He rolled himself in his cloak and lay down with his back to her.

Sleep was a long time coming.

Chapter Three

For the first time since her arrest, Maegwin slept well. She dreamt of floating on a still pool beneath a starry sky whilst benevolent eyes looked down on her. But when a sound intruded on her dreams she snapped awake and jumped from her blankets.

Rovann frowned at her from the other side of the smoldering fire. Dark stains circled his eyes and wisps of blond hair had worked free of the leather band. Had he slept at all?

He held up a stick with a fish skewered on the end. "Breakfast?"

Maegwin scrubbed at her grainy eyes and looked around. A pink glow powdered the sky. The air carried the smell of dew.

"Yes," she said. "Thank you."

Rovann spitted the meal over the fire. "How do you like your fish: burnt or well done?" He smiled thinly at his own joke then handed one of the fish to Maegwin when they'd finished cooking.

The skin was blackened but when she sank in her teeth she found the flesh inside was pink and juicy. As she ate, Maegwin breathed in the cool, still air. She was reminded of the times she had gone on retreat from the temple, spending many days and nights alone in the woods contemplating the glory of Sho-La. She had always loved the mornings. Strange then, that she now served the goddess of the night. The irony was not lost on her.

Rovann tossed his skewer into the fire. "We'd better break camp. I've a feeling it's going to be a difficult day."

They descended back onto the Kingsroad. The morning was already warm, promising another day of searing heat. They had been on the road less than an hour when they met the first travelers coming the other way. At the sight of the family laden down with possessions and pulling a bed-ridden old man in the back of an ox cart, Rovann set heels to his horse and rode down the track to meet them.

"Are you traveling from Angard?"

"Aye," answered a toothless old woman hobbling along with a cane. "My daughter lives in Mallyn. We'll stay there till the storm is over."

"Hush, mother," said a balding man, "his lordship doesn't need to know our business."

The crone paid her son no heed and didn't seem impressed by Rovann's fancy clothes. "You're going the wrong way. There'll be nothing left of Angard by this after-noon. Take the advice of an old woman and flee before the storm hits." She spoke with the weary conviction of one who had seen such things before.

"Does the governor still hold the town? Are the king's soldiers still at their posts?" Rovann asked.

The crone hawked and spat a gobbet of phlegm at Rovann's feet. "Course they are. Tried to stop people leaving, they did, like nothing was wrong. But we folk know when there's sorcery in the air, even if the nobles like to pretend it don't exist. I've seen mage storms before, back when I was a lass, and I don't intend to be around to see one again. Damn near wiped out my village, and all because of two noble lords arguing over who owned us."

The balding man tugged on her arm, making shushing noises. The family moved off down the road but the woman called over her shoulder, "You'll find nothing in Angard but death!"

Rovann's jaw tightened as he watched them depart. Without a word, he nudged his horse forward once more.

Maegwin clutched the reins hard. A strange feeling swirled in her stomach, some instinct of hidden danger. It was a beautiful morning. And yet...

Suddenly a rabbit burst out of the undergrowth. It froze in the middle of the road, staring with fearful eyes. In the next instant, a weasel darted from the hedgerow and seized the rabbit by the throat. The rabbit squealed, kicking frantically, but with a shake, the weasel snapped its neck. As the weasel dragged the rabbit away, the sightless black eyes stared right at Maegwin.

Why didn't you help me? it seemed to be saying.

Maegwin shivered. An omen. Something terrible waited for them in Angard. Was this vision a gift of the Dark Goddess? She opened her mouth to tell Rovann but then snapped her mouth shut.

Maegwin followed Rovann through villages that had fed on Angard's prosperity. Most were deserted, their inhabitants fled, their houses boarded shut. They halted in the middle of one such settlement whilst Rovann took a look around.

"Whether this storm is real or not, the people around here are taking no chances," Maegwin observed.

Rovann nodded, his wavy hair brushing his shoulders. "It's as the old woman said; the people of these parts know sorcery when they see it. When settlers first made their homes here, there were skirmishes with the Hyreni tribesmen. Their shamans are very powerful mages."

"And if the villagers are right? If a mage storm comes to Angard? What then?"

Rovann studied the settlement, his blue eyes roving over the deserted buildings. "Come, we have little time."

Why does he never answer my questions? Maegwin thought. Grumbling under her breath, she followed.

Sometime near midday, Maegwin noticed the weather begin to change. The warm air suddenly turned chilly, raising the hairs along her arms. The sky drained of color, becoming a gray, featureless blanket. Maegwin glanced at Rovann, gaging his reaction. He said nothing but a frown creased his forehead.

A group of mounted people appeared on the road ahead. The dragon banner of the king snapped above them in the breeze. Rovann hailed them when they came within earshot.

"Hold!" he cried. "Who is your captain?"

A rangy young man with red hair nodded in Rovann's direction. "That would be me, my lord. I'm Captain Shern of the fourth division."

"Have you come from Angard?" Rovann asked. "How fares the town?"

"You've heard the rumors? The governor reckons there's nothing to worry about. But rumors are hard to stamp out. There's panic in the air, sir. Even some of the soldiers are deserting, the disloyal bastards. His lordship has sent us out to track down a bunch of deserters that left their posts during the night. Have you seen a company coming this way?"

"No, only refugees."

"Then we'd better get moving. Good day, sir." The company moved on, kicking their horses into an urgent gallop.

Maegwin followed Rovann as they climbed through the gathering dusk to the top of a bald hill. At the top, Maegwin found herself looking down into a broad river valley. In the distance, a walled town filled the valley-mouth. The sky above the settlement seethed. Great banks of black cloud boiled and hissed, flashes of lightning flickering in their depths. It looked like a fist poised to smash the town to pieces.

"Mercy," Maegwin breathed. "Blessed Mother have mercy."

Something cold landed on Maegwin's face and she looked up to see rain hissing from the gray clouds. The wind howled, whipping Maegwin's hair and cloak out behind her. She sucked a deep breath through her nostrils, savoring its icy touch. She sensed a raw, wild power in the building storm. It would bring destruction, death, pain. The Dark Goddess's gifts.

A smile tugged the corners of her mouth. *Yes*, she thought. *I feel it, my mistress.*

"Yah!"

She kicked her horse into a gallop and thundered down the road. The horse's hooves clattered against the stones, the gale screamed in her ears, the rain pattered against her skin. Maegwin breathed it all in. From somewhere she heard a high, ululating cry like the scream of a hawk. With a start, she realized it came from her own throat.

"Wait!" Rovann cried from behind. He galloped up beside her, reached out and yanked her horse's reins. The beast snorted and dug in his hooves, pulling to a halt with his ears flat against his head.

Maegwin glared at Rovann. What was he doing? Didn't he feel the power? Didn't he exult in it?

"Have you lost your mind?" Rovann snapped. "We have no idea what's in there or whether the mage knows we are coming. Do as I say or I will tie you up and leave you outside the gates!"

Try it, she wanted to say. *You just try it.*

But the hard, angry look in his eyes silenced her. She had no doubt he would carry out the threat. She ground her teeth, but followed silently as he led them to the gates and passed through.

Angard, a solid town built of good stone, had become a rank, decaying place, full of fear. The cobble streets were a mess of puddles and churned up mud.

Looters had ruined the buildings. Broken windows, an overturned handcart and a child's pull-toy carelessly strewn amid the mud, bore testament to the panic that had gripped the town. But it was not deserted. Scruffy people, hollow-eyed and gaunt stared as Maegwin and Rovann rode by. They were the under-class of the town, Maegwin guessed, the beggars, thieves and whores who would normally keep to the dank back-alleys, but who now claimed the town as their own. Maegwin did not like the way the vagrants eyed her, staring hungrily at her clothes and the horse she rode.

Rovann guided his horse as if he knew where he was going. His eyes flicked everywhere, assessing. The rain intensified, rising to an incessant *pitter-pat* that drummed on the roofs and cobblestones. It slicked Maegwin's hair to her face and drenched her cloak until it became as cumbersome as a death-shroud.

Rovann came to an abrupt halt. "There."

They had reached a broad courtyard. A grand house lay opposite, a massive three-story construction with a slate roof and two statues guarding the entrance. The once grand doors hung askew and shards of glass lay strewn on the ground around the broken windows. Bits of furniture littered the area around the door: a broken chair, a rug covered with mud, a ceramic pot amazingly still intact.

"Wait here."

Rovann swung down from the saddle and walked warily up to the gaping doors. Hesitating for only a moment, he disappeared inside. Catching her unease, Maegwin's mount shifted restlessly. A crawling feeling flared between Maegwin's shoulder blades but when she glanced around the courtyard she saw nothing. Yet she knew that unseen eyes watched her through the pelting rain.

A heavy rumble cracked the sky. The black clouds flickered with lightning. Maegwin could feel the touch of the storm's energy on her skin. So much power. How could Angard and its people hope to survive such a maelstrom?

Rovann appeared from the doorway. "It's deserted," he said as he climbed back into the saddle. "The governor and his men have abandoned the town. The soldiers we saw on the road were probably the last of the garrison fleeing for their lives. We'll find no help here."

Wordlessly, they moved on. Everywhere she looked, Maegwin saw the hands of the king's engineers. The town was modern, ordered, neat. Once, it must have been a grand place. Once.

"Leave me alone! I haven't done anything!"

Maegwin jumped at the sudden high-pitched squeal.

Cursing under his breath, Rovann kicked his horse into a trot in the direction of the cry. Turning a corner, Maegwin saw that a gang of townsfolk had gathered in the street ahead, forming a rough circle around a huddled figure on the ground. Some of the men were busy kicking it.

"Hold!" Rovann bellowed.

Reining in, he jumped from the saddle and grabbed a large, scruffy man by the arm, yanking him away from the figure he'd been kicking. The man's pock-marked face twisted with fury.

"You'll pay for that!"

He threw a meaty fist at Rovann who ducked under the clumsy blow, stepped in close, and rammed his elbow into the man's face, sending him sprawling backward in a shower of blood.

Maegwin swung a leg over her saddle and slid to the ground. A tall man with a scraggly beard lumbered toward her, leering. Maegwin dropped into a crouch. He made a grab for her but Maegwin ducked low and spun, sweeping the man's legs out from under him. He crashed onto the muddy cobbles, gasping for breath. The rest of the gang watched warily, unsure of what to do.

Rovann grabbed the coat of the youth who'd been taking a beating. He was curled into a ball on the wet ground, arms wrapped round his head.

"Stop! Please!" he squealed.

"Stand up, man," Rovann snapped. "I'll not hurt you."

The youth peeked out from between his hands, his eyes full of fear. He seemed to realize Rovann wasn't one of his attackers, uncurled himself from the ground and scrambled to his feet.

A woman with matted blonde hair screamed at Rovann,

"What are you stupid bastards doing? Don't you know who that is?"

She pulled a knife and leapt toward the youth. Maegwin jumped, landing a kick on the woman's wrist that sent the weapon flying from her grasp. It landed on the wet ground, gleaming in the weak light. Maegwin scooped it up and then lunged at the woman...

The blade slid easily between his ribs. It met resistance as it reached the heart but only for an instant before it sank deep into the organ. A hot spray of blood flicked across Maegwin's face, the iron tang stinging her cracked lips. Lord Meryk Hounsey grunted in pain, his eyes wide as he stared at her in surprise.

Maegwin jolted back to the present. The blonde woman's face loomed before her, eyes wide with terror. Maegwin realized she was holding the knife against the woman's throat. Maegwin's hand trembled. All it needed was a shove. A tiny bit of pressure... Sho-La taught forgiveness of your enemies but the Dark Goddess taught death without mercy. So easy. Just a push and the woman's skin would part, her artery would open and the red gush of her life would spill onto the cobbles.

Just a push.

"Maegwin!"

Fingers like iron closed around her wrist, yanking her hand away. The blonde woman staggered backward, gasping like a stranded fish, hand flying to her throat. She stared at Maegwin in horror then bolted down the street.

Rovann tore the knife from Maegwin's grasp and dropped it in the dirt. The rest of the mob had scattered, leaving Rovann, Maegwin and the youth they had rescued, standing in the muddy street. The rain hissed against the cobbles. A gloom like twilight threw everything into shadow.

Rovann stood so close Maegwin could smell him. His

chest was heaving — in, out, in, out, water streaming down his face. In the lurid half-light, she could see the fury in his eyes. The knife glinted on the ground between them like a broken promise. *You gave your word*, his stare said. *What more violence can I expect of you?*

"You will not touch a weapon again."

Before Maegwin could reply, the youth cried, "A hundred thousand thanks, my lord and lady! Had you not arrived I fear it would have gone ill for those locals. I was just readying my strength when you appeared!"

Maegwin glanced at him. The youth was plain looking, with messy ginger hair. The green coat and trousers he wore looked as if they had once been expensive but the color did nothing for his complexion, which was a mass of freckles. One of the youth's eyes had swollen shut and a slow dribble of blood ran from his nose.

"Why did they attack you?" asked Rovann.

The youth nodded at a lute case lying in the mud. "They were arguing over who would receive my prestigious services of course! What else? And who can blame commoners for such behavior when they heard the great Leo March was in town? The land's greatest bard doesn't visit every day, does he?"

Rovann scowled, crossing his arms over his chest.

The youth cleared his throat. "Um, that is, perhaps it was merely a case of mistaken identity. They thought I was the Songmaker. Thinking about it, yes, that might be the reason after all."

"The Songmaker?" Maegwin asked, startled by the easy use of the name. "Why would they think that?"

The youth turned bright eyes on Maegwin. "Because he poses as a minstrel. They say he walks where he wills, and if he takes a dislike to you, he'll sing death down on you. He has called this storm! Ah, the power of death in a song! Can you imagine it?"

Maegwin didn't reply, turning to Rovann for some sort of confirmation or denial.

"Let's get going," Rovann said, stalking off.

As they walked back to the horses, the youth trotted after them. "Leo March is in your debt," he announced. "Are you staying in Angard? I can show you the best tavern the town has to offer. Beer so frothy you'll be wiping it out of your beard for days — if you had beards of course — meat so tender it melts like butter on your tongue, roaring fires and the companionship of—"

"Enough! Very well, lead us to this inn," Rovann said.

Leo grinned and made a flourishing bow. Hefting the lute case, he made off down the street.

The inn was not far: a large, timber-framed building. Its windows had been boarded shut but light spilled from around the cracks. After leaving the horses with the stable-man, Leo pushed through the door and led them inside. The tavern had a low ceilinged common room with a fire burning at one end. Small knots of people huddled on plank benches, talking in whispers. The patrons glanced up as the door opened and then quickly looked away. The smell of wet clothing and sweat filled the room.

If this is the best inn Angard can offer, Maegwin thought, *it doesn't say much for the others.*

The sour-faced innkeeper was busy wiping the bar with a rag. He turned wary eyes on them. "What'll it be?"

Leo leaned an elbow on the bar and gestured grandly. "Why, your finest ale and food fit for a king, my good man. These travelers are road-weary and hungry. Many have been the trials they have faced, the dangers they have encountered on the road! Now, they yearn for sustenance!"

The innkeeper scowled at the youth. "There's some beef broth left over from this morning."

"That's fine," Rovann cut in before Leo could reply. He fished out a silver piece and pressed it into the innkeeper's hand.

The only vacant table lay at the back of the room and as the trio wove their way between the tables Maegwin was acutely aware of the stares that followed them.

"How did you learn of this place?" Rovann asked Leo quietly.

"Recommended by a colleague in Mallyn," Leo replied jovially. "The innkeeper almost fell over himself to offer me my bed and supper in return for a few songs. He knows quality when he hears it, that man. What a wonderful life: roaming the land earning my keep with tales of long lost heroes! What could be better than that, eh?"

The wind suddenly grabbed the shutters and rattled them, as if it was desperate to get inside. The patrons fell silent, glancing at the windows. Maegwin saw slack mouths, glazed eyes, beads of sweat. The whole room stank of fear.

The power of the storm was growing. It tingled on Maegwin's senses, sending goose bumps up her skin, making her twitchy. And she wasn't the only one. Everyone in the inn could feel it.

"What is he waiting for?" Leo whispered, looking around with an air of dramatic terror. "Why hasn't he unleashed it yet?"

"It takes time to build a storm like this. It will be released when it's at full power," Rovann replied. He leaned toward Leo and frowned. "Your eye needs attention." He gestured the innkeeper over and asked for a bowl of water and a cloth. When this arrived, he took a pouch from his belt and sprinkled a few pinches of powder into the water.

He soaked the cloth and pressed it over Leo's eye. "Hold that. It will reduce the swelling." For a wonder, Leo did as he was told without uttering a word.

The innkeeper slapped three bowls of broth and three tankards of ale down on the table and left. Maegwin pulled over her bowl and stirred its contents idly with the spoon, watching the gray lumps of meat surface and sink, surface and sink. As she ate, she eyed the patrons. Through the growl of the storm, snatches of conversation reached her ears.

"... If we go now, we can be there before the storm hits. We're bound to be safer than here..."

"...When has the king ever cared about the likes of us? For all we know, it could be his own mage that's sent this down on us..."

"...Don't talk like that! It's those damn rebels who've caused all this..."

"...I heard that he was seen up in Harbet just last month. A noble family took him in for the night and he sang them a few songs by the hearth. Next thing, the two children took ill and died, sang into death by his songs..."

"...Ai! She's a fine specimen, ain't she? Reckon he's her husband? Perhaps he'd be willing to share her, if we asked him right..."

Glancing up, Maegwin's eyes met the hungry stares of three men seated across the room. She could tell they were men used to taking what they wanted. They had violence written in the lines on their faces.

Following Maegwin's gaze, Rovann turned in his seat and fixed the men with a hard, cold stare. *She is mine. Do not presume*, that look said. The men's grins faltered and they looked away.

Oblivious to the sudden tension, Leo slurped noisily at

his broth. "Do you have kin here in Angard, my lord?" he asked, gesturing with his dripping spoon.

"What makes you think I'm a lord?" Rovann asked.

Leo grinned, "Ah, posing as a commoner, eh?" He tapped his nose conspiratorially. "Don't worry. Your secret is safe with me. Leo March is a man of honor! You won't catch his lips flapping in the wind!"

Maegwin glanced at Rovann. Was he a lord? She had no idea.

I know nothing about him, she thought. *He tells me nothing because he does not trust me. And who can blame him? Would I have killed that woman if he hadn't stopped me?*

As she watched, Rovann's face suddenly went slack, empty of expression. His gaze flicked out of focus, as though listening to something only he could hear.

Not to be deterred, Leo turned his attention to Maegwin. "Have you ever heard *The Lay of Helena,* my lady?"

"I haven't," she replied. "Minstrels seldom visited my home."

"Ah! It's one of the most favored tales in the great houses. Perhaps I could sing it for you now?"

Maegwin raised an eyebrow, "I don't think your talents would be appreciated at the moment."

Leo frowned, looking over the common room. "You may be right. But I know some good drinking songs. Perhaps—"

His voice trailed into silence. A change had come over the air. Pressure filled the room. The air smelled charged with power. Conversation died. The patrons glanced around, eyes wide.

Outside, something detonated. A crack like the splitting of an enormous tree-trunk filled the air. The wind howled down the chimney and under the shutters, rattling them furiously. Thunder boomed and the building seemed to shake on its very foundations.

"Fates preserve us!" a man cried, burying his head in his hands.

A splintering sound echoed through the inn.

"That's the roof!" the innkeeper growled.

Everyone sprang to their feet, looking around wildly for escape but there was nowhere to go. They were trapped, held hostage by the breaking storm. The fire spat, snaking out from the fireplace in answer to the wind tearing down the chimney.

"Put it out!" the innkeeper bellowed. "It'll catch the tables!"

Maegwin threw the contents of their tankards into the fire, grabbed some from the next table and dumped them in as well. The fire sizzled then died into gray ashes that went swirling into the common room on the wild breeze. There was a crash from the street outside. A woman crept to the window and peeked between the gaps in the boards.

"The tailor's wall has collapsed! There's rubble all over the street!"

Rovann surged to his feet, sending the bowls of broth crashing to the floor. "He's here!" he muttered before staggering across the common room and wrenching the door open. The wind tore it from his grasp, slamming it into the wall. Wind and rain blasted into the inn. People screamed in terror.

For a second, Maegwin saw Rovann framed in the doorway, pale hair swirling round his face. Then he threw himself into the maelstrom and was gone.

Maegwin stared at the spot he had occupied. Should she run for it? Could she lose herself in the storm, keep running until Rovann and the king forgot her? What did she owe him? Nothing. She should run. But she had given her word and the word of a priestess of Sho-La was her bond. A sudden image flashed before her eyes. Rovann standing in the rain, staring at her with disappointment in his eyes. A knife lay on the ground between them.

She pushed her chair back and hurried to the door. Pulling in a breath, she forced her way outside. The world beyond the inn had gone wild. Angard had become chaos, a place of terrifying violence. The wind picked her up and dumped her on the other side of the street as easily as if she were a rag doll. Her face sank into ground saturated with water, filling her mouth and nostrils with stinking muck. The rain fell so hard it hammered the back of her skull like thousands of pebbles, threatening to flay her skin.

She staggered to her feet. The rain obscured everything behind a gray curtain. Dashing water from her eyes, she squinted into the gloom. How could anything survive in this? How could Rovann? How could she?

Suddenly, she spotted a shape moving through the murk ahead. Rovann. Maegwin opened her mouth to shout but the wind snatched away her voice, ripping it to shreds. She spluttered, spat and then stumbled forward. Clutching the buildings for support, she groped onward, slipping in the mud, falling to her knees, getting up again. Rovann remained out of reach, a beacon pulling her on in the gloom.

What was he doing? Did he wish to die? Did she? Why else had she gone after him?

Amazingly, she made it to the end of the street. A fallen bridge blocked the way. *By the Blessed Mother,* she thought. *What is that fool man doing?*

Rovann struggled down a wide thoroughfare into the

heart of town, following someone. A man, tall and immensely fat, was strolling as easily as if he were out taking the air. The storm did not touch him.

"Hold, mage!" Rovann bellowed, lifting his arm. Blue light bled from his eyes, his mouth. A bolt of energy sizzled through the air and struck the man between the shoulder blades. A sheet of power lifted the man from his feet and he hung in the middle of it, suspended like a fish in a tank. The storm fell out of the air. An eerie quiet descended on Angard.

Rovann padded warily toward the man and halted three paces away. Maegwin could not read his expression but the set of his shoulders spoke of fury. He reached out his hand to grab the man's wrist.

Maegwin gasped as a vision enveloped her. *The rabbit squealed, kicking frantically, but with a shake, the weasel snapped its neck. As the weasel dragged the rabbit away, the sightless black eyes stared right at Maegwin.*

It had been an omen. An omen of death.

"Don't touch him!" she screamed.

Too late. Rovann's fingers closed around the man's wrist and the air exploded. The world turned white and Maegwin was tossed aside like a piece of wreckage.

When she woke, she was lying on her back in the dirt, looking up at the gray sky. She blinked rapidly for a few moments then flipped onto her belly and staggered upright. Needles of pain stabbed her chest. It felt as though an iron band wrapped her lungs.

There was no sign of Rovann. In the street ahead, the mage still hung in the beam of blue power. But not for much longer. He was twisting, hands curling into fists and back again, fighting his bonds.

If he broke free…

Maegwin didn't finish the thought. She had to find Rovann. The explosion had ripped the street apart. Rubble lay in massive heaps on either side.

"Maegwin!"

A shape struggled amidst the wreckage. He had fallen against a wall and been half buried when it collapsed. His legs were trapped beneath a block of stone.

"Rovann," Maegwin hissed, "the mage is breaking free!"

Rovann's face was white with pain. "I know. Can you dig me out?"

Maegwin stumbled over and placed her hands under the stone. It was so heavy. She strained, and after a moment, it shifted an inch. Pins stabbed her lungs. She stopped, dizzy, and braced herself on the stone.

"I can't do it," she gasped. "It's too heavy."

A pair of hands appeared next to hers.

"Leo!" Maegwin cried in surprise.

The minstrel's face was pale, his eyes wide with terror. "Is that him?" he gulped. "Is that the Songmaker?"

"Don't look at him! Help me free Rovann!"

Leo tore his eyes from the struggling mage. Together he and Maegwin heaved on the stone. Gradually, it moved. Rovann pushed from beneath and as it gained momentum, the stone slid from its position and rolled down the pile of debris. Rovann scrambled out of his prison.

But in that instant, the mage broke his bonds.

The fat man staggered, and as he moved, the storm regained its force. Sheets of rain tore through the town. The wind howled. The mage hurled himself at Rovann, arm raised to deal a killing stroke.

Maegwin sprang at the fat man, slamming her hands, double-fisted, into the mage's chest. She should have remembered. She should have guessed what would happen. A silent concussion rocked her body. Her awareness tore wide open.

Fury, so hot it consumes him. He will have revenge. The list is long: the king, the Council, the people of the land, the air, the trees, the beasts, and the angels who dwell in the Aethyr. All will suffer as he has suffered.

Maegwin went flying through the air and landed with a teeth-juddering impact on the slick cobbles. Through hazy vision, she saw the enemy mage turn to look at her. A slow grin spread across his pudgy face. He winked and tapped the side of his nose as though the two of them shared a secret. His body writhed, dissipating as if made of smoke. In an instant, he was gone.

The storm snuffed out as if it had never existed.

Agony burned through Maegwin's chest. Her lungs were on fire. *Stand! I must stand!* she told herself. *Always meet a threat on your feet!*

She climbed upright, took two tottering steps toward Rovann and Leo, then fainted.

Chapter Four

The mud squelched as Rovann knelt beside Maegwin. A sickly yellow pallor infused her skin and her colorless lips were dry and cracked. Frowning, he pressed his palms against her chest and closed his eyes, sending his sight spinning through bone and tissue, deep into Maegwin's body. Her energies seemed corrupted. Wrongness assailed his senses like a melody played out of key. After a moment of searching he found the cause: three ribs on her left side had snapped, puncturing her lung and causing it to fill with blood.

Rovann opened his eyes and sat back on his heels. "Curse it all," he growled, scrubbing a hand through his hair.

Leo moved into a crouch on the other side of Maegwin's prone form, his forehead creased with worry. "Is she all right?"

Rovann glanced at the minstrel then back to Maegwin. Why hadn't she run? A vision appeared in his mind's eye: Maegwin pressing a knife against a woman's throat, her eyes dancing with a lurid light. Such violence. Such rage. And yet... and yet... she had come after him. Saved his life.

Now you are two, the angel had said.

"We shouldn't stay here!" Leo cried. "That mage might come back any minute!"

"Nothing is keeping you. Go if you wish."

Leo blew out his cheeks, looking to left and right, then shook his head. "Let it not be said that Leo March refused to aid a lady in need! What's wrong with her?"

Rovann sighed. "Too much. Her wounds are beyond my skill to heal."

"There was a notable healer in Angard before the storm came," Leo said, hopefully. "Maybe she stayed. Should I—"

"No," Rovann replied. "Maegwin is beyond such help."

"Nonsense!" Leo cried in horror. "We can't just leave her to die!"

"Would you let me think?" Rovann snapped, massaging his forehead. He suddenly glanced at the minstrel. "What do you mean by 'we'?"

Leo lifted his chin, meeting Rovann's eyes. "You saved my life. I won't leave your side until I've repaid that debt."

Rovann frowned. This was the last thing he needed. How could he hope to keep his mission secret with a minstrel trailing him? But he didn't have time to argue about it, and besides, Leo could help him move Maegwin. "Fine. If you want to help, fetch the horses from the inn."

Leo nodded and dashed off.

Rovann pressed his ear to Maegwin's chest. Her breathing bubbled with an unsteady 'schloop, schloop, schloop'.

Now you are two.

The bank of clouds that had towered over Angard was breaking up and sunlight flooded down, turning the puddles to silver glass. Along the street, survivors of the storm began to venture outside, talking quietly among themselves. Angard would be a dangerous place until the governor returned to restore order. It was time to leave.

Leo appeared around a corner, leading the horses. He had received a bloody nose in addition to the black eye he already carried.

Rovann climbed wearily to his feet. "What happened?"

The minstrel shrugged. "The innkeeper wanted to keep your horses. I convinced him otherwise."

"I see. I'll take Maegwin on Glynn. You'll ride the other horse."

He and Leo gently lifted Maegwin into Glynn's saddle then Rovann climbed up behind her. Maegwin's head lolled on her neck as he leaned her against him but she didn't wake. Rovann wrapped one arm around her and took the reins in the other hand. Her hair, resting against his neck, smelled of pine needles. Leo swung onto Maegwin's horse and they set off at a slow walk, picking their way carefully through the ruin.

Rovann surveyed the devastation as they wove through the muddy streets. Angard had become a place of debris and rubble. The litter of people's lives lay everywhere, as if a giant had come striding through the town, ransacking as it went.

The king must send aid, Rovann thought as his eyes roved over the destroyed homes, the wrecked bridges, the piles of flotsam. *Mallynshire declared for the king. This is the Songmaker's retribution. The king must help these people.*

With Leo guiding, they made their way toward the main gate. The paved Kingsroad was largely undamaged and the horses were able to pick up their pace. Even so, broken branches littered the road and crops in nearby fields had been flattened. The countryside was eerily silent, as though holding its breath, waiting for the next assault.

Leo remained quiet for a time, but at last, he could hold his peace no longer. "Was that the Songmaker?"

Rovann shifted Maegwin's weight against him and then shook his head. "I doubt it. The Songmaker doesn't risk himself. That mage was more likely one of his underlings."

Leo shuddered, glancing back at Angard. "Where are we going?" he asked, "Lady Maegwin needs help."

Rovann bit back his impatience. "Don't you think I realize that? We're taking Maegwin to a healer."

Before the minstrel could reply, Rovann kicked Glynn to a canter. The sun was dropping toward evening when Rovann turned off the Kingsroad and cut across country westward. Leo halted and seemed about to speak but then nudged his horse into motion and caught up. The young minstrel's face was crowded with questions but Rovann kept the pace too quick for conversation. The less Leo knew, the better.

A line of trees appeared on the horizon and as he and Leo rode closer, Rovann saw that they were tall and gnarled; ancient hoary behemoths grasping at the sky with twisted fingers. A crow, hopping around on the ground at the edge of the wood, peered at Rovann and Leo with its beady eyes.

Leo stared at the forbidding wall of trees, his mouth hanging open. "What is this place?"

"Turnang Forest," Rovann replied, watching the leaves rustling in the breeze. "Kin to Roamsford Edge."

"Then I'm glad our road doesn't run through it. The Edge has a fearsome reputation."

Rovann smiled apologetically. "Then this is not your lucky day. I hope to find the healer within the forest."

Leo looked at the black overhang of trees and then back at Rovann. "Are you sure that's a good idea?"

"You've repaid any debt you had to me, Leo. You don't have to go any further."

The minstrel scrunched his freckled nose in distaste. "I've made an oath, given my solemn word, sworn a sacred vow. I will see the lady well again, I swear it!"

Rovann closed his eyes and sent his senses toward Maegwin. Her breathing was worsening, her breath rattling in her throat like that of a dying woman. There wasn't much time.

He nudged Glynn, guiding the horse under the canopy of the trees. Inside the forest, the close-knit branches and heavy leaf-litter muffled all sound. The warm, oppressive air seemed to prohibit speech, as though speaking would break some kind of law. Rovann and Leo rode in silence. The minstrel looked around with wide eyes as they wove between towering beech and oak trees. Rovann wondered if this whole episode would end up as one of Leo's extravagant stories. The last thing he needed were tales of his journey being sung from here to Mallyn. So much for secrecy.

Night fell quickly in the forest's perpetual twilight and soon it became so dark they had to slow their horses to a walk. In the distance, a wolf's howl split the night. *Arooooo.* Leo tensed but Rovann ignored it. The wolf was many miles to the south.

"Um, are we going much further tonight?" Leo asked. "I can't see anything in this gloom."

Rovann pulled Glynn to a halt. "No. Sit still and wait."

Several moments passed. Rovann noticed Leo working himself up to speak and held up a hand for silence. Eventually, faint silver light began to glow through the trees. Rovann tapped Leo on the shoulder and pointed. The light formed into strands, glowing tendrils of mist that led off into the forest like winding paths.

"Come on," Rovann said softly. "Follow the strands."

The wolf's howl came again, closer this time and it was answered by a baying to the east. A stray branch snapped under Glynn's hoof and Leo gasped, almost falling from the saddle in his fright.

Used to soft beds and warm fires, this one, Rovann thought.

A sound reached Rovann's ears and he paused, cocking his head to catch it. The tinkling of bells.

Leo clutched his arm in fear. "Do you hear that?"

Ahead of Rovann lay a vast clearing, glowing with silver light. He sighed, closing his eyes in relief.

Thank the Realms.

A giant tree grew in the center of the clearing. The trunk was so wide Rovann guessed it would take thirty paces to circle. The tree's canopy was lost against the night sky and heart-shaped leaves festooned its branches. The leaves were the source of the light: Earthlight, a fragment of the One Light itself.

"A Sentinel," Rovann breathed. He felt suddenly small, insignificant. The tree thrummed on his senses like the mage storm had, only this time the power he sensed was filled with joy, not malice.

Leo, though, seemed not to share Rovann's sentiments. His face went slack with terror. Rovann stared at the youth, surprised by his reaction.

"What's wrong?"

"Why didn't you tell me this is what you were looking for?"

"I told you I was looking for a healer. The Sentinel is that healer."

Leo shook his head, eyes round with fear. "It's unnatural! A place of devils! I won't go near it!" He curled his fingers in the sign to ward off evil.

"What's wrong with you?" Rovann asked, feeling his patience fray. "You claim to be a minstrel – you should know that Sentinels are protectors."

"Protectors of what?" Leo cried. "Of devils and demons!"

"Have it your way," Rovann snapped. "Wait here if you prefer, but help me with Maegwin."

Reluctantly the youth slid from his horse and helped get Maegwin down from Glynn's back. A thin trickle of blood dribbled from Maegwin's mouth and a rattle sounded in her throat. Rovann carried her into the clearing.

As he passed into the Sentinel's presence, Earthlight enveloped him. Warmth washed over his skin and bells tinkled in his ears. The aura of the tree hammered on his senses, threatening to crush him. The Sentinel's power was raw and elemental.

Rovann staggered to the trunk and folded onto his knees among the massive humped roots. He held Maegwin up like an offering.

"I need your help, Great Heart."

He laid Maegwin on the forest floor and began scrabbling in the dirt with his hands. The earth was thick and soft, a heavy loam that crumbled easily. He dug out double handfuls until he had a decent sized depression in which he gently placed Maegwin. He scooped the earth back over her body, leaving only her face visible.

A strand of red-gold hair had fallen over Maegwin's face. Tentatively, Rovann reached out and brushed it away. She looked peaceful, so unlike the unpredictable, violent woman she'd been in Angard.

Who are you, Maegwin? Rovann wondered. *The angels want me to trust you, but trust must be earned.*

He slumped onto his back, fatigue washing through him. He felt battered and bruised. The mage in Angard could have killed him. *Would* have killed him if Maegwin hadn't followed him.

You are a damn fool, he berated himself. *You should have known better than to go after him without knowing who you faced. What were you thinking? Do you have a death wish?*

He didn't answer that question. He didn't like where it might lead.

One of the Sentinel's roots stuck out of the soil less than an arm's span from where he lay. He reached out, brushing his fingers against the smooth silver bark...and all sensation left him. He found himself floating above his body, looking down on the light-filled glade in which he and Maegwin lay. A surge of joy washed through him and he soared up into the sky. Below, the forest spread out, a shimmering tangle of life energies that glowed with Eorthic power. Above, a golden arc crowned the sky, indicating the border of the Realm of Earth.

Rovann knew he should return. He knew he should float back to his body, open his eyes, and take care of Maegwin. He knew how dangerous it was to Walk the Realms when his body was damaged and exhausted. But he felt the old question unfold in his mind. *Where is Istra?* It tugged at him, pulling him on.

As he rose toward the shining border, Rovann called to his mind the chants of the Eorthe, and a string of symbols formed on his tongue. He spoke the words that would give the Eorthic symbols life and a gate blazed into life in the sky. It glowed as hot as molten metal, sigils burning at each corner. Rovann passed through the gate, leaving the Realm of human existence behind.

He entered a Realm of sunlight and silver clouds. Strains of melody shimmered through the clear air. Gentle laughter sounded in Rovann's mind and he saw bright beings floating on the edges of his vision. He caught glimpses of shining eyes filled with compassion.

"Have you seen Istra?" he called.

The angels shook their heads and glided away. Rovann followed. He soared over mountains of shimmering mist, through a crystal rain that fell like drops of melody. The Realm of Aethyr was a place without time, without life or death. Only the peace of existence mattered. Rovann felt his essence evaporating into the mists, his person dissolving into the rain. Yet a thought dragged at him, anchoring him to his sense of self.

Istra is not here.

He opened a gate that shone with Aetheric symbols and passed through into the Realm of Fire.

An inferno engulfed him. The sky burned. Clouds of ash and smoke rained down. The ground was a landscape of broken rock and rivers of lava. On the horizon, a line of volcanoes spewed out their innards, choking the atmosphere with ash. Nothing could live in such a place and yet it teemed with life.

A golden salamander lounged on a rock, peering at Rovann with one great eye. Fire wraiths danced in dizzy circles, diving in and out of the rivers of magma. Mighty dragons wheeled through the sky, their scales gleaming in the red light. One of the dragons, a great queen as large as a barn, broke away from their dance and approached him, regarding him with swirling golden eyes.

"Who are you?" she asked in a rumbling voice. "You are not of the Realm of Fire."

"I come from Earth, Great Heart. Have you seen Istra?"

Smoke rose from her nostrils as she studied him. "No children of Earth walk within Fire. What you seek is not here, Warrior of the Realms. Return to your world before you are trapped."

She opened her teeth-filled jaws and blew a jet of hot air at Rovann. It sent him spinning. A gate appeared in the sky, burning with a dusky fire. Rovann spun toward it and passed through.

Darkness and silence. Nothingness surrounded him.

"Who are you?" a voice said suddenly.

"Who's there?" he replied, feeling the first icy stirrings of fear.

Soft laughter echoed. "Why have you come here?"

"Where is here?"

A pause. The hiss of breath. "Should I show you?"

The gloom lifted enough for Rovann to make out his shadowy surroundings. He stood on a plain that stretched off into the distance on three sides. On the fourth side, right by Rovann's face, reared a wall of shadow. Shapes appeared in the wall's shiny surface, outlines of creatures pressing against the barrier like fetuses struggling to break free of the womb.

Terror surged through Rovann as he recognized this place. The in-between. The border of the Outer Darkness. Beyond that forbidding wall lay the Realm of Chaos, the antithesis of life itself. That Realm had many names. The angels of the Aethyr called it The Burning. Others named it Torment, The Void.

Hell.

"Come closer!" the voice cried.

Rovann took two steps back.

"I know who you are looking for! Istra is in here with me!"

Rovann shook his head in denial. No. It couldn't be true. It couldn't. "You lie," he whispered. *By the One Light, you must be lying!*

"You suspect the truth. She is damned. She is a Sluargh now, one of the Unforgiven Dead. She will reside in Chaos for eternity."

Rovann stared at the shapes pressing against the wall. There were hands, faces, bodies. Could one of them be Istra?

"You can have her back," the voice said. "Free me and she is yours."

Istra? he thought. *Are you there?*

He raised his arm, took one step toward the wall, then another. The wall's surface shone like oil just a few inches from his outstretched hand. Just a little more, a little further and he'd see her again.

No, child. Do not do this, said a voice in his mind.

Rovann blinked as a ball of light suddenly flared before his eyes, so bright it was almost blinding. It landed on his outstretched hand. A leaf, Rovann realized, heart-shaped and spilling silver light. The leaf of a Sentinel.

He closed his hand around it and looked up at the wall of Chaos. "I will never free you."

The voice howled in fury as Rovann went spinning, spinning back through the Realms, through the gate into the Realm of Earth and landed back in his body.

Slowly, his eyelids flickered open. Above, the moon shone through the branches of the Sentinel. An owl hooted.

Agony suddenly lanced up his wrist and he realized his left hand had curled so tightly into a fist that his nails were cutting into his palm, leaking a bloody trail across his hand. Wincing with pain, he uncurled his fingers and saw what was clasped there.

A silver leaf, crumbled to dust.

Chapter Five

Rovann groaned and struggled into a sitting position. A dull ache thudded through the muscles of his legs and back. Nausea knotted his stomach. Resting his head in his hands, Rovann stared at the Sentinel. He was stupid to have Walked the Realms. What had he been thinking? If the Sentinel hadn't brought him back...

What? he thought. *What would you have done?*

He couldn't answer his own question. *Remember your duty,* he told himself. *Remember your oath to your king, your land, your people. Focus on what is happening within the Realms. It has something to do with the Songmaker.*

He noticed movement from the corner of his eye and turned to see Maegwin lift her arm and wipe a hand across her forehead, leaving a smear of dirt. While he had Walked, silky roots had covered her face like a spider's web. She brushed them aside and opened her eyes, her stare settling on the tangled net of branches above her head.

"It's all right," Rovann said. "You're safe."

She turned her head and found him with her green gaze. "Where am I?"

"Within a Sentinel's protection. How do you feel?"

"Feel?" She pushed herself into a sitting position, sending soil cascading from her shoulders, and patted her chest. "It doesn't hurt anymore. What happened? Angard?"

"Angard survived, thanks to you. Leo and I brought you here." Rovann closed his eyes and sent his senses questing toward Maegwin. Her breathing was regular and the terrible 'schloop' sound had gone from her lungs. Rovann bowed to the Sentinel, hands clasped across his chest. *My thanks, Great Heart,* he said to the tree.

"Lady Maegwin!" cried Leo, pelting into the clearing. His fear of the Sentinel seemed to have evaporated. He went down on his knees and grasped Maegwin's hands. "You're healed! Amazing! Truly awe-inspiring! Who would have thought a mere tree could do such things? This will make a fine tale." He screwed up his face in concentration. "I shall call it, *The Lady of the Tree.* No, hang on, I can do better than that. How about, *The Wondrous Watcher in the Woods?*"

Maegwin smiled. "I look forward to hearing it."

Leo showed a toothy grin then bounded to his feet. "So, what now? On to Tyrlindon and all the adventure that awaits us there?"

Rovann glanced at Leo sharply. "How did you know we're traveling to Tyrlindon? I never told you that."

If he noticed the suspicion in Rovann's voice, the minstrel didn't show it. "Where else would a lord and lady be going? The Kingsroad leads straight from Angard to the capital."

Rovann sighed, suddenly ashamed of his distrust after all of Leo's help. "Yes, Tyrlindon is our destination."

"Excellent! We can travel together. I shall take my talents to the capital and dazzle them all with my fine wit! The lords and ladies will be falling over themselves to listen to my tales!"

"Well, they'll have to wait a little longer. We'll camp here tonight and set off at first light."

The grin slid from Leo's face. "Camp? Here? So near to the tree?"

"Why not? There is no danger."

Leo frowned, considering Rovann's words. At last, he shrugged, "Perhaps I was mistaken to distrust the tree." He turned to the Sentinel and made a flourishing bow. "I beg your forgiveness, Lord of the Forest. I was wrong to doubt. You have my undying thanks." He winked at Rovann. "I'll be back with dinner shortly." Before Rovann could reply, he disappeared into the night.

Rovann watched the minstrel go. How did he expect to find food in the dark? Shaking his head, he paced around the Sentinel's clearing, picking up bits of deadwood. When he had enough, he returned to where Maegwin sat and scraped away the dead leaf-litter until he had a patch of ground in which to build a fire. He dumped the wood and soon had an orange blaze crackling in the fire-pit. Rovann glanced at the Sentinel. Unease radiated from its branches. Like all trees, it feared fire.

I will keep it contained, Great Heart, he told the tree. *You have my word.*

Maegwin scooted closer, reaching her hands out to the flames. Rovann busied himself taking off the horse's saddles and then brushing the animals down. As he worked, memories played through his head.

She is a Sluargh now, one of the Unforgiven Dead. She will reside in Chaos for eternity.

Istra? He thought desperately. *Why did you do it?*

A twig snapped and Rovann spun as Leo appeared out of the night, carrying a rabbit over each shoulder.

The youth grinned at Rovann, brandishing a slingshot. "Dinner's arrived."

"How the did you manage to hunt?"

"Practice, my good man. Being a minstrel, you can never be quite sure where your next meal is coming from. A wealthy patron can turn on you in the blink of an eye and toss you out on your ear. You learn how to find your own food or go hungry."

Rovann smiled. "Then I'm thankful you aren't a better minstrel."

Leo expertly skinned the rabbits and fixed them on spits over the fire.

Rovann slumped down with his back against the warm bark of the Sentinel. He stared into the fire but could see no answers written in the dancing flames.

———

Maegwin inhaled deeply, savoring the clean smell of the night air. Her lungs no longer burned and each breath tasted sweet. She remembered the wet street in Angard, a searing pain in her chest. And then...

Her eyes strayed to the Sentinel towering above. And then a voice whispering in her mind.

Why do you walk in the darkness, child?

The tree's power had filled her, washing away pain and doubt and anger, bringing peace instead. She felt as though she had been scoured clean.

A twig popped in the fire and she jumped.

"Maegwin?" Rovann asked. "Are you well?"

She nodded. "Thank you, Rovann."

"For what?"

"Saving my life."

Rovann smiled thinly. "I was stupid in Angard. I shouldn't have gone after that mage on my own."

"Then why did you?" *I saw the power you used*, she thought. *Why do you try to hide it?*

He shrugged as though it didn't matter. "I had to know who created the mage storm. If not for you, the mage might have killed me. That makes us even."

"No," Maegwin said fiercely. "My debt isn't yet paid. A life for a life. Don't forget, you saved me from the noose in Mallyn as well."

"The king saved you from the executioner, not I."

Maegwin scooped some twigs from the ground and began tossing them into the fire. "Of course. I'm hardly likely to forget. What does he want from me? What information does he think I have?"

Rovann shifted his position, glancing at Leo, who was engrossed in the cooking. "You can ask him yourself when we reach Tyrlindon."

"And when will that be?"

"Three days if the weather holds and we don't run into trouble."

"Done!" Leo cried.

He lifted the skewer from the fire and used his belt knife to carve the rabbits and then laid them on a bed of leaves. "Tuck in."

Maegwin stabbed a piece of rabbit with a twig. As she bit into the succulent meat, juice dribbled down her chin and she enjoyed the simple pleasure of eating: the soft texture of the meat as it came apart on her tongue, the smell of roasted flesh, the delicious taste of the liquid that ran down her throat.

Before the week was up, she would meet the king.

And then what? she thought. *Will he hang me in the public square as an example?*

Rovann said the king might pardon her, but Maegwin had learned from bitter experience that nobles did nothing unless it benefited themselves. What would the king want in return for her life? How much was it worth? Her eyes wandered to where Rovann slumped against the Sentinel's trunk.

A king's man, she thought. *A dangerous man.* In the temple the High Priestess had warned her of the perils of involving herself in the affairs of the powerful. *They will drag you in like a piece of flotsam on the tide,* she would say, *and before you know it, you will be drowning in their schemes.*

Rovann looked up and his blue gaze seemed to slice right through her. She looked away, feeling uncomfortable. Something lurked in Rovann's eyes, a shadow like the memory of old pain.

So many secrets.

She finished her meal and curled into a ball, her back resting against one of the Sentinel's roots.

Blessed Mother, guide me.

Blessed Mother, show me.

Chanting prayers, she fell into dreams filled with silver trees.

The next morning Maegwin was woken by the 'pee-wit', 'pee-wit' of a piper bird. It sat in a branch above her, head cocked to one side, yellow plume swept back, gazing at her with bright eyes. She lay still, watching the little bird. It hopped along the branch, turning its head from side to side to get a better view of this strange creature by its tree.

Don't worry, she told it. *I'm not staying in your territory.*

With a raucous cry, the piper bird took off into the forest. Dawn was starting to filter through the wood, turning the trunks from black to gray. Birdcalls filled the air. Maegwin climbed to her feet, wiping the sleep from her eyes.

She joined Rovann and Leo in a meager breakfast of bread and dried fruit then they mounted the horses. Leo and Rovann rode double on Glynn while she followed on her bay gelding. As they moved off, Rovann stopped at the edge of the glade and pulled Glynn round to face the Sentinel. He spread his arms out to the sides, bowing low. His lips moved but Maegwin couldn't make out words.

After a while, they left the forest and emerged onto the Kingsroad, the horses' hooves making clopping noises against the hard flagstones. After the gloom of the forest, the sudden brightness made Maegwin squint and she felt strangely vulnerable out in the open without the protection of the trees.

Leo though, seemed immensely happy to be leaving the forest and he whistled tunelessly as he rode behind Rovann.

Maegwin raised an eyebrow. "So, a great story-teller, are you? Let's have one then."

Leo grinned. "Anything for you, my lady." He looked around, chewing his bottom lip in thought. "How about *The Lay of Sandford Moor*? The battlefield is only a few leagues west of here. They say the soil soaked up so much blood nothing will grow on it. It's there that the King's Mage earned his nickname, 'The Slayer of Sandford Moor.'" His voice dropped in tone, becoming somberly dramatic. "He slaughtered nigh on an entire army, including all the whores and beggars that came with them. That's why Mallynshire returned to the king: they were terrified of what the King's Mage might do to them. He's eight feet tall with eyes of fire and by all accounts everyone in Tyrlindon is terrified of him, including the king."

Rovann frowned. "You shouldn't believe everything you hear, minstrel."

Leo opened his mouth to reply then snapped it shut. Perhaps he realized it would be unwise to criticize the King's Mage in front of Rovann. He was, after all, a king's man himself.

"Um, how about the legend of how Myra the Brave tamed a dragon of Fire? Now that is a heart-warming tale!" He cleared his throat dramatically and launched into his story.

Whilst Leo talked, Maegwin looked around at the changing landscape. They crossed the border into Tyrlinshire, a land of farmsteads and orchards that had grown prosperous due to its proximity to the capital.

"Ah bounteous Tyrlinshire, breadbasket of the land," Leo commented, when his story was finished. He plucked an apple from a tree that hung over the wall of an orchard, bit into it, and spoke with his mouth full. "They reckon the rebels will never take Amaury whilst the people of Tyrlinshire remain loyal to the crown. My grandmother came from round here you know." He sounded immensely proud of the fact.

"And you?" Maegwin asked. "Where is home for you? I can't place your accent."

"Me? Oh, here and there," Leo said vaguely, gesturing with his apple. "The road is my home, and wherever it decides to lead me. I spend a few weeks here, a few months there. Good minstrels are welcome in great houses the length and breadth of the land. Now, how about a poem? This one is called *Ode to a Feather Bed*."

Maegwin smiled fixedly. This was going to get tiring.

———

Three days later the Kingsroad climbed up to a wide, upland plateau. As she reined in beside Rovann and Leo, Maegwin saw a city hugging the flanks of a series of squat hills that rose up out of the plateau like the ridges of a dragon's back. A slender pinnacle rose from the center of the city, flying the dragon banner of King William of Amaury. They had finally reached Tyrlindon.

Maegwin stared. The size of the place made her feel as small and as insignificant as a flea clinging to the flank of a wolf.

Rovann kicked Glynn into a canter and they joined the crowds of people trudging down the road to the capital. As they neared the gates, Maegwin noticed that shanty towns had sprung up around the city. Shacks and crude huts clustered together haphazardly beyond Tyrlindon's thick walls. Naked children ran shrieking through mud streets and slat-ribbed dogs nosed through piles of uncollected refuse.

Are these refugees from the fighting? Maegwin wondered. *Is this what the king's protection looks like?*

"Keep close," Rovann instructed, as they were forced to slow the horses to a frustrating plod. "It is easy to get lost in the crowds."

The shanty town came to an abrupt end and they crossed a wide ring of clear ground around the city walls. Bits of broken wood and churned up mud showed the haste with which the space had been cleared. A precaution against siege, Maegwin realized, giving clear sight to defenders on the walls.

Could the Songmaker lay siege to the capital? Maegwin thought. *Is he really that powerful?*

The gate in the city walls was massive, easily big enough for two or three carts to pass through, yet even so, the crowd came to a standstill. Rovann swung down from Glynn's back and Leo and Maegwin followed his example.

"What's going on?" Leo asked. He looked around nervously and began twisting the hem of his cloak.

"Precautions," Rovann replied. "Only those with business in Tyrlindon will be allowed into the city."

Leo craned his neck to see above the crowd. "What if they don't let me in? I'll have come all this way for nothing!" There was a hint of panic in his voice and Maegwin felt sorry for the young minstrel. His dreams of making a name for himself in Tyrlindon could be shattered before they even began.

"Don't you have a commission waiting for you in the city?" Rovann asked.

"Um, not exactly. I was hoping to find a patron when I arrived."

"But you have arranged for somewhere to stay?"

Leo shook his head, ginger hair bouncing. He looked thoroughly miserable.

"Then what were you planning to do once you arrived here?" Rovann's tone was laced with annoyance.

"The same as always," Leo said. "Find a decent tavern, play there for a few nights, wait for my reputation to spread so a lord of the city will offer me patronage. It always worked in Mandrake and Silverport."

"You're a long way from Mandrake and Silverport. The guards won't let you in if you've no business here."

Leo's face turned into a look of utter horror. Maegwin thought he might burst into tears. "What am I going to do?"

Rovann's expression was stony. Then he closed his eyes and sighed. "All right. As payment for your help in Angard, I'll get you into the city and take you to a tavern I know. After that, you're on your own."

"Oh, generous lord!" Leo cried, grabbing Rovann's hand and pumping it vigorously. "A thousand blessings on you. I will write a ballad in your honor! I will sing your praises until young women weep to hear your name, I—"

"Just lead the horse and keep your mouth shut."

The crowd moved at a crawl. The sun beat down on them and Maegwin wiped sticky strands of hair away from her forehead. At last, they neared the front of the crowd. Five guards dressed in heavy chainmail and bearing the red and gold cloaks of the King's Guard barred the entrance. One of them was having an argument with an elderly man leading a donkey. Baskets of green melons were strapped to the donkey's sides.

"I've asked Master Adden and he says he's never heard of you. You aren't coming in."

"Never heard of me?" the old man wheezed. "I do his deliveries every week! I won't stand for this treatment. You fetch the guild master here right now!"

In a voice of deliberate patience, the guard said. "Sammen here will escort you back to the Kingsroad. You either go with him or spend a night in the cells. You can sell your wares in the market at Dalby. What will it be?"

The old man's face turned bright red. He jerked angrily on the donkey's rope, pulling it around in a circle. "I'd never get treatment like this if the Songmaker was in charge."

"What did you say?" the guard demanded, grabbing the old man by the shoulder.

"Nothing, captain. I said nothing."

The captain wiped his brow with a dirty cloth. "Next!"

Rovann stepped forward.

"What's your business in Tyrlindon?" asked the captain.

"If I told you that I'd have to kill you."

The captain looked up and his bearded face broke into a smile. "My lord!"

Rovann laughed and clapped the captain on the shoulder. "Captain Turner, you old bastard. You look as if you've seen a ghost!"

"Just a little surprised is all. You've caught us at a bad time, seems the whole of Tyrlinshire wants to come into the city today."

"So I see. It's not market day, is it?"

"Makes no difference. Folks don't trust the other shires no more. They'll only sell their stuff in Tyrlindon. Makes our job next to impossible, I can tell you."

"Right. Then I'd better let you get back to it."

The captain jerked his chin at Maegwin and Leo. "Who've you got with you, my lord?"

"This is Maegwin de Romily and Leo March," Rovann said. "I will vouch for them."

Captain Turner's eyes narrowed on Maegwin and Leo, assessing their threat. Maegwin held the captain's gaze but Leo squirmed, looking nervous.

At last, the captain nodded, "Welcome home, my lord."

As they passed under the lintel of the gates, Maegwin noticed words carved into the stone. *The Outer Darkness.*

"What does that mean?" she asked Rovann.

Rovann glanced up. "Queen Sophia, who built Tyrlindon, was something of a scholar. She designed the city so that each level mirrors one of the Seven Realms. You will see what I mean as we move through the city."

There was a sudden commotion ahead.

"Out of my way! I have urgent business at the gate!"

A fat man dressed in opulent clothes was pushing impatiently through the crowd. Two burly guards walked by the fat man's side and Maegwin guessed he was a merchant. "Make way!" he bellowed as he and his men shoved people aside.

Before Maegwin could move, she found herself face to face with one of the guards. He scowled, pulling the scar that crossed his face into a grotesque kind of smile. "You deaf? Move it, bitch!"

He grabbed Maegwin's shoulder and shoved her back. Maegwin's mind went blank. All thought ceased. She grabbed the guard's arm and twisted it savagely up his back. She closed the fingers of her left hand around the guard's throat and squeezed, grunting with effort. The guard gurgled, flailing at her with his free arm.

Nearby, someone was shrieking in alarm. The man's skin felt hot and sweaty beneath her fingers. His windpipe lay just below the surface. It would be so easy to press harder, just a little harder, see his eyes bulge, his tongue stick out, the pulse in his temple get slower and slower...

Something ripped her hand from the man's throat. Strong arms clamped around her chest, dragging her backward. She spun and found herself face to face with Rovann. He grabbed her chin in one hand, staring at her intently. Something brushed across her thoughts and reason reasserted itself.

Pulling in a shuddering breath, Maegwin looked around. The guard had crumpled to his knees and was busy dry-retching into the dirt. The merchant gestured wildly.

"Arrest this woman! She's a lunatic!"

Rovann grabbed Maegwin's elbow and propelled her

through the crowd, Leo following, wide-eyed, with the horses. Rovann was mumbling under his breath and the crowd closed behind them, seeming to forget their presence.

"Where did she go?" the merchant bellowed. "Did anybody see where she went?"

Maegwin hung her head, filling with shame. Yet beneath the shame lay something else: a bleak, savage satisfaction. She glanced at Rovann. He stared straight ahead, his face set in an unreadable mask. Even Leo seemed rattled, leading the horses with a grim look on his freckled face.

Soon, the stress of fighting through Tyrlindon's streets drove all other thoughts from her mind. Shops stocking every kind of commodity lined the streets: tanned hides from Mallyn, worked metal implements from Silverport. From Tyrlindon's blacksmiths came weapons: swords, axes, crossbows, halberds and armor in a hundred different styles. From Talshire came expensive clothes cut in the latest court fashions. From the north came amber jewelry, dried herbs in bunches, leather boots in all shapes and sizes. Cattle pens had been erected and noisy auctions were taking place selling pigs, horses, cattle and squawking chickens by the basketful.

This meant there was only a tiny strip left for walking, making the crowd move at a slow, infuriating trickle. The sounds, sights and smells were almost overwhelming. Maegwin longed for the cool halls of her temple.

It seemed an age until they reached the second gate. As they passed under the thick arch, Maegwin read the inscription carved there.

The Realm of Air.

The second level of the city was more spacious than the first. Instead of the endless rows of shops and stalls, here there were inns and tall, shabby houses. Sweat dripped down her back and her heart thumped as they moved deeper into the city. Her thoughts kept drifting to her impending meeting with the king. *Once we reach the palace, will I find myself thrown into a cell?*

She was a little surprised when Rovann turned into a narrow, cobbled street that twisted up the hill. Modest dwellings and alehouses lined its sides. At the top they came upon a large brick and timber building with a courtyard and stable block at the back. A sign hung over the door, painted with the stylized image of a garish creature. It sat on a lily pad, wearing a wide grin. Beneath this image were inscribed the words *The Laughing Frog.*

Without a word of explanation, Rovann led Glynn to the stable block, leaving Maegwin and Leo to follow dumbly. A young lad with messy hair and scabs on his knees came to take the horses as they entered the courtyard.

"Afternoon, my lord," he said cheerfully. "Mistress said you might be coming in today. I'm afraid to say stabling fees have gone up though, sir. It'll cost you five gold pennies to stable the horses."

Rovann reached into his pocket and flicked a coin toward the boy. The boy's hand shot out and caught it in mid-air. "You'll get one silver penny as always, Tom, and be thankful I don't tell your mistress you're trying to swindle her customers."

Tom shrugged, tucking the coin into his pocket. "Can't blame a lad for trying, can you?"

Rovann unhitched the saddlebags and slung them over his shoulder, tousling Tom's hair as he passed over Glynn's reins. "Be careful of him today, the climb through the city has done nothing for his temper."

"Oh don't you worry, sir, Glynn and me have an understanding. Don't we boy?"

With a grunt, Rovann headed across the courtyard toward the inn's back door. As she followed, Maegwin glanced over her shoulder. Tom raised his hand toward the horses and muttered a few words. The girth straps slowly unclasped themselves, the saddles lifted off the horses' backs and drifted into the tack room.

A mage, she thought. *Or at least a student.*

Suppressing a shiver, she hurried after Rovann.

The interior of *The Laughing Frog* stank of spilled ale and sweat. The plain floorboards had been worn to a shine by the passing of many feet and they creaked as Maegwin and Leo followed Rovann inside.

In the dim light from the single window, Maegwin made out shabby tables filling the common room and a tiny bar tucked into the corner. The place was sparsely populated. At one table, a shaven-headed man sat staring into a cup as though he could see his future in its murky depths. By the door, a woman in a flowing red dress sat with her feet propped on a chair, smoking from a long pipe. A skinny dog sat by her chair.

Rovann took a vacant table at the back of the common room; a spot, Maegwin couldn't help noticing, that had good views of both the back and front doors. Leo made a great show of sweeping off his garish coat and hanging it on the back of a chair. He looked around the inn with interest, no doubt assessing its suitability for his next performance.

Maegwin took a seat and sat with her hands clasped in her lap, saying nothing. A nerve in her temple throbbed. Rovann offered no explanation as to why he'd brought them to this inn.

I thought I was supposed to meet the king? she thought. *Then why haven't we gone to the palace?*

"What can I get you?" said a plump, mousy-haired woman, as she made her way over from the bar. She had a brisk, business-like manner and Maegwin guessed she must be the owner.

"What's on the menu today, Tamya?" Rovann asked.

"Soup."

"What's in it?"

The woman shrugged as though this was a pointless question. "Cabbage. Potatoes. Maybe some carrots if they weren't too moldy when cook got in this morning."

Rovann raised an eyebrow. "That will have to do then, won't it? A round of ale as well."

"Ale?" said Leo. "A cheap, nasty drink if ever I tasted one! I will have wine, my good serving woman, the finest you have."

Tamya crossed her arms beneath her ample bosom. "Silverport Blossom will cost you two gold pennies."

Leo paled, a look of disappointment melting the smile on his face. "Really? It seems things in the capital are slightly more expensive than I'm used to. Ale all round then, my good woman."

Tamya turned away, sharing a quick look with the woman by the door as she made her way to the kitchen. Maegwin noticed the look and tensed. Rovann reached into the saddlebag and took out the piece of wood he'd been carving during their journey and began whittling it with his small knife.

What are we doing here? Maegwin wanted to ask. She wanted to lean over and shake some answers from him. Instead, she remained silent. She would be damned if she would play his games.

"A lovely inn, don't you think?" Leo said. "Ashamed as I am to admit such a fault, this is my first visit to the capital and I'm pleased to say I've not been disappointed so far. You see, I'm incredibly popular in Silverport and so spent many a year under the patronage of fine lords and ladies. If you're ever in the area I would recommend Lord Martin's hospitality. Now, there's a generous man who knows talent when he sees it! Why, he once paid me six silver sovereigns just to compose a message to his betrothed."

"Wonderful," Maegwin said. "Silverport, however, is three hundred leagues to the north. I'm unlikely ever to visit the place."

"Oh really?" Leo asked. "That's a shame, but then I suppose there is plenty in Tyrlindon to keep a lady busy for the rest of her life!"

Maegwin glanced at Rovann but he didn't look up from his carving. The piece of wood was slowly taking shape under his hands and Maegwin realized it was a woman. The figurine was exquisite, showing great skill. Maegwin opened her mouth to comment but then decided against it.

Tamya returned, expertly balancing three bowls of soup and three tankards of ale in the crux of her arms and deposited them on the table without spilling a drop.

"Will there be anything else?"

Rovann didn't seem to notice the innkeeper's presence so Maegwin answered, "No, thank you."

Tamya raise an eyebrow but didn't comment as she turned on her heel and strode behind the bar, yet Maegwin was sure she saw the innkeeper share a quick glance with the woman sitting by the door once more.

What's going on here? she asked herself. *Are these people planning to rob us?*

Leo sucked his broth off the spoon, showing a surprising lack of table manners for someone used to a lord's hall. In fact, it seemed to Maegwin that he ate as though he hadn't had a meal in days. Maegwin found she suddenly wasn't hungry and swirled the contents of her bowl whilst surreptitiously watching the patrons of the inn.

The large man in the corner had downed his drink and was waving the innkeeper over for more. Maegwin could just about hear his rumbling voice.

"I'll pay next week, Tamya. You know I'm good for it."

"I don't give two shits what you're good for. You will pay now or get nothing."

The man's hand tightened around his cup. "Fine. Give me that piss-water from Mandrake then. Anything to drown this gods-cursed headache." He reached into his pocket and tossed a copper penny onto the table where it spun before slowly coming to a halt.

Tamya scooped up the coin and moved off without a word, returning a minute later to slap down a new tankard on the man's table. As if sensing she was watching him, the man's gaze flicked up to meet Maegwin's and she quickly looked down at her bowl.

The door suddenly swung open and a small, cloak-wrapped figure entered. The inn's patrons looked up, marking the newcomer's presence. The newcomer nodded to the woman in the red dress who rose to her feet and pushed the door shut behind the stranger, throwing the bolt across with a clank that sounded oddly final. The skinny dog raced to the back door and lay across it, blocking any escape that way. The shaven-headed man cursed and shoved his chair back with a scrape, surging to his feet as if looking for a fight.

"Rovann," Maegwin breathed in warning.

Rovann spoke directly to Leo. "Tamya will take you upstairs to your room. You will stay there until I tell you otherwise. You will not come down despite what you might hear. You will not try to listen. I will know if you do. Is that clear?" Rovann's voice was like steel, sharp and dangerous.

Leo looked from Rovann to Maegwin and back again, clearly frightened. After a moment in which his mouth worked uselessly he said, "Yes. Of course."

He scrambled to his feet and followed Tamya, casting a nervous look behind as he went up the stairs.

Maegwin's heart thumped against her ribs. What was going on here?

The newcomer unwrapped the cloak to reveal a small, short-haired woman with olive skin and dark eyes. Her left wrist ended in a puckered stump, marking her out as a thief. Her eyes fixed on Rovann. "It's ready."

Rovann climbed to his feet, sending his chair toppling over backward. Maegwin jumped. The shaven-headed man squared up to Rovann. He was a head taller than Rovann and the muscles on his arms looked like twisted tree roots, gnarled and wiry.

Rovann grinned suddenly. "Don't get so close, Falwin. Your breath could stun a horse!"

"I'll stun you if you don't watch that tongue of yours," the man growled. "Stone me, I would have thought you'd learned courtesy by now."

"Sorry, Falwin, on that score I'm afraid I'm a lost cause."

The big man grinned, revealing large teeth like granite blocks. He clapped Rovann on the shoulder and then crushed him into a bear hug.

"Fates curse you, you young pup, but it's good to see you home!"

Rovann laughed. "You wouldn't believe how much I've missed your ugly face, Falwin."

The woman in the red dress sidled over and Rovann turned to meet her approach. "Tiria!" he exclaimed as she folded him into a warm embrace. "I wasn't sure you got my message."

Tiria pushed Rovann to arm's length, hands on his shoulders whilst she examined him. "We didn't get your message but Syrie kept a constant watch on the astral and saw you coming down the Kingsroad."

Rovann nodded, turning to the small, dark-haired woman. "Thanks for your vigilance, Syrie."

The small woman inclined her head gravely. Suddenly seeming to remember himself, Rovann turned to Maegwin. "I thought my mission was a failure for a while there. Hounsey had done a pretty good job of covering his tracks, damn the man to the seventh hell. But I think we might have him at last. We have a witness who might be able to tell us exactly what Hounsey is planning."

All the eyes in the room flicked in Maegwin's direction and she wanted to duck her head to avoid those hard, stern gazes.

"About time," growled Falwin. "I'm tired of that snake's games. He might be an able commander but a commander turned renegade needs to be amputated like a limb gone bad. Who is your companion, Rovann? I've been nearly choking with the desire to ask since you came through the door."

Maegwin lifted her chin and stepped forward, her boots creaking on the wooden floorboards. "My name is Maegwin de Romily, priestess of Sho-La."

"And what have you got to do with Lord Cedric Hounsey?" Falwin asked.

"I killed his son."

Falwin swore under his breath. "Burn the gods, Rovann! I hope you know what you're doing. If Hounsey is loyal after all, you have just single-handedly turned him into a rebel."

"You didn't see what had been done to that temple, Falwin. There are layers of betrayal here, I can feel it. The Songmaker is involved somehow. Have you had word of what happened in Angard?"

Tiria nodded. "Refugees are arriving daily. The king has ordered the Mallyn garrison to go to the town's aid." She approached Maegwin and held out her hand. She was a large-boned woman with bushy brown hair and eyes nestled in laughter lines.

"My name is Tiria de Jarn, Third of the Council of Mages. Welcome to Tyrlindon and to my daughter's inn. Let me introduce the others. This is Falwin, Second of the Council of Mages and military advisor to His Majesty, King William. This is Syrie, Fourth of the Council of Mages and first disciple of the Eorthe. You already know Rovann, the Lord First."

Maegwin staggered, catching herself on a nearby table. Had she heard right? The Lord First? Rovann? *He is no king's messenger,* she thought as a strange feeling of betrayal stole through her chest. *He's the King's Mage, and I suspected nothing. Idiot! You have fallen into a nest of vipers. Better to have hanged on the gallows!*

The sudden urge to flee was so powerful that Maegwin rocked onto the balls of her feet. She glanced at Rovann and was surprised at how hurt she felt that he had not told her the truth. *What did you expect?* she admonished herself. *You are not friends. You barely know him. You are just a criminal who might prove momentarily useful.*

"What do you want from me?" she whispered.

"I apologize for the secrecy," Tiria said. "But until we're sure of you, it is unsafe to take you to the palace and we couldn't reveal ourselves until Syrie completed the wards. We can't risk any finding out what we do here today. "

Syrie frowned at Tiria. "Any guests tonight?"

"One. The minstrel who arrived with the Lord First but Tamya will make sure he stays in his room and I've placed a ward to prevent eavesdropping."

Syrie nodded. "Good. He'll be waiting. Let's get started."

Syrie strode to the center of the room and pushed back some tables so there was a clear space around her. Her lips began to move and after a moment Maegwin could hear faint sounds like chanting in a deep, subterranean language. A green glow formed in the small woman's eyes, growing in intensity as her chant grew stronger. The green light flared brightly before fading away as the chant fell silent.

A wind grabbed Maegwin's hair and sent it swirling across her face. It was as though a door had opened, carrying in the scent of wet earth and leaf mold. When she brushed her hair from her eyes, she realized another figure now stood in the room. A man, tall and thin, dressed as a woodsman in a long green cloak and gray tunic.

King William, ruler of Amaury, turned slowly and stared at Maegwin. He was nicknamed The Raven King and Macgwin realized why. His hair and beard were black and glossy. His sharp nose echoed the beak of his namesake and his mouth was set in a tight, flat line. He was of a height with Rovann but other than that, the two men seemed complete opposites, one with the blond hair and blue eyes of the north, the other the dusky coloring of the lowlands.

The king studied Maegwin intently, his face expressionless.

"What is your name?"

Maegwin lifted her chin, met the king's gaze. "Maegwin de Romily, priestess of the first order, follower of the Ko-Shin teachings of Sho-La."

The king nodded as if he had known this all along. "You must be wondering why I brought you here."

"I don't understand what you want with me."

"You will. Sit."

Maegwin sank into a chair and waited. The King and Rovann exchanged a long look before Rovann took a seat next to hers and the king one opposite. The rest of the Council took seats around the room, their expressions wary.

"I wish to talk about your crime," said King William. "In Mallyn you were found guilty of the murders of Lord Meryk Hounsey and three of his retainers. Is this correct?"

Defiance welled up inside Maegwin as she thought of the lordling and his hired thugs. A hot anger began to simmer in her stomach. "I never denied it," she said, unable to keep an edge out of her voice, despite whom she was addressing. "And I never fought your authorities when they took me away. And if I had my time over I'd do the same again."

The king clasped his hands in front of him and regarded her sternly. "Lord Meryk's father is a very powerful man. He wants justice for his son's murder. He says you attacked his son without provocation and deserve the noose. Is his story correct, Maegwin of Sho-La? Do you deserve to hang?"

"I've never taken a life when it was undeserved. Sho-La teaches mercy and compassion for one's enemies. But She also teaches that a debt must be repaid. A life for a life."

"And whose life did Meryk Hounsey's pay for?"

Maegwin hesitated. She had never discussed what had happened at the temple that day. Nobody had asked for her tale; the sheriff who arrested her, the judge in Mallyn, even Rovann. But now, William, King of Amaury, was asking for her side of the story. Memories stabbed at her. She didn't want to remember.

"Why do you care?" she asked. "What is it you think I have?"

"Information. Lord Cedric Hounsey says the temple on his lands burned down because of a cooking fire. He says his son Meryk was trying to save the temple when he was attacked. I don't believe him. I believe Cedric Hounsey to be a traitor who is working for the Songmaker. I think you can prove that. So I ask again, whose lives did Meryk Hounsey's pay for?"

"My order," she whispered at last. "My sisters. There were twenty of us. He burned them alive."

Rovann swore under his breath. Falwin cursed angrily. King William's face was as expressionless as stone. At last, he said, "Do you have any evidence to substantiate your claim?"

"I don't lie. I know what I saw."

"I must know if I am betrayed," the king said almost to himself. He looked up and his deep eyes bored into Maegwin. "Will you consent to a Sharing?"

The clouds outside had broken and the sun was streaming through the window directly onto Maegwin's face. Even so, she felt suddenly cold. "Do I have a choice?"

King William smiled wryly. "Perhaps not. Rovann will guide your mind into the Sharing. I will watch your thoughts."

Rovann pulled his chair forward so he was in touching distance of Maegwin and King William. He gently clasped Maegwin's hand then the king's. "Close your eyes."

Maegwin let her eyelids close. Her breathing quickened.

She did not like the feeling of vulnerability that swept over her. She was totally at the mercy of these two men, these strangers.

"Take us back to that day, Maegwin," Rovann ordered softly.

Maegwin dug deep into her mind, seeking. She was surprised at how easily the memories came, despite her efforts to bury them. They had lurked just below the surface, ready to leap out and grab her...

It was a hot day. The sky was clear and the leaves on the trees hung limp in the humid air. Maegwin came to a halt and leaned with her hands on her knees, trying to catch her breath. The Ko-Shin exercises had been more difficult this morning, perhaps because her mind was on her return to the temple. She had been on retreat for three days: just herself, the woods and the glory of Sho-La. But now it was time to return. She wiped sweat from her brow. The sun was low in the sky, almost evening.

She set off toward home and soon found herself jogging into the network of cultivated plots that surrounded the temple complex. A strange smell wafted through the turgid air. Maegwin came to a halt, feeling uneasy. She recognized the smell: burning. The crackle of flames carried on the breeze and with it the unmistakable sound of screaming.

Fear trickling through her veins, Maegwin ran. She pelted through the trees, careering over the vegetables plots, ducking under low hanging branches, splashing through puddles left by the recent rains. All the while, the smell of burning grew stronger and the screaming grew louder. She burst into the temple's clearing and skidded to a halt.

A scene of chaos met her eyes. Armed men filled the clearing. Flames licked from the temple windows. Thick wooden boards had been nailed across the temple door.

From the other side came the desperate clamor of people trying to escape. The men stood around the clearing, watching with dispassionate faces.

Maegwin stumbled, staggered by the sight. She hurled herself at the door, grasped a board and hauled with all her strength. One of the men grabbed her hair and yanked her back. She smashed her elbow into his face and ran back to the door. She had to get the boards off. She had get that door open. Her sisters needed her.

Something crashed into the back of her skull and her sight went black, the ground rushing up to meet her with a crack. She was dragged away from the burning building. Voices shouted in anger.

"You said they were all inside!"

"I thought they were! How was I to know one of them was still in the forest?"

"Because that's what I pay you for!"

"This one won't be no trouble. Slit her throat and be done with it. Why are you so worried?"

"Because, you gods-cursed fool, how do we know there aren't more of them still free? There must be no witnesses. My father will be furious!"

Maegwin's sight returned. She was lying in the middle of the clearing with a large man and a youth standing over her. The youth wore expensive sky-blue clothes and had shoulder-length black hair that had been intricately styled. He glanced at Maegwin. "Take care of her."

The guard drew his sword and advanced on Maegwin. The light from the flames made the blade glow amber in the gathering dusk. As the guard stooped over her, Maegwin rolled out from his shadow and jumped to her feet. In a fluid movement, she stepped in close and ripped the sword from his grasp. Two-handed, she slashed the blade across the man's belly. His hands flew to his mid-riff to try to hold in the gray coil of intestines that slithered from the wound.

The young lord spun around and backhanded Maegwin so hard she went sprawling into the dirt, the sword flying out of her hand.

"Bitch!" the lord shouted. "You will pay for that!" His eyes were full of hatred.

He drew his sword with a metallic ring and strode toward her. He swung the sword but as the blade descended, Maegwin rolled to her feet, snatched the fallen sword and punched it into the lord's heart. A gout of blood erupted from the lord's mouth and he stared in surprise at the sword sticking out of his chest. Then his legs gave way and he toppled into the dirt where he lay still.

Maegwin turned back to the burning temple. She must save her sisters. But the rest of the lord's men had recovered from their initial surprise. It took them only a few strides to reach her. The last thing she remembered before they beat her senseless was stabbing two more of them, then the sound of horses and the sight of the sheriff and his men riding into the clearing.

Back in the common room of *The Laughing Frog*, Maegwin gasped at the sudden pain of the memory. She jerked and Rovann tightened his grip on her hand.

Steady.

She felt the king's presence like something over her shoulder she couldn't quite see. *Why?* he asked. *What did the priestesses know?*

Maegwin delved deeper into her memory, to a time a week or so before the fire…

It was evening. Maegwin, Miriel and Tarina had been out harvesting lilies for the High Priestess's bedchamber.

The forest was still, peaceful, with only the occasional rustle of a creature in the undergrowth to disturb the stillness.

They walked in companionable silence, delighting in the beauty of Sho-La's creation and each other's company. They did not hurry, even though it was close to Vespers, but took the long route that wound through the heart of the forest, through glades thick with foxgloves and the lazy drone of bees.

Eventually the path wandered through a broad meadow with a long, low building standing at one end. It was one of Lord Hounsey's hunting lodges; small and rarely used. But this time as they approached, Maegwin noticed a light burning at a window and two horses tethered outside. Not wishing to encounter anyone, Maegwin and her companions skirted the meadow and took a trail that led them along a high hedge and round the back of the lodge. Voices came from beyond the hedge: two people talking on the porch.

"And I will get what was promised?"

"When you have fulfilled your part of the bargain."

The second voice was cold and flat. Despite her misgivings, Maegwin crept closer to the hedge and peered through its tangled branches.

Lord Cedric Hounsey stood on the veranda. He was a broad man beyond his middle years with a fringe of iron-gray hair and a beard combed into a point. Maegwin knew him by reputation only: a stern man, quick to temper and long to hold grudges. Maegwin didn't recognize the second man but he had a pinched, arrogant expression and wore a silver and ruby ring that marked him as a mage.

"Everything is in place," said Lord Hounsey. "My men are in position. We only await the Songmaker's command."

The mage nodded curtly. "You are certain you have not

been infiltrated? I've heard rumors that the Council has been sniffing round you."

Cedric Hounsey crossed his arms over his chest, looking unimpressed at this observation. "You worry like an old woman, Kaspat, do you know that? The Council are self-absorbed fools who see nothing beyond the ends of their own noses. And if they do suspect? What can they do? I have twenty thousand men waiting in the Vallen Hills. Men, I might add, that are loyal to me alone. You would do well to remember that, mage."

There was a threat implicit in the lord's voice. The mage held out his hands. "Fine. I take your word for it." He grinned suddenly, looking like a mischievous child. "Ah! Soon we will capture ourselves a most valuable prize." A twig snapped and the mage looked up, directly at the place where Maegwin crouched behind the hedge. "Who's there?" he demanded.

Maegwin scrambled back and together she, Miriel, and Tarina ran into the woods. They veered off the path and took to the cover of the thick forest. After a while, they stopped and listened. There was no sound of pursuit. They ran all the way back to the temple and went straight to the High Priestess to report what they had heard. But over the next few days nothing happened and Maegwin thought Lord Hounsey hadn't realized who had overheard his plans.

Now, as the memory tore through her like a million shards of broken glass, she realized she had been terribly, terribly wrong.

"That's enough," Rovann said. "Come with me."

The temple dwindled into the distance and Maegwin rose up, up, through the clear sky. She opened her eyes. Sunlight was streaming through the window. The Sharing had seemed to last an eternity, but the sun had hardly moved in the sky.

"Now I understand," King William growled. "You have been greatly wronged, Maegwin of Sho-La. Hounsey has been a traitor all along. What evil he has wrought—"

"The bastard has over a week's head start on us," Falwin said. "Whatever he was planning could be well under way by now."

"Why didn't our spies report this?" Tiria said, leaning her elbows on the table. "It's not possible to move twenty thousand troops in secret."

"Tiria's right," Falwin agreed. "Hounsey is a bragging idiot. He couldn't mobilize his army without us finding out. The logistics make it next to impossible."

"Not for an adept of the Eorthe," Syrie said quietly. The small woman had taken a seat on the far side of the room and although her voice was soft, it commanded everyone's attention. She scratched absently at the stump of her wrist, her eyes fixed on King William. "They could move those troops undetected if they didn't move them overland. If they moved them *under* it."

Silence filled the room as Syrie's words sank in.

"She's right," Rovann said after a moment. "There are only a handful of Eorthic adepts in Amaury. If one has gone over to the Songmaker, we are in trouble."

King William straightened, looking around at his advisors. "Right. That's enough for me. I'll see Hounsey dead before I let him march his army on Tyrlindon. Rovann, tomorrow morning you will take a squadron of soldiers and ride for the Highhold. Falwin and Syrie will accompany you. You will carry a warrant for Hounsey's arrest and a writ ceding all Hounsey lands to the crown. His commanders will be offered pardons if they agree to bring the army over to my control. In the meantime I will send units south and east to secure the Hounsey garrisons at Mallyn and Waterguard."

"So, we're making our move at last, eh?" Falwin said, sounding satisfied. "Good. I'm tired of sitting on my backside listening to rumors. We'll arrest him, Your Majesty, or die in the attempt."

"I'd rather it didn't come to that," the king said dryly. "If you find yourselves in a fight, you are to retreat. Do not engage. Is that clear?"

"We might have no choice if Hounsey has as many men as he claims."

"Syrie can get you out through the Eorthe if it comes to that."

Falwin shuddered. "Don't you worry, I'll make sure it won't come to that. Crawling through the dark with mud plugging up every orifice? No, thank you. I'll take my chances above ground."

Syrie raised an eyebrow but didn't deign to comment.

"What about Maegwin?" Rovann asked suddenly. "She was sentenced to death in Mallyn but it's obvious that her trial was a farce. We know the truth of it now, Your Majesty. I ask that she be pardoned."

Maegwin went very still, feeling lightheaded with tension. *Please,* she wanted to beg. *I have so much to do. I need to live.*

King William's eyes fixed on her for a moment and then turned to Rovann. "She still killed those men, Rovann. Am I to let that go unpunished?"

"Her actions came from self-defense. Hounsey's men attacked her first, remember. Hasn't she been punished already? She was beaten, starved and hanged, on the word of a traitor. She saved my life in Angard and has remained true to her word when she could have tried to run many times. I ask for clemency, Your Majesty."

"And you would vouch for her? You feel she poses no danger to the kingdom?"

Rovann glanced at Maegwin and she saw doubt in his gaze. *He doesn't trust me,* she thought. *And who can blame him? He's remembering my attack on that merchant's guard and that woman in Angard, attacks I can't even explain myself. He's wondering if he can truthfully tell the king what he wants to hear.*

Rovann opened his mouth to speak and then closed it again. A struggle seemed to be going on inside him. Finally he said, "Yes, I will vouch for her."

The king nodded. "It seems you have won over my King's Mage, Maegwin of Sho-La. You are pardoned and are free to leave. What do you wish to do?"

Will you abandon your vengeance?

Maegwin's heart began to thud. This was her chance. Her chance to face Hounsey and make him pay for everything he'd done to her. Her answer spilled out before she even thought about it. "I will go with Rovann, Your Majesty."

Rovann started, fixing her with an enquiring look. The king nodded. "Very well. After all, you have earned the right to see Hounsey brought to justice. Get whatever rest you can. You leave at first light."

Chapter Six

The gate swung shut with a clang and Rovann's feet crunched on the gravel path as he walked. The leaves of the trees swished gently in the wind. From somewhere came the snip-snip of shears as one of the gardeners went about their business but otherwise all was silent. Nobody else was abroad in the Remembrance Garden. It was just as well. Rovann wished to be alone with his dead.

His feet took him past tall trees marking the resting places of people many long years gone, to the furthest part of the garden where the trees were little more than saplings. Small mounds marked the graves. There were many. Too many. How many more would be added before this ended?

Rovann approached a rowan, no taller than he was, and stopped. Its smooth gray bark had the sheen of pressed silk and the young green leaves seemed full of exuberant life, reveling in the evening sunlight. When the tree was large enough a name would be carved into the trunk but Rovann didn't need any label to know who lay here.

"Istra."

He went down on his knees and ran his hands over the grass. Its vitality tingled in his fingertips, but beneath lay only bones and dust. Istra was long gone.

Gone where? The thought came unbidden to his mind. *The Outer Darkness?*

His hands curled into fists as he pushed the thought away. He would not go down that path. Not here, not now. The wind swirled and the branches of Istra's rowan rattled. The little tree bent but held firm. It was strong. It would be a mighty tree one day. Gently Rovann leaned forward and kissed the smooth bark. Closing his eyes, he uttered a prayer he had said a hundred times, more in hope than conviction.

"May the Light take you and keep you, my love."

Then he stood and moved on.

As he walked the winding paths, he passed many trees: holly, ash, oak, lime, sycamore; all marking the graves of friends, comrades, colleagues. Good people who died in a struggle not of their choosing.

How many more? he thought. *How many?*

Before him he saw a circle of trees set apart from the others. The trunks were big enough to have names carved into them. The largest and nearest of the trees bore an inscription that read: *Leonardo Sottra, King's Mage and First of the Council of Mages. Now One with the Light.* The smaller trees also carried the Sottra name: Rhea, Kari, Marissa. Leonardo's wife and daughters.

"Why did you go, Leonardo?" Rovann asked the tree above his friend's grave. "You were a better King's Mage than I. They shouldn't have chosen me. I don't want this power, this burden. I've never wanted it."

Yet it's yours, he said to himself. *Who else is there? It's your duty.*

"Have you seen Istra?" he blurted. "Do you and she walk together in the Light? Or is she...is she..."

He squeezed his eyes shut. Opened them again. "A reckoning is coming, Leonardo. I can feel it. The Song-maker meddles with the powers of Chaos. The king is sending me to arrest Cedric Hounsey but I don't think it will be enough. I suspect more to this than a rebel lord hungry for power. And then there's Maegwin. The angels want her to serve them but sometimes she scares me, Leonardo. I see something in her eyes at times, something unsettling. What would you do, Leonardo? Would you trust her?"

Rovann's eyes settled on the silver and ruby ring on the index finger of his right hand. The seal of the King's Mage. His hand curled into a fist around it. The wind gusted suddenly and the leaves whispered, sounding like a thousand tiny voices.

Why have you come? the trees seemed to whisper. *You have no cause to visit the innocent. You, who are guilty of so much.*

Rovann bowed his head and felt hot tears stinging the back of his eyes. He had much to pay for. Istra. Leonardo Sottra. Sandford Moor. On the road to Tyrlindon Leo had inadvertently used Rovann's nickname. *The Slayer of Sandford Moor.* In his dreams, Rovann still heard the screaming.

The sun was beginning to sink and bolts of orange light shone through the branches. The snip-snip of the shears came closer and the gardener was humming an old ditty. Rovann turned on his heel, strode down the path and out through the metal gate, leaving his dead behind.

The streets of Tyrlindon were still busy as it was the time when many businesses were shutting up for the night. He picked his way through the Weavers' Quarter and across Third Market Row until he arrived back at *The Laughing Frog.* The common room was filled with hungry workers and

Tamya was scuttling about, trying to keep up with demand. In one corner, Leo was diligently tuning his lute. He looked up as the door swung open and raised a hand in greeting. Rovann smiled briefly then made his way up the creaking stairs to a door at the end of the corridor. He hesitated only momentarily before he knocked.

"Come in," came the call from the other side.

Maegwin sat by the window gazing out at the street below. No candles had been lit and shadows filled the room. Rovann took a few steps then stopped. He was suddenly unsure of why he'd come.

"Your people don't trust me," Maegwin said. "Tamya has been keeping an eye on my movements all afternoon."

"These are dangerous times. The king will take such precautions until he's sure of you."

Maegwin turned to look at him. "The king gave me a pardon. In case you've forgotten, I'm a free woman. I can walk out of this inn and go wherever I choose and there isn't a damn thing you could do about it."

"So, why don't you?"

"Why don't I what?"

"Leave. Go wherever you like."

Maegwin opened her mouth but no words came out. She seemed to be struggling with a realization. "Where would I go?" she said at last. "My sisters are dead. My home burned to the ground. You and Leo are my only acquaintances in all the world." She laughed shrilly. "Blessed Mother, what does that say for my life? A down-and-out minstrel and the Lord First of the Council of Mages! Could I have picked two more disparate companions?"

Rovann noticed she'd washed and combed her hair so it fell around her shoulders like a red-gold veil. A frown pinched the space between her eyebrows as she watched him.

"Leo has taken quite a shine to you," Rovann said. "I'm sure he'd be glad of your company here in Tyrlindon. Or, if you wish it, there are many temples and religious orders throughout the city. I'm sure one of them would welcome you—"

She snorted a laugh. "You're not very subtle, King's Mage. Why don't you just say it? 'I don't want you to come with me, Maegwin.'"

Rovann glanced at the window and then back at her face. In the darkness, her green eyes seemed to shine. "My mission will be dangerous. I can't guarantee your safety—"

"I'm not asking you to. All I ask is for you let me see Hounsey face justice."

It was there again, Rovann noticed. That stain, deep in her eyes. He sighed. "The king gave you leave to accompany me. I can't stop you from coming."

"No, you can't." She rose and took a step toward him, standing so close he could have reached out and touched her. "Why didn't you tell me you are the King's Mage? All that time you played the simple messenger when the truth was wholly different."

Rovann hesitated. How could he tell her the truth? *Because I wanted to be just me! Not the King's Mage. Not First of the Council. Not the Slayer of Sandford Moor. Just Rovann. King's messenger.*

"It wasn't safe to reveal my identity."

"It makes sense now. I wondered why you were happy to escort a convicted criminal to Tyrlindon unaided. But you never had anything to fear, did you? You could have killed me with a word if you chose. Just like you could have killed the mage in Angard and stopped the mage storm."

Rovann didn't like the accusation in her voice. *Why didn't you save the town? Why didn't you use your power?* "If I had acted to save Angard, the Songmaker would have recognized me and sent a conflagration that would have killed everyone. I made the only choice I could."

She stepped closer, so close her breath tickled his neck. She laid a hand against his chest. "Even in the temple we heard stories about the terrible power of the King's Mage. Is everything they say about you true? What you did at Sandford Moor?"

For a second he was tempted to tell her. He longed to spill out every detail of that day, every appalling thing he'd done. He wanted to make her understand. But he couldn't. Gently, he lifted her hand from his chest.

"We leave at first light. Be ready."

"I'll be ready."

Rovann nodded. "Goodnight, Maegwin."

"Goodnight, my Lord First."

Rovann made his way down the stairs. In the common room, Leo was performing a bawdy song about a circus troupe who vowed to seduce all seventeen of a king's daughters. He was being largely ignored by the patrons but it didn't seem to put him off. Rovann had to admit the minstrel had a decent singing voice.

Rovann ducked out the back door into the stable yard. Tom had Glynn saddled and ready. He tossed the boy a coin as he swung up into the saddle and smiled as Tom waved his hands to make the coin disappear. The boy would soon be ready to enroll on the first year in the college. He imagined Tamya would not be pleased to lose yet another groom to her mother's classes.

Rovann nudged Glynn into a trot up the hill toward the center of Tyrlindon. It was dark by the time he reached the topmost level. Passing under the lintel which read *The One Light*, he entered an area of vast estates and formal gardens. He weaved his way through the wide, cobbled streets until he came to a walled compound at the very heart of Tyrlindon: the royal enclave. Guards were stationed atop the high wall and across the heavy gates. Rovann pulled down his hood as he approached and the guards let him through without comment.

Two buildings filled the royal enclave: the huge, many turreted edifice of the royal palace, and the long, simple building of the College of Mages. Rovann made for the rune-carved doors of the College. A servant came rushing to greet him.

"Welcome home, my Lord First."

Rovann inclined his head then swung down from Glynn's back, his feet crunching on the gravel driveway. "Is the Council ready?"

The woman bobbed a curtsey, "They await your pleasure in the meeting hall, my lord."

Rovann handed over Glynn's reins. "Very good. Take care of my horse. I'll need him ready for a long journey at first light. Use an Eorthic chant to rest him if needed."

"Yes, my Lord First."

Rovann strode up the steps and into the echoing corridors of the College. It was late and classes had finished for the day so the place was more deserted than it might be, for which Rovann was grateful. The marble floor shone in the lamplight and countless paintings of past Lord Firsts looked down on him as he made his way through the college. As he passed the dining hall he caught the usual chatter and commotion coming from within: students eating, talking, arguing, laughing.

Enjoy this time while you can, Rovann told them silently. *You might soon find yourselves fighting for your lives.*

Turning into a long gallery, Rovann saw a group of students huddled together, peering round the corner into the next corridor. They had their backs to Rovann and hadn't seen him but there was a lot of sniggering and giggling going on.

Rovann moved up behind them. Craning his neck, Rovann saw something moving down the corridor. It had the shape of a person but no substance or color. A conjuration of Air. One of the students had her face screwed up in concentration as she controlled the conjuration. The apparition moved to a door sporting a brass plaque that read, *Administrator Sindra.* The apparition knocked on the door before dissolving into nothing. The door opened and Administrator Sindra looked out.

"Yes? What is it?"

Seeing no one, she looked both ways down the corridor before crying, "Bloody first years!" and slamming the door with a thud.

The students broke into fits of hysterical laugher.

Rovann crossed his arms over his chest. "That joke was old even when I was a student."

The students jumped and spun to face Rovann. Recognizing him, the color drained from their faces.

"My...my Lord First," stammered one young man. "I... we...um...that is..."

Rovann placed his hands on his hips and the students flinched. "Could one of you explain to me what is so funny about playing jokes on Administrator Sindra?"

The students looked so scared Rovann thought they might faint. A grin pulled at the corners his mouth as he remembered the time Leonardo Sottra had caught him and some others trying to turn Deacon Ambrose's soup into dishwater. "Sindra always let's her wards lapse or she'd sense your sorcery from ten paces away. Try it on Lady Fourth, Syrie. Then I'll be impressed."

He strode off, knowing this would be all around the first year by morning. *The Lord First spoke to us! Can you believe it? The Lord First!*

The hub of the College of Mages was the meeting hall. The bright, circular room was taken up by a big round table that was hollow in the middle to leave desks for clerks and secretaries to take minutes, although tonight they sat empty. The same could not be said for the seats around the table. They were already full, the only vacancy being Rovann's own chair which sat in the place of honor at the eastern-most point of the circle.

Fifty pairs of eyes turned to watch as he strode to his seat. Men and women of all ages, from all areas of Amaury were arrayed before him. Rovann saw the long, thin braids of Chalcon, the elaborate head-dresses of Blackhowe, the flowing robes of Silverport. Around him, Rovann felt the flow of muted power.

Tiria, seated on Rovann's left, smiled warmly, her brown hair bouncing as she nodded a greeting. On his other side, Falwin sat with his arms crossed, scowling fiercely enough to curdle milk. His shaved scalp gleamed in the lamp light.

"You look like I feel," Falwin said. "Permission to cast a silence charm over the lot of them, Lord First?"

"We've not said anything about Hounsey," Tiria said, ignoring Falwin's comment, "but they know something's going on from the soldiers getting ready in the training yard. We need to tread carefully here."

Rovann heard Tiria's unspoken warning. *Not everyone can be trusted.*

Rovann resisted the urge to sigh. How he hated politics. He settled into his seat, clasping his hands on the table in front of him, and waited for the gathering to fall silent. He put the ring of authority into his voice. "I've heard rumors that the Eorthe is troubled. Do we know what this means?"

His question was directed at Syrie who sat sullenly in her chair. She frowned then dug into her pocket and held up a shining piece of rock.

"Troubled? You could say that." She tossed the rock at Rovann who plucked it out of the air. It felt warm.

"What's this?"

"Limestone. But it's been aspected. Now it channels the Eorthe. Feel it."

Rovann concentrated, detecting a strange tingling coming from the rock. He closed his eyes. Almost immediately, he sensed the pull of the myriad lines of power crisscrossing the earth. The lines of Eorthic power formed a vast invisible net, covering the land. But something was wrong. Some of the lines were moving, gathering...

"Here," he said, opening his eyes. "A convergence, right here over Tyrlindon."

Syrie nodded, her dark eyes narrowing. "Just as I've been warning for months. The power of Earth does not lie. It can only mean the Songmaker is planning to attack Tyrlindon."

There was uproar.

"Preposterous!"

"Ridiculous!"

"Let him try!"

"It would be suicidal to attack the capital!"

Rovann let the wave of outrage wash over him. As it finally died down, he held up the small piece of limestone so it was clear for all to see. "I'm glad to see you all so passionate about Tyrlindon's defense, but let's look at the facts shall we? Our intelligence has hinted at the Songmaker planning something big for months. We've known this. Why else would he increase his attacks along the eastern border, other than to pull our attention in that direction? He hoped we'd take our eye off Tyrlindon—"

"Then he's a bloody idiot!" someone cried.

"Or over-ambitious," someone else answered. "Does he think we're stupid?"

"Not stupid, just naïve."

"Who's naïve? You calling me naïve?"

Rovann growled under his breath. The candles in the chandelier flared, sending out gouts of flame before dying back to normal. The mages glanced at Rovann in surprise, falling silent.

"Yes, perhaps the Songmaker is over-ambitious, perhaps he does underestimate Tyrlindon's defense, perhaps he does think us naïve. But there is one thing the Songmaker isn't: stupid. If he's planning to attack Tyrlindon, he would only do so if he thought he could succeed."

At the far end of the table, Lord Waldrun, a mage studying to become a Water adept, took a sip of wine from a goblet and gestured languidly at Rovann with it. "My Lord First, it seems to me that we are going over old ground. We've discussed this issue again and again. Yes, perhaps the Songmaker is planning an attack on Tyrlindon. What of it? As has already been stated, any attempt on Tyrlindon will fail. It is too heavily defended. The capital will be a rock that the Songmaker will smash himself against."

Rovann ground his teeth. He would love to tip that wine over Waldrun's handsome head. He challenged Rovann's authority at every turn. "Lord Waldrun, have you heard nothing? Eorthic power is being used here. The Songmaker is bending it out of its path. Do you comprehend the significance of this?"

"Of course I do," Waldrun said. "But this wouldn't be the first time the disciples of the Eorthe have been wrong. Only a year ago they mistook a mining operation in the Telyn Hills for a convergence. We went running up there, armed to the teeth, to be confronted by a band of frightened peasants. Study of the Eorthe is never an exact science, is it? And let's be honest, the Eorthic disciples worry worse than a bunch of old women."

Syrie surged to her feet, eyes glinting with anger. "Keep a civil tongue in your head, Lord Waldrun, lest I cut it out for you."

Waldrun's full lips quirked into a smile. Rovann groaned inwardly. Syrie did herself no favors when she lost her temper. The stump of her wrist marked her out as a former criminal and noblemen like Waldrun would forever gripe about having people like Syrie among the ranks of the Council.

"Cut my tongue out will you?" said Lord Waldrun. "Is that how things are done on the streets of Silverport? And here's me thinking you'd been tamed now the king has put a collar and leash on you."

Rovann banged his fist on the table. "Lord Waldrun, you will speak civilly or I will have you removed from this gathering. Lady Fourth, Syrie, you will resume your seat. Now."

With a growl, Syrie righted her chair and sat down. Lord Waldrun held Rovann's gaze for a moment before taking another sip from his goblet.

Rovann continued, "On my journey to Tyrlindon I passed through Angard in Mallynshire. The Songmaker had called a mage storm the like of which I've never seen before. The storm contained the usual elements: Air, Water, Earth, but I felt something else as well: Chaos."

Uneasy chatter broke out around the room.

"Surely not, my Lord First," said Lord Waldrun, stroking his chin with manicured fingers. "Could you have been mistaken?"

"I could have. But I wasn't."

"Tallen," said Syrie, "you're the so-called expert on Chaos. What do you think of this?"

Tallen straightened in his chair, flicking a lock of lank black hair out of his face. "Thank you for such a ringing endorsement of my talents, Lady Fourth." His raptor's eyes raked the gathering, the candles casting flickering shadows in his gaze. "Yes, I feel Chaos bleeding into the Realms. The power of the Outer Darkness is growing." He closed his eyes, placing a hand on his chest and sucked a deep breath through his nostrils. "Can't you feel it? Smell it? Forces are mustering beyond the veil. Such force. Ah, beautiful, don't you think?"

"What's causing it?" Rovann asked.

"Chaos is always looking for a way through. The Sluargh are forever desperate to enter the Realms of the living."

"The denizens of the Outer Darkness are evil," Waldrun stated. "That Realm is not called *The Burning* without reason."

Tallen scowled and spun in his seat to stare at the Water mage. "Your ignorance astounds me. Call yourself a mage? The creatures of the Outer Darkness are not evil in the way you mean. But they are created from Chaos and Chaos is the antithesis to order. The creatures of Darkness are dangerous in that they break the laws that govern the six higher Realms."

"And could the Songmaker have found a way to tap this power?" Rovann asked.

Tallen shrugged, leaning back in his chair. "Perhaps. But he would have to be an adept of Chaos far stronger than any in history. And it's very dangerous. One misstep and the Outer Darkness will consume him."

Rovann didn't like that answer one bit. How was he to fight the powers of Chaos? Where could he even start?

"So. The Songmaker is planning an attack on Tyrlindon. We know he is using the Eorthe. He may also be using Chaos. The question is, can we repel such an attack?"

Falwin snorted. "Tyrlindon has never been taken, by sorcery or by mundane means since it was built three thousand years ago."

Syrie snapped, "So that means we're safe, does it? Idiot! We have no idea how strong the Songmaker's power is. If he breaks through our wards thousands of innocent lives will be lost. There is no choice: we must evacuate Tyrlindon."

"Evacuate? A city this size?" Falwin cried. "Just exactly how would we do that? Where would we send everyone? Talk sense, woman!"

"Roost, Blackhowe and Bridgford are all less than a day from Tyrlindon. We should send the people there."

"None of those towns could house, feed and guard such a massive influx of refugees. Tell her, Rovann."

Rovann nodded. "Falwin's right. Tyrlindon can't be safely evacuated. If there's to be an attack on the city, we'll repel it, just as we always have."

Syrie's hand curled into a fist. "Even so—"

"Fourth Syrie!" Rovann snapped. "The matter is settled."

A nerve pulsed in Syrie's throat. Finally, she nodded.

Rovann leaned his elbows on the table. "I believe we can disrupt the Songmaker's plans and stop this attack. In the morning Falwin, Syrie and I will depart on a mission to do just that." He held up his hand to forestall questions. "Don't ask where we're going. If all goes to plan, there'll be no attack on Tyrlindon. However, you must be ready to defend the capital in our absence. We need as many mages as possible to protect the city."

Falwin rubbed thoughtfully at the stubble on his chin. "If we recalled all mages stationed throughout Amaury we could easily double our numbers here in Tyrlindon. "

Lord Waldrun shook his head. "If we do that we'll leave the rest of Amaury unprotected. Perhaps this is what the Songmaker wants? If we put all our efforts into protecting Tyrlindon what's to stop him decimating Silverport or Mandrake?"

Rovann nodded, conceding the point. "I agree. So, that leaves only those present here at the college. How many students do we have who may be ready to join us?"

Veronica, the Chief Administrator, spoke in her aged voice. "We have thirty-seven final year students, my Lord First. They are due to sit their final exams at the end of term. They are competent enough to join us. Many are skilled with wardings and protective sorcery. In addition, I know of at least three fifth year students who have shown skill beyond their years. If Ranneck has no objection I would suggest we release them from their studies and allow them to join the defense as well."

Ranneck, head of fifth year, shook his head, making his jowls wobble. "Veronica, you should know better. I can't justify putting my students in danger. They aren't mages yet."

"They're already in danger, Ranneck," said Veronica. "They promised to serve with their lives when they enrolled at the college. We need those students."

Ranneck frowned. "Fine. But keep them to light duties and away from any fighting. Agreed?"

Veronica inclined her head. "Agreed."

Rovann sighed. "I've said everything I needed to say. Any other Council business can be sorted out by the Lord Second and Lady Third. Good night, all."

He pushed his seat back and strode from the room. A quick glance over his shoulder as he passed through the doors showed Tiria and Falwin staring after him, looking furious. Come the morning he would likely receive a tongue-lashing from the pair of them.

A tongue-lashing or an evening of Council arguments? he thought. *I'd choose a tongue-lashing every time.*

Moonlight fell through the high windows, covering everything in an eerie white glow. Rovann sat in a high-backed chair staring out into the night. He didn't often come to the official chambers of the Lord First, but tonight it seemed the appropriate thing to do. It was past midnight but Tyrlindon didn't sleep. Lights burned in the windows of the college and soldiers were busy preparing for the city's defense.

Rovann knew he should get some rest but there were far too many thoughts churning in his head for sleep. So instead he sat by the window, endlessly thinking.

There was a knock at the door. Rovann didn't react.

The door swung open. "You in there, Rovann?" Falwin asked.

Rovann stood and spoke a word of Aetheric power. A ball of white light enveloped his hand. The light showed Falwin and the head of final year, Ayoni, standing in the doorway. He lit a lamp.

"What can I do for you?"

They entered the room and stood, looking uncomfortable.

"Did something happen in the Council?" Rovann asked.

Ayoni cleared her throat. "I thought I'd have more time to find a solution, but you're leaving tomorrow and time grows short..." She scrubbed her hands through her glossy chestnut hair. "My Lord First, I've lost a student."

Rovann crossed his arms over his chest. "Go on."

"Jenna de Meslyn was preparing for her final exam. She was required to Walk all five of the Seven Realms accessible to us. She did not return from her Walking."

Rovann's neck prickled. "When?"

Ayoni looked down at her hands. "Three nights ago. Jenna did everything right but her wards were torn to shreds as she made the Walk between Air and Fire. Her life cord was severed. Now, her body lies lifeless in the morgue while her soul wanders the Seven Realms."

"Have you tried to trace her?"

Ayoni nodded. "I've Walked the Realms every night. My wards fail before I have time to look. If I can't find her, Jenna's soul will be trapped in the in-between for eternity, never truly part of the Realms, forever barred passage into the One Light. I can't allow that to happen to one of my students."

"No," Rovann agreed. "I'll find her. I'll Walk the Realms."

"Thank you, Lord First," Ayoni breathed, relief flooding her voice. "This shouldn't have happened should it, Lord First? I listened to what you said about the Songmaker using Chaos from within the Outer Darkness. He shouldn't be able to do that, should he? The barriers must be thinning."

Ayoni's words were like a cloud passing over the moon. The room seemed suddenly dim. A memory engulfed Rovann.

Shapes appeared in the wall's shiny surface, outlines of creatures pressing against the barrier like fetuses struggling to break free of the womb.

"Yes," he said to Ayoni. "The barrier that keeps out the Darkness is weakening. The angels of the Aethyr believe the disturbance comes from here, from the Realm of Earth. From the Songmaker."

Ayoni's eyes widened. "Then is it safe to Walk the Realms at all?"

Rovann shook his head. "I don't know. But I must try. Leave me."

Ayoni looked as if she was about to say something but Falwin took her arm and steered her from the room.

Rovann lowered himself into his seat and closed his eyes. In his mind's eye he pictured the veil of the Realm of Earth, a bright arc of silver light that capped the sky. He rose from his body, his room, the palace and toward the shining veil of silver. He built a gate from Eorthic symbols and passed through into the tranquil beauty of the Realm of Aethyr.

Angels gathered. "Why are you here, Rovann of Earth?" their tinkling voices asked. "You are not yet ready to pass to the One Light."

"I need your help," Rovann answered. "I come to find a

lost soul, a girl from the Realm of Earth. Can you help me?"

The angels gathered closer and he felt the brush of their wings, the warmth of their compassion.

"We will help you find this soul. See."

Rovann's sight sharpened, expanded, until he saw all the Seven Realms laid out before him. His vision took him first to the Realm of Air, the beautiful, swirling world of the air spirits, but here nothing was amiss, no spirit was out of place. Next he perceived the Realm of Water, the nymphs, mermaids and the uncounted other creatures that dwelled in the great oceans, all moving through their lives in blissful ignorance. Here too, nothing seemed wrong.

But then he moved on to the Realm of Fire and he felt an odd resonance, a vibration of wrongness that shook the tapestry of life within the Realm.

"She's there," he said to the angels of Aethyr.

"Then look closer," they responded. "A way will be left open for you. We will take her to the One Light."

Rovann passed through a shining gate. The peace of the Aethyr was replaced by the rage of the Realm of Fire. On the molten landscape below a group of salamanders had converged around something, drawn by the thing's obvious difference to themselves. Rovann drifted down, set his astral feet on the boiling ground, and approached the group.

A girl crouched in the circle of salamanders. She was flickering, insubstantial, a ghost. The spirit girl snarled and spat like an animal, already beginning to lose her humanity.

Silently, Rovann sent out a call for help. In the distance he sensed a vast intelligence recognize and answer him. A moment later, a huge dragon appeared on the horizon and Rovann recognized the ancient queen he had met before.

She landed on the molten ground and regarded him with her golden eyes.

"We meet again," she said. "You seem an eager visitor to my Realm, Wanderer."

Rovann bowed. "Many thanks for answering my call, Great Heart. I'm on an errand of rescue. The spirit is a girl of Earth. Her body has died and now she's trapped here. I come to guide her to the One Light."

The dragon's massive head swung in the direction of the salamanders and her eyes narrowed. "I see her."

She lumbered forward, her claws leaving great gouges in the rock. The salamanders scattered, disappearing into the rivers of lava.

Jenna's spirit gibbered, gaping up at the dragon in terror. Rovann grabbed her.

"You are Jenna de Meslyn, student of the College of Mages. A child of Earth. Remember who you are."

After a moment, the snarl relaxed from her face and her eyes lost their rabid cast. "My Lord First?" she whispered. "You've come for me?"

"I've come for you," Rovann said gently. "Do you understand that you've died? That you must go to the One Light?"

"Yes and I welcome it. After what I've seen..." Her voice faltered. She passed a trembling hand over her face before continuing. "There's turbulence in the Realms. The Sluargh of the Outer Darkness seek a way through. For a time...for a time they almost had me."

The dragon narrowed her eyes in thought and then said in a rumbling tenor. "In the oldest histories of my kind it's said that when the universe was young, the creatures of Fire were given the power to Walk the Realms. Some of them coveted the riches they saw in other Realms and devised ways to weaken the dividing barriers to allow them to pass through. After a time the barriers weakened so much they broke, the laws which governed each Realm were sundered and the cosmos descended into Chaos. Millennia passed in torment before the One Light regained control and the barriers were repaired."

She pulled back her lips, revealing rows of razor-sharp fangs. Smoke rose from her nostrils. "For their greed, the One Light stripped the children of Fire of the power to Walk the Realms. The power passed to the children of Earth, and with the children of Earth it remains. Only they have the power to meet this threat."

Rovann bowed his head. First the angels of the Aethyr and now a dragon of Fire expected him to save them from a danger he didn't even comprehend.

Why me? Why me? he wanted to shout. Instead, he said, "I hear you, Great Heart. I will do all I can."

The great dragon bowed her head. "And I will do my part. My name is Tanyaka. If you're in need, call on me. Remember, you have fire in your Realm as well. It will answer you should you need it. The dragons will patrol the border of our Realm and do what we can to keep it whole."

"My thanks, Tanyaka. The Realms are well served when they have such mighty servants as the dragons of Fire."

Tanyaka snaked out her tongue in a grin. "The children of Earth have ever been courteous. You must go. I feel the Aethyr drawing close; the angels have come to claim you."

Rovann felt a tug and Tanyaka and the Realm of Fire faded. He and Jenna were floating in the silver-clouded Realm of Aethyr. Angels surrounded them.

To Jenna, they said, "Child of Earth, we will guide you to the One Light. Are you ready?"

Jenna smiled, a smile as dazzling in death as it had been

in life and there was joy dancing in her eyes. "Farewell, my Lord First. May we meet again in the One Light."

Rovann nodded. "Goodbye, Jenna."

The angels moved off, taking Jenna with them. Rovann fought the compulsion to shout the old questions. *Have you seen Istra? Is she here?*

He saw movement beside him and realized an angel had remained behind. She was tall and graceful, with wings the color of stars. "Be at peace, Champion of the Realms."

She brushed her fingertips against his forehead. Suddenly he was falling, falling, then opened his eyes to the darkness of his room.

Chapter Seven

Maegwin glanced at the sky and yanked her hood forward. It didn't do any good. Despite her efforts, water found its way down her neck and under her clothes, feeling cold and unpleasant against her skin. It had been raining for hours. From end to end, the sky was a featureless gray blanket. Mist clung to the trail, meaning the only things visible were the ears of her mount and the brown rump of the horse in front.

They had been traveling this way since before dawn. Somewhere up ahead rode Rovann but the mist had hidden him since they set out. Maegwin found herself in the midst of the soldiers: ten hard looking men and women, grim and battle-scarred.

Her thoughts turned to the soft bed and warm common room in *The Laughing Frog*. Leo would probably be setting up right now: tuning his lute, greasing his voice with a couple of tankards of ale, preparing to entertain the lunchtime patrons.

While I'm soaked to the bone and freezing cold, she thought.

But whose fault is that? I could have remained behind but I had to insist on chasing around the countryside, didn't I? I should have stayed with Leo. How will he feel when he discovers Rovann and I have left without even saying goodbye?

Her hands tightened on the reins, making her horse snort in alarm.

I had no choice, she reminded herself. *Hounsey waits at the end of this trek. And my vengeance. A little discomfort is nothing against that.*

The horse ahead stopped suddenly and Maegwin yanked on the reins to stop her own mount blundering into the back of it. The horse snorted and stamped, flattening his ears against his skull.

"Watch where you're going," Maegwin snapped at the rider in front of her.

The soldier swiveled in his saddle and raised an eyebrow. "Me? That's the third time you've walked straight into me. Can you actually ride a horse? Next time I'll let Bellrya kick both you and your horse into the mud." The soldier was blond and handsome, which only made Maegwin angrier.

"Try it, friend, and see what happens."

"Perhaps I will."

"Go on, then!"

"Am I interrupting something?" Rovann rode up, reigning Glynn in next to Maegwin.

The soldier snapped to attention. "Not at all, my Lord First."

"Maegwin?"

She snapped her mouth and glared at him. All day they had traveled steadily southeast across Tyrlindon's plateau but now they were making their way down a muddy track through birch woodland into the lowlands.

Maegwin was wet, cold and hungry. It did not make for a good mood.

"Have it your way," Rovann said. "The border of Hounsey's land isn't far. You know the land better than any of us, Maegwin. I'd like you to look at Falwin's map." Without waiting for an answer, he wheeled Glynn and sent him cantering back up the line, mud splashing from his hooves.

"You heard the man," the soldier said, nodding after Rovann. "Off you go."

Maegwin pulled her horse out of the line and followed Rovann. She gave the soldier an icy glare as she rode by but the soldier just grinned and threw her a mocking salute.

At the head of the column, Falwin and Syrie were arguing. They sat at a crossroads. The trail to the southeast leveled out and became almost as wide as the Kingsroad. To the southwest the trail was narrow and continued to angle down into the mist.

"Blind my eyes, isn't it obvious, woman?" snapped Falwin, rubbing his scalp with a meaty hand. "We need speed! We take the southeastern road."

"And have Hounsey know we're coming before we get within ten miles of him, you damned idiot?" Syrie snapped back, gesturing with her wrist stump.

"Better that than arrive after the man has already left the Highhold!"

"And what about the river crossing?"

"We'll make the river crossing at Breakstone Pass. If we take your route, Syrie, we'll still have to cross the river, but by Catseye Ford. And with the rain it's likely to be impassable for the horses." He threw his hands up in exasperation. "Tell her, Rovann!"

Instead, Rovann reached over and pulled a map from

Falwin's saddlebag. He unrolled it. "This is the Highhold," he said, pointing at a castle marked on the map. "Hounsey's ancestral seat and where we hope to arrest him before he has a chance to mobilize his army. These are the two main roads to the Highhold. You're familiar with these lands, do you know any other routes? Any way Hounsey might sneak round us?"

Maegwin peered at the map then shook her head. "My temple was on the southern boundary of Hounsey lands. I'm unfamiliar with the lands this far north."

Rovann rolled up the map and threw it back at Falwin. He stood in his stirrups and shouted, "Captain Tyan!"

The blond soldier Maegwin had snapped at rode up. "Yes, my Lord First?"

Rovann gestured at the crossroads. "Which route would you recommend, captain?"

Captain Tyan urged his horse forward and made a big show of examining both trails. "I suggest you take the southeastern road, sir, for the best speed."Falwin raised his eyebrow at Syrie, a smug expression on his face. Syrie looked like she wanted to punch him.

Captain Tyan continued, "But about ten miles from the Highhold I reckon we leave the road and cut across country, crossing the river at the Catseye Ford. No point in letting Hounsey know we're coming, eh?"

Falwin's smug expression dissolved into a frown and Maegwin's mouth twitched in a smile. This captain was obviously used to dealing with mages.

The southeastern road allowed them to ride three abreast, and Maegwin found herself riding with two soldiers: a man and woman with white hair and freckles that marked them out as brother and sister.

"You owe me sixpence," the woman announced.

"What for?" the man replied, looking incredulous.

"I won our bet."

"What bet?"

"On the captain."

"What bet on the captain?"

The woman fixed him with a hard stare. "Hannel, don't you go trying to wriggle out of this one. A bet's a bet."

Hannel scowled. "I ain't trying to wriggle out of anything. What bet you talking about?"

"I said the captain would take us by Catseye Ford and you nodded."

"Yeah, I was just agreeing with you."

"So you weren't accepting the bet then?"

"No."

"Oh."

There was silence for a while.

"Hannel?"

"Yeah?"

"I'm hungry. When's dinner?"

"Dunno. Best ask the captain."

"I'm not asking him. You ask him."

"No way. You're the one who's hungry."

"No I'm not!"

"Yes, you are. You just said so."

Silence again, but for the patter of rain and clop of hooves.

"Hannel?"

"What?"

"She's looking at us."

"Who is?"

"That woman. The Lord First's friend."

"Oh. What's she looking at us for?"

"I dunno."

They turned to stare at her and Maegwin quickly looked away. She didn't want any more arguments. "Sorry. I didn't mean to eavesdrop."

The woman turned to her brother. "She wants our pardon, Hannel."

"What for?"

"Eavesdropping."

"Dropping what?"

"I dunno. That's what she said."

Hannel clicked his fingers. "I've got an idea. Ask her to ask to the Lord First."

"Ask him what?"

"When we're stopping to eat!"

The woman looked horrified. "I never said to ask the Lord First. I said to ask the captain!"

Hannel shrugged. "Well, get her to ask the captain then."

"You're just being lazy. You're the sergeant, Hannel. You ask him."

"Won't. Besides, she's friends with the Lord First so the captain will hardly get mad at her will he?"

"You sure?"

"Course I'm sure."

The two soldiers turned to look at her again, smiling warmly. The woman held out her hand which Maegwin shook hesitantly.

"Corporal Hesha, ma'am."

Hannel hissed and smacked his sister on the shoulder. "Wrong address, idiot! Ma'am is for married ladies and we don't know she's married, do we?"

Rubbing her shoulder, Hesha said, "We don't know she ain't married neither, do we?"

Hannel ignored her and bowed elaborately from the saddle. "Sergeant Hannel, my lady."

Hesha snorted. "My lady is it?"

"Shut up, Hesha."

"You shut up, Hannel."

"I'm Maegwin," she cut in, before this could degenerate into an argument. "And no, I'm neither a ma'am nor a lady. Maegwin will do."

"See, I told you." Hesha crossed her arms over her chest. "That's another sixpence you owe me."

"What for?"

"The bet I won."

"What bet?"

"The bet that she wasn't a lady."

"I never took no bet."

Maegwin held out her hand to forestall them both. "Look, I'm not a lady, and I'm certainly not the Lord First's friend. And I'm sorry, but no, I don't know when we're stopping to eat."

Hesha narrowed her eyes suspiciously. "If you're not the Lord First's friend, who are you?"

Maegwin opened her mouth to speak but then closed it again. What was she to say? Who was she now? "I'm Maegwin de Romily, Ko-shin priestess of the goddess Sho-La."

Hesha's mouth fell open. "You hear that, Hannel? She's a priestess."

"I heard, Hesha. I have got ears." He made a waggling gesture with the fingers of one hand. "Do you reckon your goddess could magic us up some food? Eh? Do you reckon?"

"Sergeant!" Captain Tyan trotted up to them. "Gather

the squad and post sentries. We'll stop for food in that glade over there."

"Yes, sir!" Hannel threw a salute, then wheeled his mount and began bellowing instructions to the rest of the soldiers. "Bayl, take sentry at point. Chenna, start unloading the supplies. San, get that fat behind of yours down the trail and watch for the outriders."

"Well, I never saw the like!" Hesha said as she reined in her horse. "We ask and her goddess gives! Did you ever see anything like that, Hannel? Hannel? Hannel!" But the sergeant had already ridden off. Hesha nudged her horse after him and shouted back at Maegwin, "You need anything, just ask. You hear? Just ask!"

Dinner was a dismal affair spent huddling under the trees, trying unsuccessfully to stay out of the rain. Maegwin seated herself away from the others, amidst the roots of an oak and chewed mechanically on the heel of bread stuffed with meat Hesha handed her. The mages sat together, talking in hushed tones.

Maegwin watched them. *They don't want me here*, she thought. *Especially Rovann. But I will see Hounsey dead. It's all that matters. Mistress, I will pay your blood price soon. A life for a life. I promise.*

Rovann and Falwin laughed at something. Falwin clapped Rovann companionably on the shoulder.

And when this is done? A voice asked inside her head. *What will you do then?*

But she couldn't see beyond Hounsey. When she tried to picture her life after Hounsey's death all she saw was a gray mist, as though her life ended there. Revenge. All that matters. Only that.

"Want to help me win a bet?" Hesha said suddenly.

Maegwin jumped, startled by the corporal's sudden appearance. "What?"

"Hannel reckons he can beat you at a game of six bobs but I reckon you know your way around a set of dice. How about it?" She nodded at a circle of huddled soldiers.

Maegwin smiled. "Can't let Hannel get away with thinking that, can we?" She held out her hand to let Hesha help her up and they crossed the clearing toward the group. Maegwin crouched beside Hesha and looked around.

There were three others in addition to Hannel and Hesha. Opposite Maegwin, knelt a large man whose clothes were hung with charms and fetishes. Maegwin saw coins with holes drilled through them, small bones that might have come from rodents or birds, and feathers in different colors. The charms marked him out as a member of one of the northern hill tribes but Maegwin couldn't guess which one.

The man didn't look up as Maegwin and Hesha squatted down. He nudged Hannel and said in a surprisingly high-pitched voice, "You going to throw those dice or what?"

Next to Maegwin, a woman sat cross-legged on the ground, regardless of the fact that it was soggy. Her uniform was tatty but around her neck she wore a gold torque that looked totally out of place. She was cleaning her nails with the end of an ornate dagger and had long black hair caught up in ringlets on top of her head.

"Yes, come on Hannel. It's very impolite to keep us all waiting," she spoke with the accent of a noblewoman.

Hannel frowned at her. "I'm getting to it, Lady. You've got to give a man time to work out a battle plan."

Lady raised a thin black eyebrow but said nothing. The final member of the group was a skinny, dark-haired man with a long nose and a drooping mustache. He grinned as Maegwin joined the group, showing large yellow teeth.

"Ha! Shouldn't have goaded your little sister, Hannel. Look who she's brought over." The man stuck out a hand and Maegwin slowly shook it. "Private Tallo at your service. I'm a man who can get things, if you take my meaning. You want anything, you come and see me. Liquor, redleaf, a little bit of something to help you sleep, I'm your man. At a price of course."

"Right. I'll bear that in mind."

"You played six bobs before, Gwinny?" asked Hesha.

Maegwin startled at the use of the name. She hadn't been called that since she was a child running round the temple getting under everyone's feet.

"Um, once or twice," she said, "but never in the temple. The High Priestess frowned on gambling."

Lady snorted a laugh. "Captain frowns on gambling too but knows better than to try and stop us." She flicked her dagger into the air and watched it spin before catching it and tucking it into the scabbard at her side. Maegwin spotted other knives strapped all over Lady's body. "Throw the bloody dice, Hannel, before I stuff them up your nostrils."

"Yeah, come on Hannel. My knees are seizing up here," said the big man in his high voice. "Or are you scared you're going to lose again?"

Hannel sniffed. "I will ignore that remark, Finn." He rattled a tin cup and threw six dice across the small patch of ground in the middle of the circle. "Ha! Three maidens!" he said, pointing at the three fives. "Beat that!"

Maegwin narrowed her eyes, racking her brain for the rules of six bobs. She scooped the dice into the cup and shook it. The others watched the cup as though mesmerized. She threw the dice across the ground and leaned forward eagerly. Her only pair was two fours.

"First round to me!" said Hannel, grinning. He scooped up the dice and popped them back into the cup. "Said you should bet on me, didn't I? You should all have more faith in your old sergeant. This will teach you next time, won't it?" He threw the dice again and clapped his hands together in glee. "Look at that – a pair of sixes and a pair of threes! Since I won the first round, you need four sixes to beat me! Everyone get your money ready; I'll be collecting my winnings in just one moment."

Lady scowled at Hannel and then turned to look at Maegwin expectantly. Hesha crossed her arms and did the same. Finn and Tallo shared a look that seemed to suggest they were resigned to losing their money.

Lady spoke up suddenly. "Two golds says Gwinny wins."

There was a collective gasp from the others. "Two golds?" said Hesha. "You gone daft or what, Lady? That's nearly a month's wages."

"For us peasants maybe," said Tallo, "but not for her magnificence here. Go running to daddy and she could have that money within a bell."

A dagger flew into Lady's hand and she pressed it against Tallo's throat so quickly Maegwin barely saw her move. "How long have we known each other now, private? Five years? And in all that time, have I ever used my family's wealth for anything? Yet you still insist on needling me. Do you have a death wish, Tallo?"

Tallo swallowed. "I was only kidding! Honest I was. Just a joke, nothing meant by it. I'm sorry, all right?"

Lady sheathed her dagger and returned to her place in the circle. Tallo massaged his neck with shaky hands. After a moment he said, "Sounds like a good bet to me. Two golds says Gwinny wins."

The group looked at her expectantly and Maegwin suddenly felt nervous. To her surprise, she realized she didn't want to disappoint these people.

Don't be ridiculous, you barely know them, she thought. *What are they to you?*

She rattled the tin cup and threw the dice across the ground. A four, a two, a six and three ones.

Tallo groaned. "Shit. That's a month's wages down the drain!" Pointing a bony finger at Lady, he said, "I hope you're pleased with yourself!"

Lady shrugged. "Nobody forced you to take the bet, Tallo."

"Yes, but I thought she had a trick up her sleeve! Now I'm going to be living on bread and piss-water for the next month!"

"Aren't you the man who can get things? You'll just have to put your skills into practice, won't you?"

"How am I supposed to do that when we're miles from Tyrlindon?"

"Shut up, Tallo."

Hannel grinned smugly and threw an arm around Tallo's shoulder. "Life is full of lessons and you've all learned a valuable one. You shouldn't bet against me, because basically I'm fantastic."

"You do realize he's going to be insufferable now?" said Finn.

"He'd be insufferable whether he won or not," Hesha replied.

They fell in to a morose silence, except for Hannel who began humming a tune as he collected the dice. The rain was getting heavy again and Maegwin could feel it seeping through the sodden cloak covering her back. A thought suddenly occurred to her. She remembered a time when she had watched Tarina beat Rayna at this game.

"Hang on," she said. "The game isn't finished yet. I wish to play my joker."

Hannel froze in the act of collecting up the dice. "Can't. Game's finished."

"No it isn't," said Hesha. "It was still Gwinny's turn and if she wants to play her joker, she can."

Lady laughed. "Why are you suddenly looking so scared, Hannel? Seems Gwinny knows her way around the dice after all."

"Fine," said Hannel, holding the cup out to Maegwin. "Take your second throw. You still need three more sixes to beat me. I'm not worried."

Maegwin curled her hand around the tin cup, feeling the cold of the wet metal against her skin. The squad leaned forward eagerly. Tallo rubbed his hands together in anticipation.

"I knew she had a trick up her sleeve!"

"Shut up, Tallo," growled Hannel.

Maegwin shook the cup and dropped the dice into the mud. Two fives, one three. And three sixes.

Hannel stared in silence. Lady clapped. Tallo grabbed Maegwin's face and planted a wet kiss on her cheek. Finn shook his head and fingered one of the bone charms hanging from his waist.

"I never doubted you, Gwinny!" said Tallo. "Lady can pick a winner from a hundred paces. Oh, I'll be living like the nobility for the next month!"

"How did you do that?" whispered Hannel.

Hesha leaned over and slapped her brother across the

forehead. "Didn't I tell you? She's a priestess! Her goddess must have been watching."

A shudder wriggled down Maegwin's spine. This was more than luck. This felt like the work of the Dark Goddess. Why? What did these soldiers have to do with Her plans? She scooped up the dice with shaking hands.

"This is going to ruin me," Hannel groaned.

Hesha snorted. "You could have played your joker on your own turn, brother. Overconfident, that's your problem. And don't try and make out you're destitute either. I know you've got your savings hidden in that chest under the floorboards in your bedroom."

"How did you find out about that? You sneaky little sod! How many times have I told you not to go in my bedroom?"

"You should have locked the door then!"

"Lock the door? Why should I? It's my own bloody house!"

Hannel looked like he was about to have apoplexy. The soldiers stared at him silently for a moment then Lady burst out laughing. The others followed suit and Maegwin felt laughter bubbling up inside her.

"It's not funny!" Hannel thundered but that only made them all laugh the harder.

After a moment, Hannel grinned. "Damn it all if I haven't got the worst squad in the whole army!"

Captain Tyan came over. "Glad to see you've been making the most of this rest. Now get packed up. We're leaving."

The squad's mirth cut off abruptly and they fell into well-practiced professionalism.

"You heard the man," snapped Hannel. "Finn and Hesha, get the provisions packed up. Tallo, go help Captain Tyan and the mages. Lady, get the horses ready." He turned and bellowed to the rest of the soldiers. "Sheldon get that bloody redleaf out of your mouth. Somebody kick Calwyn, he's snoring."

They moved off to their various tasks, leaving Maegwin alone in the center of the clearing. Someone coughed behind her and Maegwin spun round to find Rovann standing there. He looked uncomfortable.

Maegwin waited silently.

Rovann cleared his throat. "I just wanted to check you're all right."

Maegwin lifted her chin. "Why wouldn't I be?"

Rovann shifted his weight. "We're getting closer to Hounsey lands."

And you think I can't handle it. She thought to herself. *You're remembering what I did to that guard by the gate and wondering when I'll flip again.*

But she didn't say this out loud. Sometimes she found herself wondering the exact same thing. Instead, she shrugged. "You don't need to worry about me. I can take care of myself."

Rovann's mouth tightened at the challenging tone in her voice. "I know that, Maegwin. I just meant—"

"I know what you meant."

He was silent for a moment. "Mount up. We're ready to leave."

Maegwin watched him walk away, annoyed at herself for being disappointed to see him go.

Rovann and Captain Tyan led the way. Falwin and Syrie rode behind them with the rest of the soldiers following. Maegwin once again found herself riding next to Hesha and Hannel.

About half an hour later the rain finally stopped. The clouds broke, letting through dazzling sunshine that made the horses steam. Soon, Maegwin's clothes were saturated with the smell of wet horse. The sunlight lifted everyone's spirits and the soldier's banter returned.

"You're a coward, do you know that, Hannel?" said Hesha.

"Am not."

"Prove it."

"How?"

"Ask her."

"You ask her."

Hesha rolled her eyes. "Why should I? It's you who's interested."

"Is not. It was Lady who asked."

Hesha harrumphed. She leaned toward Maegwin and whispered, "Everyone's wondering, Gwinny. How do you know the Lord First?"

Maegwin hesitated. She glanced at Rovann riding up ahead. She wasn't sure what to say. Part of her wanted to tell the soldiers everything, have it all out in the open and be damned with the consequences.

He saved me from execution. Why? Because I'm a murderer. And now I'm riding with you all because I'm planning to murder again.

She had never framed the thought so clearly, even to herself, and it left her shaken. Would she really kill Hounsey? When she'd killed his son it had been in a fit of rage and mortal fear. She'd felt nothing but relief as she punched the sword into his chest. But could she do it in cold blood? Faced with Lord Cedric Hounsey would she be able to do what she'd done to his son?

I don't know, she thought. *Perhaps that's what I'm here to find out.*

Hesha was looking at her expectantly. She decided part of the truth would be best. "I traveled with the Lord First from Mallyn to Tyrlindon." She hoped this would satisfy them and they wouldn't probe any further.

But Hesha's questioning took a different angle. "So you were alone with the Lord First all the way from Mallyn to Tyrlindon?"

"That's right."

"Just the two of you?"

"For some of the way, yes."

From behind, Lady whistled. "Sheesh, you lucky wench. Most women in Tyrlindon would have killed to be in your place. Me included. Did you see him undressed?"

"Lady!" said Hannel sharply. "You shouldn't talk about the Lord First like that!"

"Well if you don't like it, stop listening." Lady pulled her horse alongside Maegwin. "So, did you?"

"Did I what?"

"See him undress."

"No!"

"Ah, pity. So, you didn't, you know—"

"Lady!" warned Hannel.

"She'd be lucky," snorted Hesha. "Everyone knows the Lord First has a heart of ice."

"It's not his heart I'm interested in," Lady said, grinning. "The contents of his trousers will do."

Hesha laughed and Maegwin smiled despite herself.

Hannel looked outraged. "If I talked about a woman like that, you'd punch me in the face!"

Hesha turned to her brother. "You're always talking about women like that. Just when you think I can't hear."

"Do not!"

"Do so."

Hannel frowned. "How would you understand anything about it? You've never been in love."

"And you have I suppose?"

"Of course I have." Hannel sighed wistfully. "And she was as beautiful as a summer's day."

Tallo sniggered. "You're just the old romantic aren't you, sir?"

"Well it's better than trying to get women drunk or boring them to death with false tales of your bravado. That's your normal tack isn't it, Tallo?" Hannel replied, twisting in his saddle to glare at the private.

Tallo spread his hands wide. "What's wrong with that? It works, doesn't it?"

Hannel snorted in disgust. "You are as bad as Lady."

"Hang on a minute, what have I done?" Lady asked, eyes wide with innocence.

Hannel opened his mouth for a retort but his eyes fixed on something behind them. The soldiers turned in their saddles to see what had caught his attention. A rider was coming down the path at speed.

"Shit. That's Gral. This doesn't look good."

The rider galloped straight past, pulling his horse up sharply in front of Rovann and Captain Tyan. Swearing under his breath, Hannel nudged his horse forward.

"Who's Gral?" Maegwin asked.

"One of our outriders," answered Lady. "Two to the front and one behind guarding our trail." Lady watched the urgent discussion taking place between the outrider, Captain Tyan and Rovann. Suddenly Captain Tyan whirled his mount and he and the outrider went galloping back down the road. Rovann, Falwin and Syrie watched them disappear into the distance with troubled expressions on the faces.

Maegwin felt uneasy. In an instant, the easy camaraderie of the soldiers had disappeared. Lady's hand rested on a dagger. Finn had loaded his crossbow. The group sat in anxious silence for what seemed an age before Captain Tyan and Gral returned.

The captain pulled to a halt. "Everyone off the road. We're being followed."

Rovann swung down from his horse and moved to the front of the group.

"I urge you to stay back, my lord," Captain Tyan said.

Rovann shook his head. "I need to know who's following us. Have your squad dismount and fan out into ambush formation. Be ready. If they have a mage with them, you won't get any second chances."

Captain Tyan nodded. At a quick command, the soldiers dismounted and tied the horses to the branches. They drew their weapons and spread out through a hazel thicket in an arrow formation with Captain Tyan and Rovann at its apex. Falwin and Syrie stayed where they were, ready to guard their backs.

Maegwin turned to Hesha. "I don't have a weapon."

"Then it's my guess you weren't meant to fight," answered the corporal. Reaching down, she pulled a dagger from her boot and handed it hilt first to Maegwin. "Don't tell the captain I gave you this."

Maegwin accepted the dagger and nodded her thanks. She fell into step beside Hesha as they crept to the edge of the thicket and looked out. Hannel had drawn his sword whilst Lady had two throwing knives in her hands. Finn and Tallo had their crossbows trained on the road. After a while, Maegwin heard the clop of hooves.

A sway-backed horse came into view, wide round the middle with a long, unkempt mane and great splotches of brown on its white coat. A cloaked rider clung to the saddle. Maegwin held her breath as the figure drew level with her.

The figure pulled the horse to a halt and cocked its head as though listening. Rising in the stirrups the hooded figure looked around.

Captain Tyan held out his hand palm downwards, telling his squad to hold their positions. Maegwin could make out no weapons on the figure. Perhaps it was no threat. Suddenly the figure's hand darted to its waist as though reaching for a weapon.

Everything happened at once. Crossbows twanged just as the figure looked up and the hood fell back, revealing a face Maegwin recognized.

"Leo!"

Then Rovann was bursting from the thicket, his hands making weaving gestures. The crossbow bolts veered, one flying harmlessly into the bushes, another grazing Leo's cheek. The minstrel yelped, throwing his hands up and falling off the back of his horse to land in a muddy puddle with a squelch.

"Scout formation!" ordered Captain Tyan. "Three north, three south."

The soldiers swarmed out of the thicket, fanning out across the road, weapons ready.

Maegwin scrambled from her hiding place and ran to Leo. The minstrel sprawled on his back in the muddy puddle. Maegwin dropped Hesha's dagger and knelt beside him.

"Leo! Are you all right?"

"Mercy!" wailed the minstrel. "Mercy! Take my horse! Take my purse, just please don't kill me!"

"Leo, it's me. Maegwin."

The youth's eyes settled on her face and the fearful expression melted into one of relief. "Maegwin? Really?" The cut on his cheek was dripping blood down his face although Leo didn't seem to notice. He clambered up and threw his arms around Maegwin, splattering her with mud.

"Realms be praised!"

Maegwin pushed him gently away and looked him in the face. "What are you doing here, Leo?"

"I—"

Before he could finish the sentence, Rovann grabbed the minstrel by the tunic and yanked him to his feet. "What are you playing at, you fool? You could have been killed!"

Leo worked his mouth but no words came out, "I... I..."

"Rovann, you're scaring him," Maegwin said.

"Scaring him? I just saved his miserable life!" He flung Leo away, who went staggering to his knees in the puddle.

"I'm sorry!"

"What are you doing here?" Rovann snapped.

Leo shrank back, his face white with terror. "I'm sorry!"

"That doesn't answer my question!"

"I came to find you! So I can chronicle your quest and write some songs about it. I didn't mean any harm."

Rovann stood over him. "How did you know where we were?"

"I followed you."

"Only the Council knew we were leaving today. How did you find out?"

"I could tell you were up to something with those secret meetings. Then, when Lady Maegwin got up so early this morning, so did I. I saw the soldiers come and collect her from *The Laughing Frog*, so I hired a horse and followed.

Rovann didn't look appeased. For a moment Maegwin was sure he was going to strike Leo. But then his shoulders sagged. "Get up. Syrie will give you something for that cut." Rovann wandered away and sat down on the grass at the roadside. All the fight seemed to have gone out of him.

Maegwin pulled Leo to his feet and ushered him over to where Syrie waited. The olive-skinned woman said not a word, but her eyes were stony as she took some supplies from a pack and began bathing the wound on Leo's cheek.

"What did I do?" the minstrel asked. "What did I do?"

"You mean you don't know?" Syrie replied, smothering salve on Leo's cheek none too gently. "You, my idiotic friend, may have just ruined our whole mission."

"What do you mean?" asked Maegwin. "He's not done any real harm. We've lost a couple of crossbow bolts, that's all."

Syrie snorted and fixed Maegwin with the glare that could have melted stone. "Idiots, the pair of you! You understand nothing. Nothing."

Maegwin bridled at Syrie's tone. "So why don't you tell us?"

"The Lord First used sorcery to save this miserable wretch's life. There's a good chance it will have been detected."

The import of Syrie's words slowly sank in. "So Hounsey—?"

"Probably knows we're coming."

Maegwin looked over to where Rovann sat. Captain Tyan knelt beside him.

"I think he's alone, my Lord First," Captain Tyan said. "The outriders couldn't find any signs of others on the trail. However, to be sure, I suggest we circle back on ourselves across country. It'll take time but—"

"No," Rovann said, rising to his feet. "There's no need. He's alone."

Captain Tyan frowned at this. "You sound very sure."

"I know him," Rovann admitted. "He was a companion on the road when I was bringing Maegwin to Tyrlindon."

The captain turned to regard Leo. "So what do we do with him? We can't spare anyone to escort him back to Tyrlindon and we certainly can't leave him here. They'll probably be Hounsey patrols out looking for us now."

Falwin hawked and spat into the dirt. "You should have let the soldiers shoot him, Rovann."

"Thanks, Falwin. That's really helpful."

"What then?" Falwin grated.

"He'll have to come with us," Rovann replied.

Falwin's eyebrows rose. "You're joking, surely? How many of your waifs and strays do you want to bring on this mission? We can't take him with us: he's a liability."

"Do you have any better ideas?" Rovann snapped. "If we leave him to make his own way back to Tyrlindon he's likely to be picked up by a Hounsey patrol. At least if we take him with us we still have the chance to catch Hounsey unawares."

"The chance of that died when you used sorcery to save the stupid bastard."

Rovann closed his eyes and took a deep breath. "I know that, Falwin. It's my fault he followed us. I should have had Tiria keep a closer eye on him."

Captain Tyan placed his hands on his hips and looked over the group. "So it's decided. Let's get mounted up and moving. We'll cut across country. If Hounsey does know we're coming he'll be sending patrols down all the major roads leading to the Highhold. Let's not make it easy for the wily old bastard eh?"

Rovann nodded. "Agreed."

They were mounted and moving within minutes, a miserable Leo riding by Maegwin's side. A gloomy silence descended on them, led by Rovann's dour presence up front. At Captain Tyan's suggestion, they traveled up the road for a couple of miles until a stream cut across it then turned their horses into a thick woodland and followed the stream deep into the trees. They were forced to move in single file and at a slow plod Maegwin found frustrating. Now she knew Hounsey was waiting for them she somehow felt more alert, as though she was riding into battle, rather than to quiet murder.

"At least it's not raining," someone said behind her.

"Shut up, Hannel."

"I was just saying."

"Well don't."

The woodland was dense and the going slow. Mid-afternoon came and went as they slowly picked their way between the trees. The stream they'd been following angled off to the north so they turned away from it and found their own path using Syrie's knowledge of the Earth's power lines.

By early evening Maegwin's clothes were almost dry but she was bored and restless. She was glad when Captain Tyan called a halt for the night. They made their camp beneath the spreading boughs of huge oak tree and, as Maegwin looked up, she was reminded of the Sentinel that had healed her. That whole episode seemed a lifetime ago. Laying her hand against the tree's rough trunk, she whispered. "Greetings, Old Heart."

"I didn't know you had skill with the Eorthe."

Maegwin spun to find Syrie watching her, head cocked to one side.

"I don't."

"You've just given the ritual greeting to the tree."

"I...I heard Rovann say it, that's all."

Syrie's eyes were like hard black pebbles as she stared at Maegwin. "I sense the Eorthe in you. You've been touched by a Sentinel, haven't you? I can see it shining inside. But it battles with something else."

Maegwin shifted uncomfortably. "What else?"

"I'm not sure. Sometimes it seems…Nothing. It doesn't matter." She strode away.

Rattled by Syrie's words, Maegwin stepped over to her horse and began taking off the saddle and bridle. Leo led his horse over. "You're not angry with me are you? I didn't realize this mission was secret or anything. If I had I wouldn't have come."

"Yes you would, Leo," Maegwin replied, straightening to face the minstrel. "Since I've met you, you've been set upon by a mob, caught in a Mage Storm, beaten up by an innkeeper and escorted to Tyrlindon by the King's Mage himself. Am I sensing a pattern here?"

Leo chewed his bottom lip. "Hmm. I never thought of it like that." His face brightened. "It actually makes me sound rather heroic doesn't it?"

"Heroic? More like idiotic."

Leo glanced at Rovann who was brushing Glynn down. "Do you think he'll stay mad at me for long?"

Maegwin frowned. "Who knows? I couldn't claim to understand the Lord First."

"Perhaps I could write him a song?" Leo said hopefully. "That might soften his heart toward me?"

He looked so enthusiastic that Maegwin couldn't help smiling. She realized she'd missed Leo's mindless banter. He was something familiar in a world of strangeness. Now Leo was here, Maegwin didn't feel quite so alone.

They finished brushing down the horses and hobbled them for the night. Hannel stood in the middle of camp, looking around with his hands on hips. He counted the number of people and then frowned at the tents.

"Bloody hell."

"What's up with you?" asked Hesha.

"Not enough tents."

"Eh?"

Hannel nodded at Leo. "Where's our new recruit gonna sleep?"

"Oh, don't worry about me," Leo said expansively. "I'll sleep under the stars with the moss as my bed and the leaves as my blanket!"

Hannel grunted. "That sorts that out then."

"You can't let him do that!" Hesha said indignantly. "It looks like it's going to rain again. He will catch his death."

"So?"

Hesha fixed him with a hard stare.

Hannel sighed. "Fine. He can share with me and Tallo, although three of us in that tiny thing is going to be a tight squeeze."

Tallo dropped his saddlebags in front of a tent. "Hardly matters, seeing as we're all taking turns on guard duty tonight."

Leo made a flourishing bow. "Thank you, kind sirs! You kindness humbles me. I shall write a poem in your honor."

Tallo and Hannel shared a long look. "Poem is it? Can't say I've ever had anything written about me before," said Hannel.

"Well, nothing repeatable anyway," said Lady.

Hannel pointed at the tent. "You can put your bed roll in there. But you'd better not snore."

"Of course not, you won't even notice me."

"Good. Otherwise you'll be out on your ear, rain or no."

Maegwin clambered into the tent she was to share with

Lady and Hesha. The tent was so small her bed roll was a mere inch from Lady's and the rough fabric of the tent wall was next to her face. It made her feel enclosed, almost as if she was sitting back in the cell.

Don't be stupid, she chided herself. *They've shown you kindness. Would you rather be sleeping outside?*

She laid out her meager possessions and made her way back out. Finn, Tallo, and Lady were on sentry duty. Maegwin spotted their shadows on the edges of the camp and the glint of drawn weapons. On the far side of camp a larger tent had been erected which Maegwin guessed must belong to the mages. Leo, Hannel, and Hesha were crouched together in a circle by Hannel's tent. The other soldiers were scattered around the camp. Maegwin squatted by Leo's side. Hannel was talking and Leo was listening avidly, nodding at intervals.

"So, you got that? Triples beat pairs but two pairs will beat one triple. Full house beats all and you get one joker. Got it?"

Leo nodded. "Got it. It's not too dissimilar to a game the lords of Silverport indulge in. Nine Maidens it's called. The noble folk used to often sit and play whilst I was entertaining them with my songs. I'm sure I picked up the basics."

Hannel grinned. "Excellent. How about we make it a little more interesting? Say, five silver pieces to the winner?"

"Don't take the bet, Leo," Maegwin warned. "He's trying to fleece you."

Hannel widened his eyes in mock hurt. "You do me an injustice, Gwinny. I was merely trying to make the man feel at home."

"And win what you owe to Lady and Tallo so you don't have to dip into your own pocket," said Hesha.

"Such accusations are like a knife to my heart!" said Hannel, placing one hand on his chest dramatically.

"Alas, I could not take such a bet in good faith," said Leo. He unclipped his purse and upended it on the ground. A copper piece, two buttons and a small brass counting weight fell to the ground with a splat. Leo shrugged apologetically. "My talents haven't been best appreciated of late."

Hannel raised an eyebrow. "All right, if I win you have to brush down my horse and saddle him in the morning. How about that?"

Leo grinned. "Agreed!"

Maegwin found herself a relatively dry patch of ground and sat down, leaning back against the trunk of a silver birch. Her eyes strayed to the mage's tent. She hadn't spoken to Rovann since Leo arrived. Maegwin told herself it didn't bother her but her eyes kept straying to his tent.

Falwin and Syrie sat by a small, smokeless fire, Syrie poking it absently with a stick. Rovann was nowhere to be seen. Maegwin realized she hadn't seen him at all since they'd stopped for the night.

Maegwin climbed to her feet and approached Captain Tyan. "Where is the Lord First, captain?"

Tyan shrugged. "He went off somewhere but didn't say anything to me." His jaw tightened in annoyance. "In fact it makes my job a lot bloody harder when these mages don't tell me when they've got something planned. How am I supposed to keep everyone safe if they don't tell me where they're going?"

Maegwin didn't have an answer to that so she sat down by the silver birch once more. Night came quickly in the forest and soon Maegwin could make out nothing beyond the ring of low firelight in the center of camp. Maegwin kept her eyes on the mages. Where was Rovann? Why had he gone off without telling her?

Syrie suddenly looked up and Falwin scrambled to his feet. A shadow emerged from the trees. Rovann. He stumbled, Falwin darting forward to catch him. The big man said something and Rovann nodded. Syrie lifted Rovann's cloak and Maegwin gasped. Rovann's tunic was covered with blood. Syrie looked around quickly and then she and Falwin bundled Rovann into the tent. Nobody else seemed to have noticed, or if they had, they were pretending they hadn't. Maegwin itched to run to the mage's tent but forced herself to stay where she was. She suddenly felt cold. Her heart thudded in her chest.

Rovann was hurt. She doubted she would get much sleep tonight.

Chapter Eight

The tent's ceiling didn't get any more interesting no matter how long he stared at it. Rovann had been doing so for hours. Beside him, Falwin and Syrie slept. Rovann shifted, trying to get more comfortable, but as he did so, pain pierced his left side. He grunted, squeezing his eyes shut against the searing agony.

Although Syrie had washed and stitched the wound, the muscle beneath remained torn where a knife had slid between his ribs. The blade had missed his heart by the barest fraction. He'd been lucky. Very lucky. But it hurt when he moved. It hurt when he sat still. It hurt when he even breathed.

His thoughts drifted to earlier in the evening. As dusk was falling he'd slipped into the woods to scout for danger. Weaving silently through the trees he headed south, eyes roving the shadowy woodland, senses thrown wide. Nothing. He felt only the vibrations of forest creatures.

After walking several miles, he stopped. Something wasn't right. Where were Hounsey's patrols? Crouching by the smooth trunk of a copper beech, he closed his eyes, opening his senses to the Eorthe. Around him shimmered the life energies of the wood: trees, birds, animals. Rovann himself. To the north lay the shimmering glow of their camp. That was all.

Reluctantly he drew power from the Realm of Aethyr. His sight sharpened. His senses deepened. And then suddenly he saw...something. A mile to the east a disturbance rippled through the life energies of the wood. The vibrations flickered as though not wholly present. Or as if shielded by something. Rovann's eyes flew open and he surged to his feet, taking off into the wood in that direction. As he neared his destination, he slowed to a walk.

From up ahead a voice spoke. "You sure we can't have a fire? I'm sick of cold rations."

"Shut your mouth, idiot! Do you want to bring the King's Mage down on us?"

Rovann ducked behind a tree. That was one question answered: Hounsey did indeed know they were coming. Rovann peered around the trunk and saw three men sat in a circle munching on strips of dried beef. They wore simple woodsman's clothes but carried too many weapons for the disguise to be convincing. Something shimmered around the men. It was almost invisible to the naked eye but to Rovann's heightened senses it appeared like heat haze, distorting the air as they moved. Rovann's breath hissed through his teeth. He recognized the touch of the Outer Darkness. Chaos.

One of the men flung his piece of dried beef away in disgust. "How long are we supposed to live like this? Creeping around the woods like animals? Not five miles from where we sit lie three of the king's mages, unprotected and unsuspecting. We should attack them! But instead we sneak through the woods to get *around* them, like a bunch of sniveling cowards!"

A man with a gold hoop through his ear hissed, "And that is exactly why you aren't the leader of this mission, Tendry! Realms, are you a complete idiot? It's the King's Mage you're talking about, not some backwater hedge wizard. If we followed your advice, we'd be dead before the sun rose!" The man curled his lip at Tendry to show his disgust, "And besides, you know his lordship's orders. We're to deliver this and no more." The man tapped the pocket of his tatty coat.

Tendry scowled, unrepentant. "And if the King's Mage should discover us while we're sneaking around?"

"Why should he? He's not looking for us; he doesn't know we're here. We'll just let him go on blundering down to the Highhold thinking he's being oh, so clever while Lord Hounsey's plans ripen nicely."

A shiver of unease squirmed down Rovann's back. What was going on here? What was Hounsey up to? Common sense told him to return to camp and tell the others what he'd seen. But he wouldn't get a second chance to discover what these men were supposed to deliver.

Pulling in a deep breath, Rovann sprang from his hiding place, calling up Air as he did so. Two of the men looked up in alarm but didn't have time to cry out before tight bands of air caught and held them. But Gold Hoop threw up his hand at the last minute and a shield of sorcery surrounded him.

A mage, Rovann thought. *A mage, and I didn't even notice!*

His sorcery snapped back at him and he had to throw up his own shield, releasing the flows of air that held the two other men. They sprang at him, knives flashing. He ducked under a slashing blow from one man, danced away from the jab of another, and threw himself at the mage, chanting Fire.

Light and heat erupted across the clearing. It slammed into the men and took them off their feet. The mage recovered in only a moment. Jabbing his hand forward, a wave of force picked Rovann up and threw him against a tree. With a grunt, he slid down the trunk onto his knees, winded.

Calling on the Eorthe, Rovann wove a symbol in the air. Gold Hoop froze as Eorthic power seized his limbs, turning them as immobile as rock. The man's eyes tracked Rovann as he climbed to his feet and padded toward him.

Rovann hadn't forgotten what happened when he touched the mage in Angard. He'd not make the same mistake. Drawing on the Realm of Aethyr, he channeled a sliver of Aetheric power and wrapped it around Gold Hoop.

"Take off your coat," Rovann commanded.

The mage bared his teeth in a snarl, but, helpless to do otherwise, took off his coat and flung it to the ground. Rovann knelt on the soggy leaf-litter and rummaged through the coat's pockets. His fingers closed on a smooth, flat packet. A letter. Rovann drew it out, ripped it open and scanned the contents. Rows of carefully written symbols filled the page, none of which he could decipher.

He curled his fist in frustration, crumpling the letter into a ball. A coded message. Whatever it contained must be important. Very important.

A footstep behind him. Rovann whirled just as the man called Tendry stepped close. Rovann could smell the man's sour breath as he punched a knife into Rovann's chest.

Rovann grunted as white-hot fire lit his body. Tendry ripped out the knife ready for another blow but Rovann screamed a word and a wall of blazing sorcery burst forth.

It carved into Tendry, into Gold Hoop and the other man. For one horrible moment, Rovann watched as their bodies contorted with agony before the flames burned inwards, consuming them utterly.

Rovann staggered, heaving in long, steadying breaths. Pressing one hand against his wound and holding the letter with the other, he stumbled back through the forest toward camp.

Now, as he lay in the tent trying to sleep, he wondered if he'd made a terrible mistake. He should have captured those men. Instead, he'd killed them and he might never find out what they were doing. He sighed. It was no good. Sleep wouldn't come. Rovann climbed carefully to his feet and tottered outside.

Clouds covered the moon, thickening the shadows and promising more rain. Rovann crossed the camp and paused by Maegwin's tent.

Now you are two.

What had the angel meant? Did they really mean for Maegwin to serve them? Didn't they recognize the volatility within her? She was unpredictable and that made Rovann nervous. He shook his head, incredulous at the turn of his own thoughts.

Unpredictable? Volatile? he thought. *Is she any different to you? You have killed three men this night. They don't call you the Slayer of Sandford Moor for nothing.*

Hand clamped against his side, Rovann strode out of camp. Once beneath the trees he breathed in the scent of damp wood and listened to the rustling of animals in the undergrowth. A white owl alighted in a branch above him, staring down with eyes like saucers. Rovann circled the camp, weaving silently between the gray trunks.

"You couldn't sleep either?"

He whirled. Maegwin stood behind him, a frown pulling her eyebrows. Rovann gasped in pain and staggered as his knees buckled. Maegwin rushed forward, taking his weight on her shoulder and Rovann leaned into her, drawing breaths through his bared teeth until the agony subsided.

"What are you doing here?" he growled at her, more harshly than he intended.

"Stopping you from falling flat on your bloody face by the looks of it!" Maegwin snapped.

Rovann pushed away from her support and took two tottering steps. Maegwin crossed her arms and glared at him, her eyes full of anger.

"You shouldn't walk the woods at night," Rovann said. "It could be dangerous."

"Thanks for the advice," she replied. "One rule for me and another for you, is it?"

Rovann didn't rise to her bait. "What are you doing here, Maegwin?"

She shrugged. "I told you, I couldn't sleep. I heard you get up and followed." Her eyes strayed to where his hand clamped over his chest. "I saw you come back last night and I was... worried about you."

"You don't need to be. I'm fine."

Maegwin snorted. "Looks like it. What happened?"

Rovann slowly straightened. "I ran into some trouble."

"Meaning you don't want to tell me."

"Meaning it's nothing you need worry about."

Maegwin sighed and threw up her hands in frustration. She picked at the hem of her tunic. "We're in trouble, aren't we?"

Rovann winced as fresh blood flowed over his fingers. "Yes, Maegwin. I think we are." He opened his mouth to say more but a sudden stab of pain sent him staggering.

Maegwin yanked his hand from his chest and examined his wound. She hissed. "Who dressed this? It looks like a butcher's been at it!"

"Syrie's bedside manner can leave a little to be desired."

"Obviously. This needs tending, Rovann. It looks serious."

Rovann shook his head. "I don't have time. I need to finish checking the camp."

"What you need is treatment and rest!"

"Later. I need to find out what Hounsey's up to. Go back to bed. "

Maegwin growled. "Damn you, Rovann! You may be the Lord First but you're still a fool! If you go on blundering around you'll bleed to death!"

Rovann's chest felt like it was being squeezed by an iron band. "Fine. Then help me."

"How?"

"I need to sit."

Maegwin wedged her shoulder under his armpit and helped prop him against a tree. Waves of dizziness threatened to make him blackout. Gritting his teeth, he waited one, two, three heartbeats until the light-headedness passed.

"I'm going to travel the astral so I can get an idea of what's going on around us. Can you guard my body?"

She frowned at him, clearly unimpressed. "Fine. I'll treat your wound while you're gone."

Her hand, where it rested against his chest, felt warm. "I didn't know you had medical skills."

She smiled crookedly. "There's a lot you don't know about me."

He returned the smile. "Yes, I suspect there is."

He closed his eyes. After a few moments his breath fell into an even pattern. Rovann gathered his awareness and shook off his body, rising up, up, through the branches, into the sky.

The pulsing life energies of the forest were laid out below. Everything seemed in its place: nocturnal animals going about their lives, birds roosting high in the trees, the members of his expedition sleeping. Nothing appeared amiss. No, if he was to discover anything, he must head closer to his enemy's stronghold.

But weakness suddenly washed through him, making his astral body flicker like a candle flame. Looking down, he saw himself slumped against the tree. Maegwin worked feverishly on his wound, tearing strips off her tunic to dress it but blood was oozing down his chest where the stitches had burst. Frailty swept through his body. It snatched his power, turning him as insubstantial as a wraith.

Rovann looked south toward the Highhold. He had to get there somehow. Closing his eyes, he willed his strength to come. It didn't. He felt as stretched and brittle as a pegged-out hide.

Am I dying? He wondered as his thoughts began to fragment. *Is this it?*

Stillness filled him. A quiet peace. His power ebbed away and he didn't fight it. His eyes drifted softly closed.

Then a sound intruded on his lassitude. A voice floated on the astral, singing.

> I walk by the side of the Mother,
> Through forests and valleys fair.
> I walk by the side of my mistress,
> Knowing She'll always be there.

Rovann's eyes snapped open. He gasped as strength flowed into him. Thought and awareness returned.

We walk in the shadows of moonlight,
We sing by the light of the dawn.
I'll always sing with my mistress,
From Her side I'll never be torn.

Rovann's eyes widened in shock. Maegwin. She'd wrapped her arms around his chest and cradled his body as she sang. Her voice was beautiful, temple-trained to sing the glory of her goddess. The shimmering notes floated into the night, into Rovann's body. And from that song flowed a power Rovann recognized.

A Sentinel, he thought in awe. *She sings the power of a Sentinel.*

Rovann let out a whoop of joy and sped across country, watching the land flash by below, until many miles to the south, he approached the Highhold.

The castle crouched atop a sheer cliff like some snarling beast. From this distance its turrets looked like black claws raking the sky. It was an intimidating sight.

Rovann drifted closer. Suddenly his astral form was rocked by a silent detonation. Everything flashed white. He was blinded. For a second he hung there, unable to move, unable to think. As the light faded, his vision returned and he gasped.

A wall of shimmering darkness now enveloped the Highhold. It circled the fortress like a giant curtain and Rovann could see nothing beyond it.

He cursed himself for an idiot. He'd blundered straight into a ward, triggering the latent sorcery placed around the Highhold. Hounsey must command powerful mages indeed to be able to construct such a conjuration. Rovann sensed strange energies within the shadowy curtain. They swirled and danced, wrapping around each other and breaking apart. With a shudder he realized that the ward was composed of both Earth energies and Chaos. No wonder he hadn't sensed it.

Fighting a growing panic, he turned his back on the Highhold, sped back to the camp, dropped into his body and opened his eyes. Physical sensations crashed back in. A cramp in his shoulders. An itch in his elbow. The hardness of the tree-trunk against his back. A dull pain wrapped his chest but it was bearable. As he pulled in slow, steady breaths, he was relieved it no longer hurt to breathe.

Looking around, he realized it was not yet dawn. Darkness filled the forest. Maegwin had curled up next to him with her head resting on his chest. Her body felt warm and the weight of her leaning against him was oddly reassuring. How long had it been since he'd been this close to anyone? He could barely remember.

Maegwin's hair brushed against his neck, tickling the skin. She shifted in her sleep then settled again. Tentatively, Rovann curled his arm around her shoulder and she instinctively leaned into his embrace. But after a moment he blinked suddenly as though waking from a deep slumber and shook Maegwin's shoulder until she jerked awake, looking around wildly.

"What is it?"

"Time we were gone."

A succession of emotions flickered across her face. Embarrassment. Annoyance. "You're back at last."

Rovann climbed wearily to his feet. He pulled up his tunic and inspected his wound. A wad of cloth was pressed against the puncture with a row of tiny, neat stitches holding together the skin.

"Leave it," Maegwin said. "I made a salve from comfrey

and yarrow which should stop infection. Try not to burst the stitches again."

"I'll do my best, oh mistress."

Maegwin frowned at him, unsure if he was mocking her. She stood. "Did you find what you were looking for?"

"More than I expected. None of it good."

Maegwin didn't reply. Instead, her eyes moved, tracking something behind him. Turning, Rovann saw a white owl sitting on a branch, its saucer-eyes glowing in the gloom. Maegwin watched the bird, her fists clenching and unclenching at her sides.

"What is it?" Rovann asked.

She didn't answer. She cocked her head, almost as if listening to a silent conversation. After a moment, the owl took flight, disappearing into the gloom of the forest like a ghost. Maegwin cried out and sped after it.

"What are you doing?" Rovann called but received no answer.

Cursing, he ran after her, weaving through the trees and ducking under branches but Maegwin was soon out of sight. Gasping with effort, he followed as best he could and came upon her so suddenly he almost ran into her. She stood beneath the heavy boughs of an oak in which the white owl perched. But Maegwin wasn't looking at the owl. Her eyes were fixed on the base of the tree.

"What is it?" Rovann asked, stepping up beside her.

She pointed. The tree's roots formed a shallow bowl filled with water. Rovann saw the sky reflected in it.

Maegwin glanced at the owl, at Rovann, then the pool. "Don't you see?"

Rovann shook his head. "See what?"

She gestured irritably. "It's an omen."

"What are you talking about?"

"Look at the pool," she snapped. "What do you see?"

"Just the sky. The stars."

"Which stars?"

In the gloom, the pool looked like a black void into which the stars had fallen, glittering like tiny shards of glass. One of them seemed to shine more brightly than the others. And it glowed red.

"That's not possible," he breathed.

She nodded. "I know. The Bale star. It shouldn't be visible at this time of year. It's an omen, Rovann. The owl led me here to witness this warning. We mustn't ignore it. In the teachings of Sho-La, the Bale star signifies choices or the answers to riddles. Something awaits us at the High-hold, some kind of reckoning."

Rovann shook his head, unwilling to accept her explanation. "How can you know this?"

"I just know. It's a message from Sho-La. You have to trust me."

Rovann hesitated, watching her. Was her vision really a message from her goddess? Or was it connected to the Chaotic powers he'd seen at the Highhold? How was he supposed to know?

Now you are two, the angel had said.

At last, he nodded. "Then we'd better warn the others."

A smile lit Maegwin's features, her green eyes sparkling.

Rovann held out his hand. "Come on, let's get back."

Maegwin clasped his hand and they made their way back to camp through the slowly lightening wood. Maegwin was silent, matching his stride.

"Maegwin?"

"What?"

"Thank you."

A smile quirked the corners of her mouth. "You're welcome."

A voice spoke suddenly. "Don't move or I'll run you through."

Rovann saw the glint of naked steel and the silhouette of a man on his left.

"Private Tallo?"

"Who's asking?"

"Tallo," Maegwin said, "are you seriously threatening to stab the Lord First?"

"What?" Tallo moved to get a better view. "Shit. I mean, er, sorry, Lord First, I didn't realize it was you. Apologies." He sheathed his short-swords.

"Apologies for what? Doing your job?" Rovann replied. "Rouse the camp, Tallo, we need to get moving."

"Aye, sir."

Syrie and Falwin stood waiting outside their tent as Rovann and Maegwin emerged from the trees. Falwin's eyebrows shot up and Syrie's mouth pressed into a tight, flat line.

"We have to hurry," Rovann announced before they could speak. "Something strange is happening at the Highhold."

"Eh? What are you talking about?" asked Falwin.

"Hounsey has set Chaotic wards." He glanced at Maegwin but didn't tell them about her omen. He wasn't sure what they'd make of it.

"How do you know?" Falwin said.

"Because he's walked the astral," Syrie answered. She moved to stand in front of Rovann. "I can smell the Eorthe on you still."

"You idiot!" Falwin exploded. "We agreed it was too

dangerous to walk the astral this close to the Highhold! Or don't those rules apply to you?"

Syrie watched him, her dark eyes intense. "What's going on, Rovann? What did you find?"

"Darkness," he replied. "And that's what worries me. The ward around the Highhold is so strong I could see nothing beyond it."

"Curse that man," growled Falwin. "What is he playing at?"

"That's what I hope to find out. With any luck Hounsey won't have had time to gather his army at the Highhold. If that's the case, we'll enter the fortress, using sorcery if we have to, and arrest him."

"And if Hounsey *has* gathered his army?" Falwin asked. "We can't fight our way through twenty thousand soldiers."

"If that is the case," said Syrie, "I will get us into the castle using the Eorthe."

Rovann nodded. "Agreed. Once we've secured the Highhold and arrested Hounsey, we'll offer pardons to his officers if they bring their forces over to the king. You have the paperwork, Falwin?"

The shaven-headed man nodded. "Just waiting for your signature."

"Good. Any questions? No? Then let's get going."

The soldiers clicked into a slick, professional routine. In less than half an hour, the party had left the clearing, leaving behind little evidence they had ever been there.

Rovann rode with Captain Tyan and Maegwin. As the sun rose, the rain clouds cleared, leaving the sky blue and sparkling. As the day grew hotter vapor began to rise from the mulch, filling the space between the trees with mist.

Rovann didn't like it. Everything seemed too quiet. Too still. There were no bird calls. No squirrels chirruping in the trees. No insects buzzing in the undergrowth. It seemed as if life had fled from the land around the Highhold.

They travelled in wary silence, hands never far from weapons. After four tense hours of riding, Captain Tyan suddenly held up his hand and the company halted. In silence, they dismounted and crept carefully forward. The captain pointed.

The company stood at the top of a rise. On the other side of the valley, clinging to its rocky plateau, rose the black edifice of the Highhold, center of Lord Cedric Hounsey's power.

Maegwin's pulse quickened. She had never seen the Highhold in the flesh but had dreamt of it often. Strangely, the place was exactly how she imagined it. In the morning light the black stone glistened like oil. The windows stared like empty eye sockets. It had an ancient look, as though it had sat for eons, staring down at the land around.

"Hounsey," she breathed. "I'm coming for you."

Captain Tyan made a silent gesture and they moved back into the cover of the trees. They tethered the horses in a thicket and then gathered in a circle. Maegwin hunkered down next to Rovann.

Captain Tyan did not look happy. A frown pinched his forehead and he drummed his fingers on his knees. "This isn't right."

"No," Rovann replied.

Maegwin looked at him sharply. What was he talking about? They'd reached the Highhold unmolested. Hounsey was in reach. Wasn't that what they wanted?

"Where is everyone?" Tyan said.

Rovann shook his head. "I don't know. This area should be crawling with Hounsey patrols. The villages of South-mark and Talstead lie a little over a mile away, yet there is no chimney smoke nor any sign of villagers on the roads or in the fields. I saw no guards on the Highhold's battlements. It looked empty."

Falwin snorted. "It's a trap. This has 'ambush' written all over it. The second we approach the gates I guarantee Hounsey soldiers will pour from the Highhold's every orifice."

"Falwin's right," Syrie said. "We mustn't approach by the main gate."

"What alternative is there?" Rovann asked.

"Let me take us in through the Eorthe. Hounsey won't be expecting that."

Rovann chewed his lip as he thought. Finally, he shook his head. "No, Syrie. The more I think about it, I realize it's too dangerous. We don't know what affect the Chaotic magic might have on your use of the Eorthe or whether you'll even be able to use it. Hounsey has Chaotic wards around the castle, remember."

"Then what?" Syrie snapped. "We just walk up to the door and knock?"

Rovann sighed. "Captain Tyan, what do you suggest?"

Maegwin ground her teeth in frustration. Why didn't they make a decision? Hounsey was just on the other side of the valley and they sat around talking instead of acting!

She rose to her feet and kicked at some dead leaves in exasperation, watching them go flying into the air to be caught by the wind and sent skirling into the branches of the trees. Maegwin watched them fly up and then gasped as her eyes alighted on something sitting in the tree above her.

A white owl.

Maegwin went very still. The owl stared at her, eyes unblinking. After a moment it stretched its wings and silently flew into the forest.

Without thinking, Maegwin sped after it.

She wove in and out of the tree trunks and jumped over undergrowth, desperately trying to keep the bird in sight. The owl landed at the top of a holly bush and sat staring down at her.

Maegwin skidded to a halt, panting. The holly bush grew at the top of a squat mound that was almost conical in shape and did not look like a natural part of the forest. She noticed that tangled lengths of ivy hung down the mound's nearside and were gently moving in the breeze as though the space behind was hollow.

Maegwin pulled the curtain of ivy aside. Beyond was a black space like a cave but Maegwin caught a glimpse of steps receding downward.

"What's that?" said Leo behind her.

She spun. She hadn't heard the others catch up.

Rovann stepped forward, peering at the opening. "It's a bolt-hole. And I'll bet it leads right into the Highhold."

The tunnel was dark, damp and stank of mold. Thin silver roots snaked down the walls, gripping the spaces between the mortared stones. As she walked, Maegwin's boots kicked through puddles and the light from Rovann's torch showed spiders and rats scurrying away. Maegwin didn't like it one bit. The weight of all that earth above was oppressive. It reminded her of the cell in Mallyn.

She ground her teeth and tramped behind Leo as the company moved silently through the cloying darkness. They walked in silence but their thoughts seemed loud to Maegwin. She could guess what they were thinking.

Was it luck that led us to this passageway? Or is it part of Hounsey's trap? What will we find at the end?

Maegwin couldn't answer any of those questions.

It seemed like they walked for hours until Rovann halted and held up the torch. A stout wooden door stood in their way. The door was rotten, riddled with wood-worm and collapsed into splinters when Rovann set his shoulder to it.

Beyond lay a long-forgotten cellar. Crumbling wooden crates and piles of putrid vegetables stood haphazardly around the perimeter. Maegwin wrinkled her nostrils at the stench of decay.

"Are we within the ward?" Captain Tyan asked Rovann.

"Yes. Don't worry, captain. It manifests only on the astral. It won't harm us here on the physical plane."

Tyan nodded, apparently pleased with this answer. Sergeant Hannel stepped up to his captain.

"It's all clear, sir. There's nothing down here. Perhaps Hounsey really has forgotten the tunnel."

The captain did not look convinced. "Perhaps."

Maegwin took her place behind Rovann as they made their way up a set of dusty, winding steps. At the top was another door. Tyan gave signals to the soldiers and everyone quietly drew their weapons. Maegwin hefted the short-sword Hesha had leant her.

Behind, Leo whispered, "I haven't got a weapon!"

"Then make sure you don't get in a fight!" Maegwin replied.

Captain Tyan held up three fingers then dropped them one by one, counting down. As his last finger curled he slammed his shoulder into the brittle wood, throwing the door open and sending them all tumbling into the room beyond. Adrenaline pumped through Maegwin's body. This was it. Finally, she could begin taking her revenge.

But the room beyond was as silent as a crypt. It looked to be part of the kitchen with a long oaken block in the middle whose surface was gouged with many long scratches. A butchering block, perhaps, where the castle's cooks would prepare meat for Hounsey's table.

A shiver of unease tiptoed down her spine. Hounsey must know they were coming so where were his people?

"Perhaps they're all upstairs?" said Leo hopefully.

Rovann made a shushing gesture then padded over to an archway leading into another room. He shook his head. Nothing.

Captain Tyan led the way as they stole through the kitchen. Pots and pans hung from the wall and two ovens filled a wide fireplace. The tables and benches had been scrubbed clean, everything put away in its place. Even the floor had been swept. But there was no sign of any servants.

Beyond the kitchen they came out into the castle proper, a series of interconnecting corridors and chambers based around a central courtyard. Pausing outside the kitchen door, Maegwin cocked her head. Silence. But on the edges of her perception she felt…something.

"What's that?" she whispered.

Rovann looked at her sharply. "What's what?"

"I feel something strange. Almost like a vibration," she tapped her chest "in here."

"I sense nothing." He raised an eyebrow at Syrie and Falwin, asking the question. The two mages shook their heads.

Rovann turned a quizzical expression on her. "When did you notice this?"

"Just now. It's difficult to explain. It's like when you feel an earth tremor coming up through your feet."

Syrie narrowed her eyes at Maegwin. "Perhaps it's the ward?"

"I don't think so," answered Rovann. "If that was the case I'm sure we'd feel it too. Maegwin, if you detect any kind of change, let me know."

She nodded, not trusting herself to speak. She suspected she was sensing Hounsey's presence. At least, that's what she hoped.

"We need to reach the Great Hall," said Falwin. "That's where we'll find Hounsey."

"Agreed," said Captain Tyan. "Ambush formation and keep swords drawn. Got that?"

They moved along the corridor, their feet making no sound on the thick carpet. Leo fell in beside Maegwin, looking around with terror-filled eyes.

They reached an intersection with four corridors branching off. All were empty. They turned left, into a long gallery with doors on either side. As they crept towards the nearest one, Maegwin noticed it was open. Inside was a records office with shelves full of ledges and a set of brass scales on the desk. But nobody was within. Along the corridor all the doors stood open, revealing the rooms to be neat, ordered and empty.

At the end of this corridor they reached a flight of wide stairs that swept grandly upward. The banister gleamed as if recently polished and a red and gold carpet covered the treads.

"Perhaps we'll have more luck on the second level," observed Falwin.

Warily they climbed the stairs. At the top they found themselves among the living quarters. Large sitting rooms and halls filled the space. All empty.

Captain Tyan called a halt while they assessed their options. Whilst the captain and the mages gathered to confer, Maegwin walked a few paces and looked around. On her left stood a stout wooden doorway with a crack in the mortar around one edge. She frowned, sure she'd seen this before.

She shoved the door open and poked her head inside. Beyond lay the kitchen, just as they left it.

Cursing, she jogged back to the others. "You'd better look at this."

"I don't believe it," said Rovann as he stepped into the kitchen. "How is this possible? We're back where we started!"

"But we went up the stairs!" said Leo. "How come we're back down here? It doesn't make any sense!"

"This has the stench of Chaos to it," said Falwin.

Suddenly a piercing scream split the air. Maegwin jumped as the sound cut through her then ran after Rovann as he sped down the corridor to another room. A woman lay slumped in the corner with a hand pressed against a bloody wound in her stomach.

Rovann threw himself to the woman's side. "What happened?"

The woman fixed glazed eyes on Rovann's face. "I didn't know anyone was in here, sir. Honest I didn't. When I opened the door, he came at me."

"Who came at you?"

The woman gestured feebly. "That man."

"Where did he go?"

She pointed at the corridor and tried to speak but her

hand suddenly flopped to her side. Her breath rattled as it escaped her mouth one last time. Rovann gently closed the woman's eyelids then straightened and addressed the others.

"So the castle isn't empty after all. We need to catch whoever did this."

"Sir!" came Hesha's urgent cry.

"What is it?" Rovann said, running to where Hesha waited at the end of the corridor.

"I thought I saw a man dressed in black crossing the landing down there."

Rovann's face folded into look of steely determination. "Come on."

As they turned a corner Maegwin caught a glimpse of a figure disappearing through a doorway.

"There!"

But as they followed, they found themselves back in a familiar place.

"The bloody kitchen again!" hissed Sergeant Hannel. "What the bloody hell is going on here?"

Maegwin jumped as a blood-curdling scream suddenly rent the air. Just as before, a woman lay in the corner of a room with her hand pressed to her stomach. Same woman. Same wound.

Rovann's eyes glinted with suppressed fury. "He's playing with us. This is some sort of elaborate game."

Captain Tyan rubbed at his stubbly beard. "Soldiers I can fight. Guards I can overcome. But this is sorcery at work. This is up to you, my lord."

Rovann glanced at the captain, an unreadable look passing across his face. "I can't combat what I can't see. Like Falwin said, only the power of Chaos can bend the rules of reality. Time has been bent so we see this woman dying again and again. Space has been bent so that no matter where we go in the Highhold we arrive back at the kitchen." He kicked a flagstone in frustration and leaned both hands on the wall, head hanging down, hair hiding his face.

"Why would Hounsey go to all this trouble?" Maegwin asked. "Wouldn't it be easier to use his power to capture us? Kill us? Why would he bother with trickery? What does it achieve?"

Rovann shook his head. "I don't know..." His head snapped up. "Unless..." He spun, eyes going wide.

"What?" Maegwin asked. "What is it?"

"Unless Hounsey isn't here at all. Unless he's never been here. Unless this is a trap designed not to capture us, but to delay us."

Maegwin felt the blood drain from her cheeks. "But that means—"

"He's gathering his army elsewhere. It might already be too late."

Bellowing at the others to follow he ran back to the kitchen

"What's going on?" yelled Falwin.

"We must get out!" Rovann shouted.

Feeling bewildered and shocked, Macgwin allowed herself to be swept up by soldiers as they formed a ring around the three mages. How could this be happening? Hounsey had eluded her. Did he not have the courage to face her?

They thundered down the spiral stairs to the basement, their boots thudding on the stone. Maegwin jumped the last two steps down into the cellar — and found herself back outside the kitchen door.

She staggered a few steps and was caught by Hesha who

helped her back to her feet. Maegwin turned in a slow circle. This was not possible. Surely, it was not possible? The wooden door to the kitchen was on her left with the same crack in the mortar she'd first noticed.

Looking at the faces of her companions, Maegwin saw dread and confusion in their eyes. Leo wrapped his cloak around himself and hugged his arms over his chest.

Maegwin leaned against the wall and slowly slid into a sitting position with her knees drawn up to her chest. Rovann conferred with the two mages whilst Captain Tyan ordered his soldiers to move out along the corridor, keeping watch for the man they had seen fleeing earlier.

A few seconds later another scream echoed through the castle but this time nobody moved to answer it. They knew what they would find.

Maegwin closed her eyes and tried to clear her thoughts. In her chest she felt that strange vibration again. Could the man they'd seen have something to do with this? Was that Hounsey? And if so, could she somehow track him?

"Hannel?" whispered Hesha.

"What?"

"Are we trapped?"

"Don't be daft. The Lord First will get us out."

"He doesn't look too confident. I reckon we're trapped."

"You're such an optimist, Hesha."

"Just being realistic, is all."

"Well, don't. Be quiet."

An uneasy silence fell, punctuated by the low murmuring of the mages. Under her breath, Maegwin began to chant her morning prayers in an effort to focus her mind. Her thoughts settled on the words and all other distractions receded. Eventually she fell silent, allowing her attention to hone in on the vibration.

Yes, it was definitely closer. Maegwin opened her eyes and stood. She took two steps down the corridor and felt the tremor grow stronger. She walked until she reached the wall. It was featureless, made of tightly mortared stone with no doors or windows. And yet, the strange sensation came from beyond it.

"What is it?" asked Leo.

She didn't answer. Instead, she reached out, expecting her fingers to brush against the coarse texture of stone. But they didn't. They carried on through, sinking into the wall as though it was made of treacle. Leo gasped and shouted for the others.

Part of her screamed this was dangerous, she should wait for Rovann but another part of her screamed that she might find Hounsey beyond. Her fingers tingled but she didn't let this break her concentration. Taking a deep breath, she stepped through the wall.

A concussion rocked the Highhold. A rumble like thunder grated beneath her feet and the illusion snapped. The wall disappeared, the corridor disappeared, the kitchen disappeared. Instead, Maegwin found herself gazing into a large oblong room filled with tables sporting arcane equipment.

A man dressed in black velvet looked up from where he leaned over a table, his eyes going wide. In the next second, he threw out his hand and a wave of sorcery flashed toward Maegwin.

She threw an arm up and cried out just as Rovann pushed her out of the way and flung up his own wall of sorcery which shredded the attack to pieces. Rovann's power formed a shimmering aura around the man, cutting him off from his sorcery.

The man snarled and rushed to a door at the back of

the room. Something silver flashed through the air and a knife thudded into the door with a thud, pinning the man's sleeve to the wood.

"You're not going anywhere," said Lady, hefting another knife.

She and Tallo crossed the room and grabbed the man by the arms, dragging him back.

"Who are you?" Rovann demanded.

The man had a pinched, arrogant expression. "You really think I'll tell you? Then you're more stupid than I thought."

Rovann stepped close. "One more chance. Who are you?"

Maegwin peered at the man. Something about him nagged at her. Suddenly she gasped in recognition. She remembered that day so many weeks ago when she'd overheard Lord Cedric Hounsey talking to a man about the Songmaker's plans. Talking to this man. This mage with the arrogant, pinched expression. This mage who played a part in the burning of her temple.

With a wild shriek she flung herself at him, fingers clawing at his eyes. "I'll kill you!"

The man grunted in surprise as she crashed into him and they both went toppling to the floor. Maegwin managed to get her fingers around his neck but a second later Lady and Tallo yanked her away.

"What are you doing?" Lady asked. "Have you gone mad?"

"It's him!" Maegwin panted, struggling to reach the mage. ""He's the one!"

Rovann laid a hand on her shoulder. "Did this man have something to do with your temple?"

She nodded, unable to speak.

Rovann's expression turned grim. "Then he has already condemned himself." He knelt by the man's side and looked him over. "I assume by the fact that nobody has come to your aid that you are here alone. Am I right?" The man's eyes fixed on Rovann but he didn't reply. "I'll take that as a yes. Which means Hounsey left you to create these illusions to keep as trapped here. Why?"

"You're the Lord First aren't you? Work it out for yourself."

"Because Hounsey wants to delay us."

"Give the boy an apple!" The mage sneered. "And you fell for it. The mighty Lord First and the Second and Fourth of the Council, supposedly three of the most powerful mages in the land and you fell for my illusion."

"But Maegwin didn't," Rovann pointed out.

The mage's eyes snapped to Maegwin's. "And why is that? Why can she detect Chaos when you cannot? Ask yourself that, my Lord First."

"Let me kill him, Rovann" Maegwin whispered hoarsely.

Rovann glanced at her and then back at the mage. "Where is Lord Cedric Hounsey?"

"I'll never tell you!"

Rovann sighed and a glow enveloped his palm which he held directly above the mage's forehead. "You know I can make you tell me. It would be easier if you volunteered the information."

The man's eyes flitted from side to side, a look of fear passing across his features. Then, before anyone could move, his hand darted to his waist where he unsheathed a small knife. He plunged the blade into his own heart. With a gurgle, his head smacked onto the floor and a soft hiss escaped his lips.

With an exasperated cry, Rovann yanked out the knife and pressed his hands on the wound. But it was too late. The mage's eyes rolled back in his head, staring sightlessly at the ceiling.

"No!" Rovann said. "Curse you!"

Maegwin sagged in Tallo and Lady's grip. Her revenge fluttered away, leaving her empty. When would she get what she desired?

"Perfect! Just bloody perfect!" Falwin growled, kneeling on the mage's other side. He unbuttoned the dead man's coat and began feeling around in his pockets. After a moment he pulled out a small leather book. "What's this?" He thumbed the pages. "It looks like some kind of code."

Rovann's head shot up. "Code? Give me that!"

He snatched the book leafed through it. After a second he reached into his own pocket and pulled out a parchment which he unrolled and placed on the floor, pegging it down with bits of equipment from a table.

"I took this letter from those Hounsey scouts I came across last night. But it's coded and I couldn't read it. But maybe…"

Maegwin could hear the excitement in his voice and saw the glint in his eye as he placed the book by the side of the parchment and began running his hand along the symbols then looking up the meaning in the book.

"Falwin, write these down as I read them out."

The minutes ticked past. Maegwin chewed her nail while she waited. Leo cracked a joke but fell silent when nobody responded.

Finally Rovann reached the end of the parchment and turned to look at Falwin expectantly. The big man peered at what he'd written, his eyes scanning the words. As he read, two spots of color formed on his cheeks and his eyebrows pulled slowly down into a frown.

"Fates preserve us," he whispered.

"What is it?" Rovann asked. "What does it say?"

Falwin's eyes flicked up to Rovann's. Maegwin didn't like the dread that seemed to fill his expression. "These are details of Hounsey's plan. You were right, Rovann. He is in league with the Songmaker and it's far, far worse than we thought. Listen to this. *You are to take Carrow Crossing. Descend on the citadel in full force and secure the bridge. This will give us access to the capital and I will bring my forces to meet yours at Bleaklow Point. My plans for the Hawk are in place. My soldiers will ambush him at Turnstone on the Sarth Road. He will become my puppet. My plans are ripening and soon we will have what we desire. But you must play your part. Take Carrow Crossing. Do not fail me.*"

Angry muttering broke out amongst the soldiers. Lady swore and drew her throwing knives. Finn made the sign against evil. Clearly this name was known to them.

"Who's the Hawk?" Leo asked, echoing Maegwin's thoughts.

Sergeant Hannel answered, "The Hawk is a military title, named after the legion of elite cavalry he commands. The Hawk is Prince Owen, King William's son and heir."

Leo's mouth fell open. "And the Songmaker is planning to kidnap him?"

"So it appears," Rovann answered. He'd been staring at Falwin the whole time, and now he addressed the mage directly. "What is Prince Owen doing on the Sarth Road? He's supposed to be in Silverport."

Falwin shook his head. "That was a ruse. Prince Owen has been in Argania for the past two months, brokering an alliance with Grand Duchess Briallyn. But I don't understand why he's coming by road. He was supposed to be traveling back to Tyrlindon by river."

"The river routes may be impassable," Syrie snapped. "Particularly the Carrow. It's prone to flooding and with all the rain we've been having…" her voice trailed off as the implication of her words sank in.

Falwin shook his head. "No. I don't believe Hounsey has that kind of power."

"But the Songmaker does," Maegwin found herself saying. Memories flooded her mind. Howling wind. Driving rain. A destroyed town full of fear. "You didn't see what he did to Angard."

"We've been tricked and led like lambs at every turn!" Syrie snapped. The small woman's skin was slicked with sweat and anger blazed in her eyes. "Call ourselves mages? A bunch of schoolchildren wouldn't have fallen for this trickery!"

"Calm yourself, Syrie," Rovann said. "We still have time—"

"Time?" she spat. "Time for what? His army marches on Tyrlindon, the capital is not warned, and he has captured Prince Owen! We have no time at all!"

Rovann placed his hands on her shoulders, forcing her to look at him. "Hounsey laid a trap to delay us here. That means his plans are not yet ready. Thanks to Maegwin, we have sprung the trap. There is still time if we act quickly."

Syrie scrubbed her chin with the stump of her wrist. "Then what are we going to do?"

Rovann sucked in a deep breath, closed his eyes, opened them again. He seemed to visibly gather himself. "Falwin, you will ride back to Tyrlindon immediately. You will warn the king and the college that Hounsey is marching on Tyrlindon. You will spread word through the countryside and evacuate as many villages as possible that lie in the army's path. You will make sure Tyrlindon is prepared for siege."

Falwin's face twisted into a scowl. "Yes, I'll go. Hounsey won't sneak up on Tyrlindon while there's still breath in my body. You have my word on that."

Rovann nodded then turned to Syrie and Captain Tyan. "The rest of you will go to Carrow Crossing. Hold Hounsey's forces for as long as possible. We must give Falwin enough time to reach Tyrlindon and warn the city."

"Carrow Crossing is over fifty miles to the north," Captain Tyan pointed out. "How will we get there in time?"

"I'll do it," said Syrie. "I'll take us through the Eorthe."

Rovann frowned at her. "That is a lot of people to carry, Syrie. It will be dangerous for you."

"Is there any alternative? No, I thought not. And you? What is your part in this?"

"I will go after the prince. I'll be damned if I'll leave him to become the Songmaker's puppet."

"Take some of the soldiers with you. You shouldn't go alone."

"He won't be," said Maegwin, pushing herself from the wall. "I'll go with him."

Rovann met her gaze and nodded. "I know the Sarth Road but I've never heard of the ambush site. Turnstone, wasn't it? Anyone know it?"

Leo nodded. "Yes, my lord, I've passed through before. I spent many a night at the lady Maria's manor in Furrow, not three miles from Turnstone. I can show you the way!"

Rovann frowned at the minstrel, clearly reluctant to let him accompany them. But there really wasn't much choice. "Fine. Let's get moving."

Wait," said Syrie. She fumbled in her pocket and

brought out a smooth round stone which she pressed into Rovann's hand. "This has been aspected. Once you have the prince, use it to escape through the Eorthe. And be careful."

Rovann closed his hands around the stone and nodded his thanks to the Fourth. Taking one last look at the gathered company he squared his shoulders.

"We know our tasks. Let's get to them."

Chapter Nine

"Are you sure this is the place?" Rovann asked.

Leo chewed his lip as they stared down at the Sarth Road. Maegwin understood why it was perfect for an ambush: narrow and hemmed in by steep, wooded hills, a traveler wouldn't know an enemy was there until they attacked.

"Well?" Rovann asked.

"Um, yes, I think so." The young minstrel's eyes wandered up and down the road. "Yes! I remember now. Turnstone is that way, not far at all."

Rovann frowned at Leo as if not convinced but nudged his horse into a trot through the trees, riding parallel with the road below.

They had ridden hard for hours, until their horses were lathered and blowing. At the moment the road was empty, stretching into the distance with no sign of either Prince Owen's traveling party or of Hounsey's men. Maegwin chewed her nail and glanced at Rovann where he rode Glynn four paces from her. She sensed the tension radiating from him. His blue eyes were icy, his jaw tense. He looked like a man itching for a fight.

"I'm sure it's just up here, my lady," Leo said to Maegwin. "I'm sure of it."

"I believe you, Leo," she replied, smiling at the youth.

"I don't think Lord Rovann does," he replied. "He's still angry with me for following you, isn't he?"

"Is that why you volunteered to guide us? To impress Rovann?"

Leo shrugged. "I must make it up to him somehow. At least this way I can prove I'm not totally useless."

Leo's normal good cheer had evaporated and the expression on his freckled face was thoroughly miserable. Maegwin guessed this grand adventure had not exactly turned out how he'd hoped.

"Think of all the material you'll get from this," Maegwin said, trying to cheer him up. "You've ridden with the Lord First, broken into a traitor's stronghold and are on your way to rescue a prince! You could make endless songs out of that. And what's more, they'll be uniquely your own. Patrons will be falling over themselves to hear them!"

A slow smile spread over Leo's face as he thought about this. "You're right. Original material. How many minstrels can claim to have been part of the songs they sing? Yes! I can picture it now: the inns and taverns of Tyrlindon packed to the rafters, all wanting to hear *The Lay of Leo March!*"

Maegwin raised an eyebrow. "*The Lay of Leo March?*"

His cheeks flushed red. "A working title, only. Until I come up with something better." He began humming under his breath.

Maegwin smiled to herself.

Rovann held up a hand and they pulled the horses to a halt. "Is that it?"

Leo moved forward and peered through the trees. "Yes, that's Turnstone."

"I don't see anything," Maegwin said. "Just some old farm buildings."

Leo nodded. "Yep. Turnstone."

"I thought Turnstone was a village."

"No. A farmstead. Although, by the looks of it, it's abandoned now. Can't say I'm surprised. The land round here was never good for farming."

Maegwin realized what he meant. The farmhouse sat looking forlorn amidst an overgrown garden. Many of the windows were broken and she could see holes in the thatched roof. Around the farmhouse were several outbuildings, equally dilapidated. The whole place looked deserted.

"Where are Hounsey's men?" Maegwin asked. "Where is the prince?"

"That's what we're here to discover." Rovann fixed Maegwin and Leo with a stern gaze. "Listen carefully. I don't want either of you involved in any fighting. I'll warn the prince and his men, then we'll all flee using Syrie's stone. Clear?"

Maegwin shook her head. "You're likely to end up in a fight. Who knows how many men Hounsey has sent? How will you best them alone?"

Rovann didn't answer but the hardness in his gaze sent a shiver down Maegwin's spine.

With sorcery, she thought. *You are the Lord First. They won't know what hit them.*

"You and Leo will watch the road and warn me of anything approaching behind me. Got that?"

"I can help you fight, you damned idiot!" Maegwin hissed. "Surely two blades are better than one?"

"No, Maegwin," he replied, shaking his head. "I can't be worrying about you when I go after the prince. Guard our escape. Please."

Maegwin held his gaze for a moment. "Fine," she said at last. "Leo and I will do as you say."

They rode slowly and carefully toward Turnstone, keeping under the thick cover of the trees. There was no movement within the farmstead and Maegwin began to wonder if this was another one of Hounsey's games.

But then a sound came to her on the breeze: the clop of hooves and the creak of wheels. A cart trundled round the bend. Its bed was filled with sacks and two men sat on the board. Perhaps twenty mounted men rode at the wagon's side, dressed in the rough garments of peasants.

The cart came level with the farmstead and everything seemed to happen at once. A roar sounded and armed men suddenly poured out of the buildings. In response the men with the wagon drew swords and faced the oncoming attackers. The two forces crashed together and battle erupted.

"Is one of those men Prince Owen?" whispered Leo.

Maegwin nudged her horse a step closer and squinted. Her eyes were drawn to a black-haired man whose fighting skills surpassed the others. His sword moved in a blur as he fought against a warrior with a sword and flail. The defender ducked under a wild swing from the flail and then spun around to catch its backswing on his blade. Using his double-handed broadsword more like a quarter staff, the man allowed the flail to tangle itself around the blade and yanked it, pulling Hounsey's soldier from his horse. The black-haired man drew a dagger and threw it into the man's throat. Without pausing, he swung back into the fighting.

Prince Owen, Maegwin guessed. Hounsey's men had obviously realized it too, as they were congregating around the black-haired man.

"Wait here!" Rovann commanded.

He sent Glynn thundering down the slope.

Maegwin's eye was caught by something further down the road. Two mounted figures emerged from the trees and sat calmly watching the battle. A man and woman, toward their middle years, and wearing fine clothes.

Mages, Maegwin thought with a shudder. *And Rovann hasn't seen them.*

"Yah!" she cried, setting heels to her horse's flanks. She clung on grimly, trusting the horse to keep its footing. In only a few heartbeats she cleared the last of the trees and came out onto the level terrain of the road.

The enemy mages stood in their stirrups. The woman extended her arms to either side.

"Rovann!" Maegwin screamed. "Watch out!"

He turned at the sound of her voice, eyes going wide as he spotted the mages behind him. The ground in front of Rovann exploded. Maegwin's horse whinnied and stamped, fighting Maegwin for control. She sawed on the reins, forcing the terrified beast on. Earth showered down on her, smoke obscured her vision. As it dissipated, she saw Rovann picking himself up.

"Get back to Leo! I'll deal with the mages!"

His hand flew out and the enemy mages were plucked from their horses and thrown through the air. They landed in the dirt with a crunch.

Maegwin glanced from Rovann to the battle. Part of her wanted to stay close to Rovann but another part longed to join the fighting. She was sure of one thing: she would not hide in the trees like a coward. Those were Hounsey soldiers over there. Revenge was close. So close. Wheeling her mount, she sent the beast thundering toward the prince's men.

Maegwin's mount hit the line of soldiers with an impact that smashed her teeth together and almost ripped her from the saddle. She was enveloped in dust, noise and confusion. Soldiers bellowed. Horses whinnied. The smell of sweat and fear filled her nostrils. It was intoxicating. Maegwin drank it all in, letting it deluge her senses.

A Hounsey soldier spun toward Maegwin, a long spear aimed at her face. Instinctively she ducked under it then swiped at the man with her sword, taking away half his face. Maegwin had never been trained to fight but the horse beneath her and the sword in her hand felt right, natural. As if she'd been born to it. Something cold settled into Maegwin's bones, locking her emotion away, leaving her icy calm.

I am yours, my mistress, she thought. Deep inside, she heard gleeful laughing. *A life for a life. Revenge, at last.*

Maegwin stopped seeing people. Faces no longer mattered. She saw only Hounsey colors. Only that. Sound drifted away. Movement seemed to slow. Two Hounsey guards spurred their horses toward her. In answer, Maegwin dug her heels into her mount's flanks and sent the beast hurtling at them. Her horse collided with the first beast. Its rider, a woman with spiky hair, lost her grip on her spear and sawed savagely on the reins, trying to bring her mount under control.

Maegwin ducked in time to evade the slashing blade of the other soldier. The man's slash took his arm wide, leaving his side exposed. Maegwin leaned low in her saddle and thrust her sword into the man's armpit. Bright red arterial blood spurted out. Maegwin grinned in delight.

The spiky-haired woman recovered, yanking a short-sword from its scabbard. Maegwin pulled hard on the reins, forcing her mount round to meet her attacker. The woman's arm swung and Maegwin watched as the sword blade came hissing toward her stomach. Then a knife suddenly blossomed from the woman's eye. She fell from the saddle like a stone. One of the prince's men sat on his horse ten paces away, arm still raised. Maegwin nodded her thanks. The man bobbed his head in response then whirled back into the fighting.

To Maegwin's left she saw an archer taking aim at the prince. She kicked her mount, sending it crashing into the man. His shot flew wide, the quarrel burying itself in the wagon with a 'thunk'.

The Hounsey solider bellowed in fury and swung his bow, catching Maegwin across the chin with a crack. Her head snapped back, agony exploding through her face. It was so intense for a moment she could barely think. She leaned forward, pressing her face into her horse's mane and pulling in long breaths as dizziness swamped her. She steeled herself, expecting to feel the blow of a sword or flail against the back of her neck. But the blow didn't come and the faintness passed. Maegwin looked up. The archer sat on the ground in front of her, his head missing.

"You all right?" asked a soldier, reining in beside her.

"Fine," she muttered, feeling her bleeding chin.

"Who are you? Where have you come from?"

Maegwin gestured behind her. "With...the Lord First... come for...the prince."

The man's gaze narrowed on Rovann's battle with the

enemy mages and he started in suprise. "Here, take this. That pig-sticker will get you nowhere."

He handed her a broadsword carved on the pommel with the bear's head of Hounsey. It had twice the reach of the sword that Hesha had leant her. Maegwin hefted the weapon, gaging its weight. It seemed fitting to slay Hounsey men with a Hounsey blade.

"Thanks."

The man glanced up. "Watch out!"

Maegwin saw a ball of flame arcing toward them. A concussion rocked the earth. Maegwin's horse reared and she fell off, landing face-first in the mud. Her ears rang. Flecks of blackness flitted across her vision. A heartbeat later, her sight cleared. Mud and trampled grass lay by face, and maybe a pace away, a severed finger. She groaned as she rolled slowly onto her side, feeling broken teeth grind in her jaw.

She looked around wildly, searching for Rovann. Had he been caught in that blast? Finally, she spotted him locked in battle with the enemy mages. Sorcery played in the air around them but neither side seemed to be able to land a blow, their spells countering the other with little effect.

Maegwin clambered onto her hands and knees. Three paces away lay the prince's soldier and his horse. The stunned beast had rolled onto the man's leg and he was trapped beneath the stocky brown mare. Maegwin crawled over and grabbed him beneath his armpits. Gritting her teeth, she pulled. The man didn't budge. The horse was still alive, lying on its side, nostrils wide with its panicked breaths. Maegwin approached slowly, hands held out to the side.

"Shush. Easy, girl." The mare watched with wide, fearful eyes.

The saddle strap had twisted around the man's leg. Maegwin grabbed the loose end and pulled but the buckle was stuck. Mud and dried blood had crusted on it, making the mechanism stiff and unyielding. Suddenly Leo knelt down next to her.

"What are you doing here?" she demanded. "You were told to stay in the trees."

"What fun would that be?" Leo replied, smiling through the grime that covered his face.

They pulled together and the strap came free. The saddle slid slowly off the horse's back and the prince's man crawled free, massaging the blood back into his leg. Maegwin remembered another time Leo had helped her free a trapped man. That time it had been Rovann in the rubble of Angard.

"You're making a habit of this, Leo," Maegwin said, clapping the young minstrel on the shoulder.

Leo grinned, pleased with himself. "More material for my songs! I never knew life could be so exciting!"

"And dangerous. You should get out of here while you still can."

"What, and be called a coward? I promised to make it up to Lord Rovann and I meant it! Let it not be said that Leo March does not keep his word! Surely Lord Rovann will forgive me when he finds out how bravely I've fought?"

Maegwin opened her mouth but before she could speak, Leo surged to his feet and threw himself back into the fighting. He had picked up a spear from somewhere and waved it around wildly. The fool was going to get himself killed. With a growl, Maegwin retrieved the broadsword the prince's man had given her. She dug the point into the ground and used it to lever herself up. Her ears still rang from the explosion.

Looking around, she saw people and horses strewn across the site. A shaven-headed man rose from the mud with a bellow, swinging a sword. Maegwin stabbed him through the neck. Blood showered, spraying across Maegwin's face. A rush of elation tingled through her body. She licked her lips, tasting the iron tang of the man's blood.

A life for a life.

Sword raised, she looked around for her next opponent. The Hounsey guards were regrouping under the command of a tall man bellowing commands. They formed into tight fighting lines and advanced.

She reached the prince's cordon. Four steps to her left Prince Owen fought fiercely. He had the same dark hair and eyes as his father and his jaw was set with determination. He was bleeding from several cuts to his arms and face but barely seemed to notice.

"Stand your ground!" he bellowed at his men. "Hold the line!"

Maegwin set her back to the cart, taking a place next to Leo. The minstrel had taken a blow across his forehead, leaving a bloody gash. He looked pale and a little shaky but wielded the spear with admirable determination.

Together she and Leo faced a man fighting with a double-handed ax. Maegwin threw herself to the left as the gore-smeared weapon swung at her. The blade embedded itself in the wagon and stuck fast. Leo darted in and hamstringed the man whilst Maegwin stabbed him in the stomach.

She wiped sweat from her eyes. Somewhere in the distance she heard the boom and crash of the mages' battle but the cart blocked her view. Fear clutched her belly. If anything should happen to Rovann…

A crossbow bolt suddenly thudded into the cart by her head.

"Archers!" bellowed Prince Owen. "Load crossbows!"

Maegwin crouched, shielding herself with her arms as the zing of arrows filled the air. When she looked again, Hounsey's bowmen lay dead in a line across the road. Hounsey pikemen replaced them.

"I don't like the look of those weapons," said Leo beside Maegwin. "I bet they could skewer a wild boar."

Maegwin fixed her eyes on the advancing line. It didn't matter what weapons they used. They would still die under her sword. She dropped into a crouch and felt something bubbling inside her. Words spilled between her lips.

> I go to war to break my foe,
> To shed their blood, to feed their woe,
> I go to war to rend and slay,
> To wreak revenge and make them pay.

She had no idea where the song came from. *Sho-La? Mistress? Is this you?* she thought. *Are these your words?*

The song filled her with power, with delight. Swinging the sword high, she brought it down in a two-handed diagonal slash that opened a man's belly. She yelled in triumph as he toppled to the ground clutching his entrails. A spear hurtled toward her. She twisted and the spear grazed along her back, lighting her spine with fire. She smacked the flat of her blade into the stomach of the woman who had thrown the spear. As the woman doubled over, Maegwin punched her, hearing her nose crack with a satisfying crunch.

The woman crashed onto her back, one hand clutching her face, the other reaching toward Maegwin imploringly.

"Don't," she whimpered, eyes wide with fear. "Mercy. Please."

Maegwin leant over, sword raised. Then paused. The woman had startling blue eyes and black hair that tumbled free of her bear's head helmet. A white scar ran across the bridge of her nose.

Who awaited this woman back home? Did she have children? A husband? Were people anxiously watching for this woman's return?

A voice whispered in Maegwin's head. *A life for a life. Take it.*

Maegwin raised her sword. But suddenly the battle chant died on her lips. Something else stirred inside her. Another song. One that sang of healing and peace and mercy. The Sentinel. In her mind's eye she saw a golden tree and a gentle voice spoke.

Mercy, Maegwin.

She was a priestess of Sho-La and her goddess taught forgiveness of your enemies. But she was also a priestess of the Dark Goddess who taught vengeance.

Maegwin blinked once, twice. Then she staggered back, her sword falling from nerveless fingers. Seizing her chance, the Hounsey woman scrabbled up and dashed away. Maegwin leaned against the cart. Around her, the battle raged. Inside she felt strange, as if she had reached the edge of a cliff...and taken a step back.

She looked up, realizing she could no longer hear the sounds of the mages fighting. She scrabbled onto the cart and looked around, not caring if she became an easy target for archers. Where was Rovann? Where was he? Her eyes settled on a collapsed shape lying in the mud. Her heat thudded.

Rovann!

Where were Hounsey's mages? Surely they would not have fled? They had come here to capture the prince and wouldn't leave without their prize—

She spun around to scream a warning just as she felt a rumble in the ground beneath the cart. Too late. The air around the prince suddenly shimmered and the two enemy mages flickered into existence beside him. The man grabbed the prince by the throat and whispered something. Prince Owen went as limp as a rag doll. The woman crouched low and flung out a surge of power that knocked the prince's defenders from their feet.

Maegwin clung on as the cart bucked and watched as a portal ripped open the air behind the prince. It swirled with shadowy energies.

"Stop them!" Maegwin screamed.

The mages backed toward the portal, pulling the prince with them. Then suddenly a sword tip erupted from the female mage's chest. She gurgled in surprise before collapsing on her face in the dirt, revealing Leo clutching a bloodied sword and looking terrified.

The other mage shouted something in a strange language, yanked the prince through the portal and disappeared.

"Leo!" Maegwin screamed.

The minstrel threw himself after the prince. He stepped into the portal and it flared brightly. As the light died, Maegwin saw Leo hanging suspended within it, like a fly trapped in ointment.

Leo's eyes widened. Around him, the portal began to collapse like a slowly contracting bubble. Leo's eyes found Maegwin's. They were clouded with pain. The minstrel screamed once, a sound that set Maegwin's hair on end. Then the portal collapsed and he was gone.

"Leo!"

Rovann woke with a start. Cold drops of rain splashed against his skin and ran down his neck. He blinked, trying to figure out where he was. Memory crashed back in. Fighting. Prince Owen besieged. Enemy mages unleashing terrible sorcery. Darkness that broke Rovann's wards. Then nothing.

Groaning, he rolled onto his stomach and raised his head. Maegwin stood atop the wagon, shouting something at the prince. Beneath Rovann, the ground trembled.

No, he thought. *No.*

Hounsey's mages appeared behind the prince and a portal split the air.

Get up! Rovann shouted at himself. *Get up!*

But his body wouldn't obey. He watched in horror as Leo killed the one mage, as the other dragged the prince into the portal and Leo followed. The portal was like a hole ripped in the fabric of the world, sucking out all light. Chaos, Rovann realized.

And Leo was trapped within it.

As Rovann watched, the portal contracted. The young minstrel wailed in pain, a sound that pierced Rovann's heart. Leo had risked his life to help Rovann in Angard and now he'd done the same for Prince Owen.

Rovann stretched his arm out and tried to summon something, anything, to aid the minstrel. But Rovann had nothing. He was as empty as a burst waterskin.

Come on, curse you! he screamed at himself.

Faintly, the Aethyr stirred within him, like a tiny trickle breaking free of a dam. Summoning as much energy as he could muster from his exhausted body, Rovann began shaping sorcery into a spell to cut Leo free. But the words had barely formed on his tongue when, with a snap that sent a shockwave across the area, the portal closed. Leo was gone.

"Leo!" Maegwin's scream ripped the air.

Rovann stared at the place where the portal had been. Leo was dead. Prince Owen was in the hands of the Songmaker. He'd failed.

Slowly, every muscle protesting, Rovann climbed to his feet.

The soldiers formed a perimeter around the wagon, weapons drawn, but the rest of Hounsey's soldiers turned around and fled. The prince's soldiers seemed stunned by the sudden disappearance of their lord. Rovann staggered toward the group and Maegwin ran to meet him.

"Rovann! You have to go after him! You have to save Leo!"

Rovann glowered at her. "Go after him? That was Chaotic power, woman! Leo is dead!"

Her eyes widened and something shifted within them. "But...but..."

Rovann turned away, swaying like a drunken man. The road had become a scene of carnage. Men and horses lay strewn around like bits of flotsam. Some were dead, some struggled to stand.

Rovann pinched the bridge of his nose and then scrubbed a hand through his hair. How could the Songmaker have harnessed Chaos? Nothing living had to power to wield the Outer Darkness. Nothing.

He staggered up to the prince's men. "Who is in charge here?"

A tall, scarred woman stepped forward. "Lieutenant

Andra, my lord." She swallowed thickly. "My lord, where is the prince? Who were those people?"

"Traitors, lieutenant. Prince Owen is now in the Songmaker's hands."

"Fates preserve us!" she whispered. "What will he do to him?"

"The Songmaker wants Amaury, whole and intact. Prince Owen will become his puppet king."

"We have to go after him!" Lieutenant Andra hissed. "We have to rescue the prince!"

Rovann's eyes came to rest on the road where it wound into the distance. He felt like a game piece being moved across a board. But who was moving the pieces? Who were the players in this game?

Why must you always do the right thing? Istra had once asked him. *Why must you put your duty before everything? Others could carry this burden.* And he'd answered, *there are no others, Istra. I am the King's Mage. The burden is mine.*

Istra might be gone, but his words were still true. Steeling his determination, he turned back to the lieutenant.

"Lieutenant Andra, what is the state of your soldiers?"

"Bad, my lord. We've lost Charyn, Marlow and Getty. Ander has taken a blow on the head and can no longer fight."

Rovann rubbed his chin as he considered. "Detail one of your men to take the wounded back to Tyrlindon in the wagon. Lay the bodies over there."

"What about the prince?"

"Even now Lord Cedric Hounsey is marching on Carrow Crossing. I've sent a force there to secure the citadel and we'll join them. We will hold Hounsey at Carrow Crossing and do what we can to discover the prince's fate."

The lieutenant saluted and began shouting orders.

Rovann watched the soldiers move with practiced efficiency. He approached the line of bodies and saw sightless eyes staring at the sky, mouths stretched open in pain, gaping wounds black with blood.

How many more? he asked himself. *How many?*

Opening himself to the Realm of Fire, he held out his hand and white hot flame enveloped the bodies. After only a few minutes nothing remained but ash that floated gently on the breeze.

"Let's get going. Form a circle," Rovann instructed, cupping his hands over his heart. "And hold hands."

Maegwin stood off to one side, staring at the spot where Leo had disappeared.

"Join us please, Maegwin," Rovann called.

Maegwin turned and walked listlessly toward them. She did not look at Rovann as she took her place next to him in the circle.

Chapter Ten

Maegwin watched the spot where Leo had disappeared. How could he be gone? One minute full of life, the next, nothing. Wiped from existence.

Just like your sisters, said a voice in her head.

She should have saved Leo. She should have done...something. Rovann stepped closer and his hand gripped hers. She clung on tightly.

"Are you all right, Maegwin?"

She nodded, even though it was a lie. Rovann's eyes were full of concern. And guilt.

Yes, she thought. *We should have saved him. We both failed.*

Rovann nodded, as if sensing her thought.

Maegwin wanted to throw her arms around him, bury her face in his shoulder and feel his strong arms circling her. But she didn't. She stood with her back straight and eyes fixed ahead.

Rovann stepped into the middle of the circle and clasped the round stone Syrie had given him. In a deep voice, he began to chant. The words made no sense and

Maegwin guessed they were in a language that no human could understand. The chant reverberated deep inside her chest.

"My lady," said someone at her side. She turned to see the soldier who'd given her a sword. "I'm sorry about your friend. He was brave to do what he did."

Maegwin nodded, not trusting herself to speak.

"We'll say a prayer for him. When we get the time."

A prayer? Maegwin wanted to ask. *What good will that do? Vengeance is what I want. For Leo. For myself.*

Rovann's head snapped up. "It's coming. You won't be able to breathe for a time but try not to panic, you'll be perfectly safe."

"What does he mean 'we won't be able to breathe?'" said one of the soldiers with a hint of panic in her voice.

The lieutenant shrugged. "He said we'll be safe."

"Hang on, I never agreed to being suffocated! I think we should—"

The soldier's words cut off with a strangled cry. The woman was yanked downward. Maegwin had a second to register this before something grabbed her feet and pulled with incredible force. She was suddenly drowning in mud. Soil smothered her like a blanket. It filled her eyes, nose, ears, mouth. The musty smell of earth permeated her nostrils, the cold of it pressing against her skin. She couldn't breathe. She couldn't hear. She couldn't see. But there was no pain. Her lungs no longer worked but that didn't seem to matter. She remembered Rovann's warning.

Despite the sensation of drowning, Maegwin forced herself to relax. A strange power held her. In Maegwin's mind's eye it conjured images of rocks and rushing rivers and growing things. It spoke of still lakes and deep caverns where no light shone. It whispered of shimmering mist and the flight of birds. Of the slow lives of trees and the rustle of small creatures in the undergrowth.

The power of the Realm of Earth. The Eorthe.

Maegwin lay suspended in it for what seemed an age but finally the sensation receded and she opened her eyes. A light rain fell from a gray sky. A bird of prey circled far above, its piercing cry splitting the air. With a grunt, Maegwin rolled over and staggered to her feet. She took a few tottering steps, fighting down a ripple of dizziness and nausea. Blinking, she looked around. She stood on a hillside, overlooking a broad river valley filled with trees. Mud covered Maegwin from head to foot. Her hair was a matted tangle, her clothes unrecognizable.

But she was alive. And miles from where they'd started.

Maegwin scanned around for Rovann and saw him sitting a few paces away, a dazed expression on his face. She hurried over and helped him stand.

Some of the soldiers stood with hands on knees, retching into the dirt.

"That was horrible," someone muttered. "I'm never doing that again."

Rovann made his way round the group, checking everyone was accounted for. When he was satisfied he said, "Fourth Syrie's calculations were perfect. I estimate we're perhaps two miles from Carrow Crossing. We should be ahead of Hounsey's army but we'll have to travel quickly. Ready?"

Everyone nodded, too tired for words.

"Right. Let's go."

They moved off at a steady jog, a pace that trained soldiers could keep up for hours. Maegwin ran at Rovann's side. He stayed silent but his face was ashen, his hand clamped to the wound in his side.

The path came out onto a wide road, paved and neatly kept like the Kingsroad. Maegwin got her first look at Carrow River.

She had never seen anything like it. There had been rivers on the temples lands but nothing to equal this. The river was so wide that its far bank lay shrouded in haze, lost in the spume rising from the raging torrent. The Carrow's near bank was sheer, almost a cliff, with straggly bushes clinging to its side. Rocks jutted out of the river at intervals, the water swirling white and vicious around them. An angry rumble filled the air.

Maegwin swallowed. The river's power thrummed on her senses. It was like the Sentinel, primal and uncompromising.

Maegwin understood why the river was impassable. Any boats that tried to traverse these waters would likely be smashed to pieces, its occupants dragged to the bottom by the current. This must be why the massive iron and timber bridge that spanned the river was so strategically important. With no other river crossings for miles, whoever controlled this bridge controlled all traffic wishing to approach Tyrlindon.

On this side of the river the bridge entrance was guarded by a gray citadel that squatted on the road like an ugly toad. The citadel's gates stood open. People milled around in the market outside the walls.

Rovann called a halt and they surveyed the citadel from the cover of the trees.

"Where are the guards on the battlements?" growled Lieutenant Andra. "Where are the soldiers on the gate?"

"This is a trader road," Rovann replied, "and the citadel more of a trade outpost than anything. Hounsey and his men can't be that far behind us. What worries me more is that there is no sign of Syrie or Captain Tyan."

People recoiled at the sight of this group of mud-splattered soldiers but they made it to the main gate without challenge.

An armored guardsman who'd been leaning against the wall came to attention and held out a halberd to block their way.

"State your name and business."

"I must speak to your commander right away," Rovann replied.

The guard raised an eyebrow. "Then state your name and business."

Rovann held out his hand, showing the guard the large ruby ring on his finger. "My name is Rovann de Lacey, First of the Council of Mages and King's Mage to William II of Amaury. And my business here is to stop you all being slaughtered by an army that's close behind us! Now take me to your commander!"

The guard swallowed thickly. "Ah, you're one of them. You'd better come with me."

Rovann ground his teeth in frustration as they followed the guard through a tunnel with murder-holes in the roof and emerged into a large courtyard.

They walked into the middle of a stand-off.

Captain Tyan and his company stood in the courtyard. Facing them were a group of guards wearing the king's livery. No weapons had been drawn but Rovann could taste the tension in the air.

"List to me, you stupid bastard," Tyan growled. "Enemies are marching here right now! Fetch your commander and rouse the garrison before you're all slaughtered!"

The man Tyan addressed stood his ground "I've told you what Commander Charis said. Yore not to be allowed in. He's received no message from the king—"

"Take a look over your battlements and that should be all the bloody message you need!"

Rovann scanned around, looking for Syrie. At last he spotted her lying on the ground. Corporal Hesha knelt by the mage's side, mopping her brow with a bit of cloth. Syrie's eyes were closed, her skin pale.

Cursing, Rovann ran over and went down on his knees on the wet cobbles.

"My Lord First!" exclaimed Hesha. "Thank the Fates!"

"What happened?" Rovann asked as he placed his hand on Syrie's forehead.

"Don't know, sir. She took us under the ground and when we came out, she just collapsed. We ended up further away than we wanted and we've only just got here. These fools won't let us in!"

Rovann closed his eyes and sent his senses questing toward Syrie. She was exhausted, all her energy spent. Carrying so many people through the Eorthe had been too much for her. She'd not had the use of her channel stone, which she'd given to Rovann instead. As a result, she'd poured almost all her life-force into getting the soldiers here.

Rovann opened a gate to the Realm of Aethyr and let it flow from his hand into Syrie. He felt her heartbeat strengthen, her pulse quicken, vitality rush through her veins. The paleness left her skin and two spots of color suffused her cheeks.

Rovann withdrew his hand and gripped Syrie's shoulder. He eyes fluttered open.

"Rovann?"

She sat up, looking around. "The prince?"

Rovann shook his head and a look of horror passed across Syrie's' face. "And Leo?"

Rovann swallowed. "Lost."

Syrie didn't say anything, shock showing on her face. Then her expression hardened. "Hounsey will pay for this. The Songmaker will pay for this."

"Yes," Rovann agreed. "They will."

He held out his hand, helped Syrie to her feet and turned to where Captain Tyan was facing down the garrison captain.

"Do you recognize this? He asked the man, brandishing his ruby ring,

"I…um…" stammered the captain.

"There's no time for this," Rovann growled. He flicked his wrist and a wave of sorcery rolled out, knocking the garrison from the feet. Rovann turned to the gate guard who'd accompanied him into the citadel.

"What's your name?"

"Corporal Tanner, sir,"

"Well, Corporal Tanner, the citadel is now under my command. You will rouse the garrison and give Captain Tyan here any assistance he requires."

Corporal Tanner saluted, "Yes, sir!"

"What is the complement of the garrison here?"

Tanner shifted his feet. "Most are assigned to guarding the treasury, sir. We're mostly infantry with a few archers. About fifty, all told. The commander reckons that's all we need to run this place properly."

Rovann frowned. "Captain Tyan, Lieutenant Andra has fourteen soldiers, to add to our company. Take command of the defense as you sit fit."

Captain Tyan nodded. "Aye, sir."

He led the soldiers up a set of stone steps onto the battlements then disappeared into the tower. Rovann watched them go. With a squawk a crow landed on the battlements, a piece of carrion dangling from its beak. The bird moved its head from side to side, black eyes glittering in the gloomy light.

Rovann shivered. "Come on."

Maegwin and Syrie followed as Rovann pushed open the wide, ornate doors into the inner keep. Their feet echoed on flagstones as they hurried down a corridor lit with lamps and through another set of doors into the room beyond.

Rovann found himself in a large hall. A long table filled most of it, with a cold fireplace at the far end. A man sat at the head of the table, staring at them. He had a chicken leg in one hand and juice dribbling down his chin.

"What's the meaning of this?" he yelled, pointing at Rovann with the chicken leg. "Who let you in?"

Rovann crossed the room, placed his palms flat on the table and stared at the man. "Corporal Tanner let us in, commander. And right now, he's rousing your garrison. A task you've sadly neglected."

The commander ripped a piece of chicken from the leg and chewed noisily. "How I run my garrison is no business of yours. You might be a trader, and a rich one judging by that ring on your finger, but if you want to cross the river I suggest you speak to me in a more civil tone!"

Rovann fought down an urge to slap the man. "If you hadn't been holed out here, growing carbuncles on that fat backside of yours, you'd recognize that the ring on my finger is that of the King's Mage."

"King's Mage is it?" said the man, dropping the chicken

bone onto his platter and picking up a large slab of bread which he proceeded to sweep around his plate, mopping up the chicken juice. "What brings you here? I've had my tax inspection this year and everything was in order. I have the tallies if you want to check them—"

Rovann slammed his palm onto the table, making the crockery rattle. "Commander, there is an army marching to your gates, led by Lord Cedric Hounsey. You must close the gates, bring everyone inside the citadel and be ready for siege."

The commander shook his head, making his jowls wobble "An army? What rubbish! There is no way an army could sneak up on us without me knowing about it."

Syrie's temper snapped. She marched up to the commander and grabbed him by the collar. "Listen to me, you fat bag of piss. If you don't close those gates, an army will be marching on Tyrlindon by sundown three days from now. People will die and you, I promise, will be the first among them!"

"How dare you threaten me?" shrieked the commander, pushing away Syrie's hand. "I am Lord Commander Charis, of house Sylen. I will not be spoken to in such a manner!"

"And I am Syrie, Fourth of the Council of Mages and you will do as I ask!"

The commander's lip curled in a sneer. "I have entertained some of the land's most powerful people in this very hall. Only last month the Alurian ambassador took dinner with me. Your titles don't impress me, Fourth of the Council of Mages. Now remove yourselves and let me finish my dinner in peace!"

Syrie goggled, heat flushing her cheeks. Rovann began to speak but paused as an almighty clanging shook through the great hall. It took a second for Rovann to realize what it was: the warning bell.

The commander's eyes widened. He moved his mouth like a stranded fish but no words came out.

Rovann stared at the commander, giving him a chance to take charge. But the man just sat there, staring like a bewildered child. With a growl, Rovann whirled and strode out into the courtyard. The commander stumbled behind them, his napkin tucked into the top of his chainmail shirt.

"What's happening?" he said, looking around as though lost. "What's happening?"

Rovann grabbed the man's shoulder. "Do you have message birds?"

The commander nodded. "Yes, old Spinnow keeps them in the tower."

"Then dispatch all of them for Tyrlindon. Warn the king that Hounsey has turned traitor and that we'll try to hold his army here at Carrow Crossing."

The commander swallowed thickly and stumbled toward the tower.

Rovann sprinted across the courtyard and up the stone steps that led to the battlements. At the top, the wind was stronger, ripping at his hair and clothes. The warning bell clanged from the tower.

Captain Tyan leaned on the wall, surveying the approach to the citadel. He turned as Rovann approached. "Corporal Tanner's estimate was slightly optimistic. One of the squads was sent over to the Marlin garrison and wasn't replaced. We have forty-six soldiers, including my own. When fully manned, I suspect this citadel could hold off an army indefinitely, particularly with the supply route of the river at its back. As it is," he shrugged, "who knows?"

Rovann leaned on the battlements and looked out.

Below, panic had erupted amongst the stallholders. They were running toward the gates, some clutching their wares, others carrying only what they wore on their back. Tallo and Lady moved through the crowd, swords drawn, moving the people along. Raising his eyes, Rovann noticed the cause of the stallholders' concern. A wave of silver crept through the trees toward the citadel.

Light glinting off armor, Rovann realized. Realms, how many men did Hounsey have?

"Hounsey doesn't know the garrison is under-manned," said Rovann. "We must make him think we have a full force defending this citadel."

"Agreed," replied Tyan, scrubbing a hand through his stubbly beard. "We have to hope that Hounsey, in his arrogance, hasn't bothered to scout this area. The soldiers will man the walls with a small reserve in the courtyard, should the gates be lost."

Beside him, Syrie whistled under her breath. Her almond-shaped eyes narrowed on the approaching army. "It won't be enough. Hounsey is no fool. He'll realize the walls aren't fully manned. As soon as he does, he'll charge the gates and we'll all be dead before the sun sets tonight. Somehow we must force him to lay siege. It's the only way to give Tyrlindon time to prepare."

"How do you plan to do that?" asked Tyan sharply. "Unless you can magic soldiers out of thin air, I don't think we have any choice."

"Do they have an armory here?" Syrie asked.

"They do."

"Then arm the civilians. The stallholders, the cooks, the chambermaids. Realms, arm the bloody stable boys if it comes to it! Anyone strong enough to bear arms must man the battlements."

Captain Tyan's mouth set into a flat line. "Asking them to fight would be a death sentence."

"There is no choice!" snapped Syrie. "If we don't convince Hounsey to lay siege and hold him here, the capital will be taken unawares. Then how many innocents will die?"

Captain Tyan studied her for a moment. Rovann could see the thoughts moving behind the man's eyes. It was a terrible choice. Should he sacrifice the lives of a few to save many? Rovann understood the weight of such choices. At last, Captain Tyan nodded.

"Corporal Hesha!" he shouted. "Arm the civilians and get them onto the battlements. Teach them how to stand as though they're soldiers and do it quickly. We don't have much time before the army arrives."

Hesha saluted crisply, "Yes, sir!"

Tyan leaned over the battlements and bellowed, "Tallo! Lady! Get yourselves in here now! Close the gates and bar them!"

On the road below Tallo and Lady pushed the remaining civilians toward the gate. Behind them, Hounsey soldiers emerged from the trees, spilling across the road in a sea of silver. The bear's head banner of Hounsey snapped above them in the breeze.

"Everyone to the battlements!" shouted Captain Tyan.

There was a clang as the gates closed and an influx of soldiers came pelting up the steps onto the battlements taking position and drawing weapons.

Rovann stared out at the sea of men. Where was Hounsey? Where was the prince?

He pulled in a deep breath. Closed his eyes. Opened them.

It was time.

Maegwin stood on the battlements beside Rovann, watching Hounsey's forces surround the citadel. Along the riverbank, across the open ground between the citadel and the surrounding woodland, Hounsey's forces approached from all directions, sweeping in like a vast silver tide.

And they were utterly silent.

No war cries, no challenges, no drums beating out their march. Just silence and ruthless precision.

A few faint screams echoed from the far end of the market but were quickly strangled. Maegwin hardened her heart against the sound. Perhaps a merchant, too greedy to leave behind his wares, or else an eager thief seeing an opportunity in the abandoned stalls. Either way, they'd learned the cost of their folly.

The tide of soldiers swept toward the citadel…and stopped. A shiver went through the ranks.

"Out of range of our archers," Captain Tyan growled. "They intend to lay siege."

There was relief in Tyan's voice but Maegwin didn't share it. She wanted battle. She wanted shouting, screaming, sweat, noise. She wanted Hounsey's face slack with fear.

"Our ruse won't fool them for long," Rovann said. "We can't hold the citadel."

It was said quietly, out of hearing of the traders and market-goers being ushered onto the battlements by Hesha. They wore borrowed armor and carried borrowed weapons. Although they stood straight under the careful direction of Hannel and Hesha, Maegwin could smell their fear. If Hounsey's forces had come a few steps closer, they could have smelled it too.

"Perhaps we're doing the wrong thing," said Syrie. "Perhaps we should just rescue the prince and make a run for it across the bridge. If we torch the bridge once we're safely across, we will stop Hounsey from crossing."

"It's not that simple," Tyan replied. "Hounsey has engineers. If they gain access to the citadel's landing stages on the river, they could build a floating bridge in no time."

Syrie growled in frustration, wrapping her cloak tightly around her as though suddenly cold. "I know you're right. But I can't just sit here whilst Prince Owen is in that traitor's hands. We have to get him back. I can use the Eorthe to get us close to Hounsey, then we snatch the prince from under his nose." Syrie's voice was tight with emotion and Maegwin remembered what Rovann had told her of Syrie's fierce loyalty to the king. She seemed to be taking the loss of the prince personally.

Maegwin watched Rovann closely. *Yes,* she urged him silently, *strike against Hounsey. I'll go with Syrie and deal such destruction—*

"No," Rovann said. "It's too dangerous. If you were killed there would be one less mage defending Tyrlindon, one less adept of the Eorthe to stand in the Songmaker's path. You're too valuable, Syrie."

She hissed like a cat. "So we do nothing?"

"No. We defend this citadel for as long as we can—" he held out his hand to stall Syrie's answer. "And we don't even know if Hounsey has the prince."

"Of course Hounsey has him! You saw the mages who abducted him! They were with Hounsey soldiers, Rovann."

"But we don't know where they took the prince," Rovann replied, fixing his icy gaze on Syrie. "Think about it. If you had captured such a prize would you send that prize somewhere it would be at risk? I don't think so. In fact, I don't think Hounsey holds Prince Owen at all."

"Then who—"

Syrie's words fell away as realization dawned. Silence descended between the two mages and in that silence Maegwin saw a single name written.

The Songmaker.

Him again. The rebel mage's schemes seemed to dominate her life. Ever since that terrible day at the temple.

The Songmaker.

A name that carried so much. Yet Maegwin knew nothing about him. Nothing beyond the vague dread his name inspired. Nothing beyond the hazy image of some faceless enemy. The spider in the shadows.

Rovann was fighting a war against this man but it was not Maegwin's struggle. When she thought of the Songmaker she felt nothing at all. It was just a name. She wanted Hounsey. He was the one who had killed her sisters, destroyed her life, driven her into the arms of the Dark Goddess.

A breeze blew across the battlements, lifting Maegwin's hair from her shoulders, sending it streaming out behind her. She watched the motionless army.

"What are they waiting for?" she wondered aloud. "Why don't they attack?"

What did those soldiers feel as they stared up at the intimidating walls of the citadel, Maegwin asked herself. Hatred? Anger? Or was it fear? Would they have rather stayed at home in peace? Were they just following orders the way Maegwin followed the orders of the High Priestess?

Not good enough, a voice whispered inside her head. *There is always a choice. You live or die by them. Meryk Hounsey was following his father's orders when he burned your sisters alive. Does that make him any less guilty?*

No, my mistress, she answered. *It does not.*

A sudden sharp pain made her look down. She realized she had curled her hands into fists, digging her nails deep into her palms. Slowly, she forced herself to relax, uncurling her fingers and resting them on the coarse stone of the wall.

Patience.

Sergeant Hannel ran over to speak to his captain. "We're surrounded on three sides, sir," he reported. "A group of sappers have gone down the riverbank on ropes. I reckon they're trying to undermine the citadel's foundations, or else create enough instability to make us panic."

Captain Tyan nodded. "Send someone to keep an eye on them. If it looks like they're getting anywhere, we'll station people in the north tower and wash those sappers off the bank with boiling oil. For now, just keep watch."

"Aye, captain." Hannel strode away.

"Why don't they do anything?" asked Syrie. "Why are they just standing there staring at us? Isn't there a protocol to this sort of thing? Shouldn't they come forward and demand our surrender or something?"

"Hounsey won't parley," said Maegwin, surprising herself by speaking. "He expected to catch this citadel unawares but instead he's found the gates closed and soldiers on the wall. That means they were warned. And who would have warned them but us? Hounsey knows we're here and he knows we won't surrender."

Captain Tyan straightened suddenly and Maegwin saw movement among the army. The first two lines of infantry stepped back to be replaced by a line of archers.

"Shields ready!" bellowed Tyan.

Maegwin heard the thuds of bowstrings just as Rovann cannoned into her, sending her sprawling. An arrow zinged through the space she'd occupied. Rovann landed atop her, his weight pressing down on her chest, his hair brushing her neck. Maegwin breathed deeply, savoring the scent of him. After a moment, he levered himself up, hands planted on either side of her face. He looked down at her, his face inches from her own.

"Are you hurt?"

His eyes were blue like the sky in summer. Maegwin stared into them, feeling her heartbeat quicken. The world seemed to disappear. There was just her and Rovann. Nothing else. She pictured herself reaching up, tangling her fingers through his thick hair...

Rovann blinked and the spell was broken. He moved away, pulling her into a crouch behind the wall.

"Stay down," he muttered.

Arrows hissed through the air, some striking the battlements, others thudding into hastily raised shields. Ten paces away an arrow slammed into the throat of a stallholder. The man's hands scrabbled wildly at the shaft, before he toppled off the parapet and landed with a crunch in the courtyard below.

Captain Tyan bellowed, "Archers! Return fire!"

The 'whump' of bowstring sounded. Maegwin peered over the top of the wall. Hounsey's front line was pulling back from the rain of arrows and forming up again out of range. They didn't fire another volley.

Sergeant Hannel lofted his sword, the afternoon sun glinting off the blade. In response, the defenders raised a shaky cheer, calling out their defiance.

Hounsey's men were not done yet. A commotion passed through the army as something moved to the front. Almost like something being disgorged from the mouth of a beast, a group of heavily armored soldiers emerged carrying a massive battering ram. One end of the ram had been clad in metal and shaped into a mailed fist.

Captain Tyan bellowed an order and the citadel's archers and crossbowmen stepped forward, weapons trained on the advancing soldiers. Maegwin counted forty soldiers carrying the battering ram. Every second soldier carried a heavy oblong shield made from dull metal and almost as tall as a man.

"Fire!" yelled Captain Tyan.

Arrows and crossbow bolts sped down. The huge shields snapped up to cover the advancing soldiers in a roof of solid metal. The soldiers didn't miss a step. Not one of the defenders' arrows found its mark.

"Reload and fire!" came the order, although Maegwin suspected that they already knew it was futile.

Captain Tyan swore under his breath, scratching his beard with a grimy fingernail. "Hesha, take your company to the murder-holes above the gate tunnel. Corporal Tanner, you and your men take position in the courtyard. If they break through the gates you must hold them. Understood?"

The two officers saluted and ran off to carry out their orders.

Maegwin watched, mesmerized, as the ram inched toward the gates. Arrows fell on the attackers like deadly rain. A crossbow bolt found its way through a gap in the shield wall and took a man in the chest with an explosion of blood. The man collapsed into the mud but his comrades just marched over him relentlessly, like a machine.

Maegwin watched Rovann. He faced away but she saw his tension in the set of his shoulders and the way his fingers gripped the stone. She shared his frustration. Maegwin felt helpless. She wanted to fight, not cower behind a wall like a coward.

Let them break through the gates, she thought to herself. *And then I'll show them what I can do.*

Slowly, she drew her sword.

Rovann stood, turning to look beyond Maegwin. Following his gaze, she saw two people standing on the battlements directly above the gates. She recognized the flowing black hair of Lady and the mustache of Tallo. Behind them, Lady's squad waited nervously. New recruits Maegwin guessed, thinking they had an easy posting to this trader citadel.

"Hold, curse you!" Lady snapped at them. "You won't move until I tell you!"

The battering ram was only ten paces away now.

What are you up to, Lady? Maegwin thought.

Lady watched the approaching ram intently. She was motionless, body tensed, a predator preparing to pounce.

But she'd left it too late.

That metal fist would smash into the gates, sending splinters of wood flying everywhere. Then the enemy would pour through the breach and there would be carnage in the courtyard.

Maegwin's heart thudded as the soldiers swung the ram. She braced herself for the impact.

Lady let out an ululating cry.

And everything happened at once.

Three of her squad staggered up, carrying a massive iron cooking pot. They up-ended it over the edge of the battlements and a sheet of black oil splashed over the ram and soldiers carrying it. Tallo straightened holding a longbow with an arrow nocked.

And the tip of the arrow was on fire.

Maegwin caught her breath as the arrow sped down, aimed not at the heavily protected soldiers, but at the oil-soaked ground beneath their feet. The ground erupted in a sheet of flame. It enveloped the battering ram and the soldiers.

Lady and Tallo's timing was perfect. They gave the soldiers no time to react, no time to avoid the devouring flame.

The men burned like candles. Screaming echoed off the citadel walls as the soldiers staggered around, desperately trying to put out the bright tongues licking their bodies. The ram became an inferno, burning with hungry yellow flames. The fire climbed higher, reaching for the gates.

Blessed Mother! The gates will catch fire! Maegwin thought. *Lady, what have you done?*

But the flames licked at the gates and then died, unable to find purchase on the slick wood.

They've soaked it, Maegwin realized, remembering the barrels she'd seen Tallo rolling across the courtyard earlier. *They soaked the gates in water. It won't burn.*

The last of the burning men's screams died away. Heavy silence fell, punctuated only by the hiss and crackle of the conflagration by the gates. Hounsey's army stood like statues...waiting.

Maegwin felt a surge of triumph. They had seen off the first attack, and bloodied Hounsey's nose into the bargain.

Didn't expect that did you, you bastard?

Captain Tyan leaned on the wall. She could see his eyes flicking in all directions, taking in the deployment of the army and assessing their next move.

"So what comes next?" Maegwin asked.

Rovann glanced at her then away. He seemed to be looking into the far distance to where the army disappeared on the horizon. "This was a feint, Maegwin. A half-hearted attack to gage our strength. When they next attack, it will be for real."

Maegwin moved to stand beside him. Following his gaze, she squinted into the distance, and saw it. Squatting in the middle of the army, a large black tent with a banner flying from its peaked roof.

Hounsey.

Her hand tightened on her sword. She imagined Lord Hounsey standing outside that tent, watching them even as they watched him. What thoughts were running through his mind? Was he afraid?

He should be, Maegwin thought. *He should be.*

Maegwin had never been so close to Hounsey. So close to her revenge. Only a sea of armed men stood between her and her goal. She could almost taste the bitterness of his blood on her tongue. She could almost feel the muscles of his neck beneath her squeezing hands.

"Why doesn't he use sorcery?" Syrie said suddenly.

"Because he knows we're here," Rovann replied. "He would have to risk himself against us. And why do that when he has an army at his command?"

The sun was beginning to set. The river glinted orange and red. The gloom between the trees began to thicken.

Sounds of hammers and saws drifted to them on the still air. A copse to their left was suddenly full of activity.

"Siege towers," growled Tyan. "When they're ready, we'll be overrun. But at least it gives us a few hours to prepare some tricks." Turning away, he shouted. "Hannel! Lady! To me! Show me everything we've got in the armory and I want a report on how those damn sappers are doing on the riverbank. Don't let them see you and leave them be for now. Their actions may give us a clue to Hounsey's plans." He strode away, leaving Maegwin with Rovann and Syrie.

"How far do you think Falwin is from Tyrlindon?" asked Syrie quietly.

"Too far," answered Rovann. "Hopefully some of the message birds the commander sent will get through but we can't count on that. Somehow we must hold off Hounsey through tonight and all tomorrow if possible." He turned to look at the small, dark-haired woman. "I want you to go with Tyan. Do what you can to bolster the defense. Perhaps we can slow Hounsey down if we prepare some surprises. What can you do with the Eorthe?"

Syrie crossed her arms and smiled suddenly. It was a fox's smile, full of cunning. "Much. Tyan may have a few tricks in mind but I have quite a few of my own. Hounsey will not take us easily."

Rovann laid his hand on Syrie's shoulder. "I don't doubt it. But you must guard yourself, Syrie. Don't exhaust your power in this citadel's defense. When it comes to it, you must be able to escape back to Tyrlindon. We'll need you to defend the city."

Syrie held his gaze for a long time then sighed. "Yes, my Lord First."

Maegwin found herself alone with Rovann. He didn't look at her, instead staring out at Hounsey's army.

"What do you want me to do?" she asked him.

"You're not a soldier, Maegwin," he replied. "I can't command you to do anything."

She didn't like the tone of his voice. It sounded oddly cold. She grabbed his arm, forcing him to look at her. "What are you talking about? I came here to fight Hounsey and that's what I intend to do!"

"I know," he said softly. "There's a barracks at the far

end of the courtyard. Hannel has put together a duty roster. Those not on duty are being sent to the barracks to rest while they can. I suggest you join them."

She recoiled as if he'd slapped her. He was sending her away. After all they'd been through, he still didn't trust her.

Rest? she wanted to shout at him. *You want me to rest when my enemy is at the gates? You think I could sleep? That man killed my sisters, killed Leo, and you want me to rest! Why are you sending me away? I want to stay with you!*

But she didn't say any of this. Instead, she turned and stalked down the steps, leaving Rovann alone on the battlements, staring into the distance.

Chapter Eleven

Maegwin drew her knees up to her chest and hugged them. Despite the summer heat, cold seeped into her skin. She shifted, trying to find a more comfortable position on the narrow bed.

Muted conversation filled the barracks but nobody spoke to Maegwin. Perhaps she made them nervous, sitting with a naked sword laid out on the bed beside her. Once or twice she caught people looking her way and heard whispers, "She's the Lord First's friend."

Maegwin wanted to laugh. *If I were his friend, would I be sitting here? He sent me away.*

She glanced at the window. Night had fallen and the citadel was busy. The sounds of soldiers carried on the air; the tramp of boots, orders shouted back and forth. Inside the barracks, the air smelt of fear.

The duty roster was a bad idea, in Maegwin's opinion. Captain Tyan should be keeping these people occupied, not leaving them here to chew on their terror. Instead of sleeping, the civilians sat huddled together talking about mundane things, as if it would keep anxiety at bay.

Maegwin had sat here since sunset and felt something building inside her. She had seen nothing of Rovann since she'd left him on the battlements and that in itself had helped her come to a decision. Rovann had never wanted her here. Well, if she was not part of the mission she wasn't tied to its objectives. She owed the mission, and the people undertaking it, absolutely nothing.

Which meant she could do what she liked.

Three hours had passed since sunset and Hounsey had not attacked. Clouds had rolled in and the moon had not yet risen, making the night murky and thick.

It was time.

Maegwin scrambled off the bed and dragged a pack out from underneath which she swung over her shoulder. She grabbed her sword and strode out the door, letting it slam behind her.

She stood for a moment in the shadows of the recessed doorway, looking out into the courtyard, then took the steps to the battlements. At the top she turned left, skirting the base of the tower and onto a narrow walkway giving access to the curtain wall on the far side of the citadel, against the river.

Leaning on the wall, Maegwin looked down to a shallow ledge that tumbled away into the cliff of the river's western bank. She pressed herself into the shadows as a sentry approached, halberd in one hand, sword sheathed at his hip. The sentry passed within three paces then suddenly turned, looking directly at her.

Maegwin jumped from the shadows and rammed her elbow into the man's face. The man crumpled, out cold.

"Sorry," Maegwin mumbled, as she stepped over him and approached the parapet.

Maegwin unslung the pack, pulled out a coil of rope she'd taken from the stock room earlier and looked over the parapet. The wall was so high the bottom was lost in gloom. Maegwin struggled to make out the small shelf of cliff-edge she would be making for. If she missed the ledge she would tumble down the cliff and be swallowed by the river.

But it was a chance she must take.

From somewhere below came the tap and scrape of the enemy sappers. They'd attached themselves to the cliff beneath the citadel's walls and appeared to be trying to dig holes in it. She was pretty sure they wouldn't notice her.

Maegwin uncoiled the rope and looped it around a merlon, knotting it and tugging to make sure it was secure. She threw the rest of the rope over the edge and watched it spool out down the length. Gritting her teeth, she grabbed the rope with both hands and set her foot onto the parapet.

"Where are you going?"

Maegwin spun, dropping into a fighting crouch. A shape stood in the gloom at the tower's base, watching her.

She tensed for an attack. Then Rovann stepped out of the shadows.

Maegwin's heart stuttered. What was he doing here?

He stepped forward warily, as if she were a skittish animal. Fixing her with his ice blue eyes he said quietly, "What are you doing, Maegwin?"

"Don't waste my time with pointless questions," she snapped. "You know exactly what I'm doing."

His gaze took in her defensive stance, the sword at her hip and the length of rope tied to the battlements. "I guessed you'd try tonight."

"You guessed right," she hissed. "Don't tell me I can't go. You have no right to give me orders, *my Lord First.*"

If he noticed her sarcasm he didn't show it. Instead, he smiled wryly.

"Order you? I think I've learned my lesson on that score."

She narrowed her eyes at him suspiciously. "Then why are you here if not to stop me?"

"I'm coming with you."

Maegwin started in surprise and her belly fluttered with excitement. A second later, anger twisted her mouth. "Why? You told Syrie she mustn't try to rescue the prince. You said she can't risk herself because she's needed to defend Tyrlin-don. You are the Lord First. Surely you are even more vital? Or don't your own rules apply to you?"

Rovann winced and Maegwin knew her words had hit home. "Some things are necessary."

"An easy excuse, Rovann."

"Perhaps. But we both know I'm right. I can't abandon the prince, regardless of the dangers. Syrie knows this. If everything goes wrong tonight, she'll know what to do."

A shiver ran down Maegwin's spine. *If everything goes wrong tonight.* If that happened, both she and Rovann would die.

Am I going to my death, mistress? Are you waiting to bring me home?

"Then we'd best get moving."

She grabbed the rope but Rovann placed his hand on her shoulder.

"Not like that. One slip and you die." Rovann leaned out and hastily pulled the rope back up, leaving it anchored to the merlon. "Tie it around your waist. I'll lower you down."

Maegwin looked at him for a long moment. He met her gaze. *Trust me*, he was asking. *Trust me.*

She nodded. "Don't let go."

"I'll do my best."

Rovann planted his feet and ran the slack around his back and under his arms, clasping it in front of him to give himself purchase.

Maegwin vaulted onto the parapet and then slowly lowered herself over the side, clinging to the rope and leaving her feet dangling. It took a moment of wild scrabbling to get her boots planted flat against the wall, but when she'd finally done it Rovann let out some of the rope, allowing her to lean back.

In this manner, she slowly walked down the wall, body almost horizontal with the ground. Above, Rovann strained to hold the rope. It must have been shredding his hands but he made no complaint.

Gratefully, she jumped the last five paces and landed on the thin strip of ground at the base of the wall. She quickly untied the rope and tugged it to tell Rovann she'd made it safely down.

As Rovann pulled the rope back up, she pressed her back against the citadel wall. Her legs were shaky. She closed her eyes, drawing in breaths to steady herself, and then looked out.

Perhaps eight or nine paces ahead was a dark void where the cliff fell away sharply. Beyond, came the roar and crash of the river. To the left, hidden in the night, came the tapping and scraping of the enemy sappers.

The rope suddenly snaked down beside her and Rovann descended hand over hand, feet scrabbling down the wall like some street urchin. With a jump, he landed beside her.

"How do we get the rope down?" Maegwin asked.

"Leave it. We'll need it to get back into the fortress."

Maegwin looked at him and saw the lie in his eyes. He knew they'd be unlikely to be coming back but she didn't shatter this eggshell hope. She nodded. "Come on."

Keeping her back pressed to the wall she took a few steps to the right before Rovann grabbed her arm.

"Wait."

"What is it?"

She could barely make him out in the darkness. His eyes looked like tiny blue lamps. "There's something I have to do first. Wait here. I won't be long." Without waiting for an answer, he shuffled along the ledge.

"You're going the wrong way!" she hissed at him, but he'd already disappeared into the night.

Cursing under her breath, Maegwin followed.

From up ahead, Maegwin heard the 'click-click 'of picks working on stone and the low rumble of muted conversation. Hounsey's sappers. Rovann was heading straight for them.

Another thirty paces and the sappers finally came into view. They had somehow set torches into the cliff face under an overhang so they weren't visible from the citadel. Six men hung suspended on ropes and appeared to be excavating a row of small holes in the stone. One of the sappers had a pack around his waist, from which he scooped a white, spongy material which he pushed into the holes.

Maegwin crouched, pressing herself into the shadows. "Rovann!" she hissed. "They'll spot you!"

He ignored her. He crept along the ledge until he was directly above the overhang shielding the sappers. There was a flash, a strangled cry, and six black specks went tumbling into the churning river. The ropes swung uselessly, suddenly empty.

Maegwin gaped at the spot the sappers had occupied. Rovann hurried back and hunkered down beside her.

"What are you waiting for? Let's get moving."

Maegwin glanced from Rovann to the vacant ropes and back again. "What did you do?"

Through the gloom she caught a flicker of unease in his eyes. "We don't have time for this. Come on."

She didn't move. Grabbing his arm, she hissed, "What did you do?"

"You know what I did. What choice was there? Would you rather I let them blow the cliff apart and kill us all? I had no other choice." He snatched his arm back and stomped past her.

Choice? she thought. *There is always a choice. Where is the justice in killing an enemy who doesn't even know you're there?*

She wanted Hounsey to know she was his killer. She wanted his last sight to be the look of triumph on her face.

But not this. Not this killing in the shadows.

Maegwin hurried after Rovann. For reasons she couldn't quite explain, she was suddenly furious with him. "That's not good enough," she hissed at his retreating back. "This wasn't supposed to be about killing soldiers. This was about Hounsey and the prince."

"What do you want from me?" he demanded, spinning around to face her. "A promise that Hounsey is yours? Well, I can't make such a promise. You will just have to trust me."

"Why should I? You demand trust and then turn like the wind. You're like a double-sided coin: on one side the high and mighty Lord First, above reproach, fighting only for what is right. But on the other side is another face. A face that stalks the darkness. A face that kills without warning."

"That's enough."

"Enough? You sit in judgment on me when you're no

different! I never denied I'm a killer. But you do. You hide behind your title as though it gives you the right to make decisions over other people's lives. Leo called you the Slayer of Sandford Moor. Now I understand why."

All emotion drained from Rovann's face and Maegwin couldn't make out what took its place. He appeared suddenly cold and remote. She knew by the set of his jaw he was furious.

"You have no idea what you're talking about," he whispered.

Maegwin was acutely aware of the drop at her back. And she was also acutely aware of how quickly Rovann could kill her if he chose. His shoulders were hunched and tense, his fists clenched at his sides. Maegwin's stomach churned in sudden fear.

"Then why don't you help me understand?"

He said nothing, staring at her for a long moment. Then all the fight seemed to go out of him and he sagged, sliding down the wall until he sat on the ledge.

"You're right, Maegwin. There is always a choice," he said. "And the choice I had tonight was a simple one. The lives of six soldiers or the lives of forty or more, many of them innocent civilians. An easy choice? Some might say so. But who has the wisdom to decide such things? I certainly don't. And yet, I must. Such decisions can fall to no one else. I have to make them so others don't have to." His voice was raw with pain.

Maegwin knelt beside him. Gone was the King's Mage. Instead, he was Rovann, just a man. A man struggling to do his best under the terrible weight of his duty. She clasped his hand.

"I'm sorry."

He smiled wryly. "Don't be. I'm glad you're honest with

me. Sometimes I need to hear it." He reached up and brushed his thumb across the tip of her nose.

He sat so near she could hear the soft hiss of breath escaping his lips. Feel the warmth of his skin where his shoulder touched hers. Smell the scent of his hair. She cupped his cheek with her hand, lifting his face. He didn't flinch. His blue eyes bored into hers. She bent her head and pressed her lips against his. After a second, his arm circled her waist, pulling her against him.

Heat flashed through her body as his lips moved against hers, as she felt the firmness of his body pressing against her. She wrapped her arms around his neck and kissed him hungrily. She lost herself in the smell of him, the feel of him, the taste of him. Her thoughts drifted away. Nothing mattered. Only this moment. Here. With Rovann.

Something detonated behind the citadel. They both jumped. Maegwin sprang up, looking around wildly.

"What was that?"

Rovann climbed to his feet. In his eyes she saw him drawing away from her. The mask descending again. "Sorcery."

"Ours? Or Hounsey's?"

He shook his head. "I don't know. Come on."

He moved off at a jog and Maegwin followed.

They crept along until they reached the corner of the citadel where the south wall met the east and they crouched in the shadows, looking out.

Beyond lay Hounsey's army.

All Maegwin could see was a sea of campfires, beginning perhaps a hundred paces away and continuing in all directions.

"So many," Rovann breathed.

Another detonation sounded, making the earth rumble.

Twenty paces from the citadel gates the ground erupted in a shower of mud and rubble. The front lines of Hounsey's army scattered back in terror. On the walls, Maegwin thought she could make out the form of a small, dark-haired woman.

"Syrie," Rovann said. "She's creating a diversion. She knows what we intend."

He was silent for a time, eyes scanning the enemy camp. At length he said, "I don't have Syrie's skill with the Eorthe but I can use Air to form a shield so none will witness our passage."

Maegwin looked at him sharply. "No. If you do that, Hounsey will know we're coming."

"His mages will have sensed the sorcery I used on those sappers," Rovann pointed out.

"So? The attack might easily have come from the citadel. He has no reason to assume anyone has left the citadel."

Rovann thought about this. "Even so, I think—"

"No!" Maegwin hissed. "Syrie is creating a diversion. We have to take advantage of it."

Rovann frowned at her. "What do you suggest?"

Maegwin smiled. "Follow me."

She slid out of the shadows and moved off in a low crouch, keeping close to the edge of the riverbank. Rovann followed silently. Clouds had covered the sky, for which Maegwin was thankful. Any soldiers who happened to glance their way would be night-blinded by the light from their campfire.

Nevertheless, as she and Rovann crept along the river-bank toward a thick copse, sweat slid down Maegwin's back. Her heart hammered in her chest. A sudden break in the clouds or a soldier glancing their way and they'd be caught.

As they finally entered the copse, she sank into the shadows and let out a slow breath. Rovann touched her arm and pointed. Two silhouettes stood nearby. The first line of pickets.

Silently Rovann pointed at her and then to his right. He tapped his own chest and pointed to the left. Maegwin nodded. As he moved off, keeping low to the ground, Maegwin crept in the other direction, circling behind the pickets. She searched the darkness, alert for other pickets or obstacles she might accidentally trip over and give away her position. When she was level with the guards she froze behind a bush. The men had spears planted in the ground and were silently searching the woods. Well trained. And disciplined. Maegwin flattened herself into the muddy ground as the guards' gaze passed over her hiding place and then breathed out as it continued on.

Rovann suddenly darted from behind a tree and smashed his elbow into one man's face. Cursing, Maegwin threw herself at the second guard. Her sword hissed from its scabbard and took the man across the forehead with the flat of the blade. The guard grunted, sank slowly onto his knees and fell face forward in the mud.

Rovann knelt over the guards and muttered a few strange words. "They won't wake for hours. You take that one's clothes," he instructed as he began undoing the cloak and tunic from one of the guards.

"I won't wear Hounsey colors!" Maegwin snapped.

"You will if you want to get through this alive."

Maegwin ground her teeth and then slammed her sword back into its sheath. She knelt in the mud and turned the second guard onto his back. She quickly undid the cloak and then dragged his blue Hounsey tunic over his head. The tunic came almost to her knees so she rolled up the bottom half and tucked it into her trousers, hoping the cloak would hide the ill-fitting clothes.

"Ready," she said.

"Take the spears, and when we move, hold your head up and walk like you're supposed to be here. We're just two Hounsey guards doing a round of the pickets. If anyone challenges you, don't lose your temper. Let me do the talking."

"Fine," Maegwin replied. "But let's get going before somebody comes."

They moved off, Rovann taking the lead. Maegwin followed close behind.

Rovann led them through the trees toward the heart of Hounsey's camp. Maegwin was content to let him lead. She watched him moving ahead of her, listened to the rustle of the clothes against his skin, watched the way his shoulders pulled the tunic tight across his back when he walked. She remembered the heat of his lips against hers, the sensation of his arms wrapped around her. She wanted to feel it again.

No, a voice spoke in her head. *Remember what you're here for. Remember your vengeance. It's all that matters.*

Rovann held up his hand and froze. He pointed into the woods and Maegwin spotted the second line of pickets. "They're more widely spaced," he whispered. "We have to take out the first guard without alerting the others. That should leave a gap in the line we can sneak through."

Maegwin trod silently at his side as they took a game trail that wound toward the line. Rovann indicated for her to wait as he snuck up behind one of the guards and cracked him over the head with a branch. He caught the man as he crumpled to the ground. Leaving her hiding place, Maegwin strode forward, drawing her sword which she raised up high and swung at the unconscious man's face.

Rovann grabbed her arms, halted the blade inches from the man's throat. "What are you doing?"

She looked at him and it took a moment for her eyes to focus. "Kill him," she rasped. "He might give away our position."

"No," Rovann said, shoving her back. "Weren't you just lecturing me about killing those sappers?"

"This is different. Those sappers weren't a threat to us."

"Nor is this man."

He stared at her, his gaze uncompromising. With a snarl, she sheathed her sword, turned and continued on the trail.

The trees ended and Maegwin found herself amongst the army proper. To the left stood a corral of horses, ahead, a team of men working a portable forge. Tents and campfires stretched into the distance in neatly ordered rows.

"Where are all the guards?" said Maegwin. "This is too easy."

"Yes," Rovann agreed, skirting around a cold campfire. "And that makes me nervous."

Maegwin turned in a slow circle, scanning the camp in all directions. In the blackness she couldn't make out Hounsey's tent. But she sensed... something.

"It's this way."

Maegwin led them through a maze of tents and guy ropes and onto a wide thoroughfare. Rovann strode by her side, ignoring the few soldiers they passed.

"Halt!" A voice spoke suddenly from the darkness.

Maegwin froze.

A tall woman stepped from the shadows. She was dressed for riding, with the bear's head of Hounsey emblazoned on her chest. The bars on her shoulder marked her as a lieutenant. "You're not from my unit. Where are you going?"

"What's it to you?" Maegwin snapped.

The lieutenant's eyes narrowed. "I will have your name and unit, soldier, and then I'll have you flogged for insubordination!"

Rovann cleared his throat. "Sappers Thren and Sara, sir. Bin over at the wall and it's been a hard day, see. Sara didn't mean nothing by it, did you lass?"

Maegwin glowered at her feet and murmured, "No. Sorry, sir."

The lieutenant frowned. "Sappers eh? How goes it over at the citadel? You cursed idiots gonna bring that wall down for us or what?"

Rovann grinned. "Keep watching, lieutenant. Keep watching. Captain will be wanting a full report so we best be going."

The lieutenant stepped back to let them pass. "Go on." As Maegwin moved off, the lieutenant caught her by the arm. "Just make sure you learn some manners, soldier."

Maegwin forced a servile tone into her voice. "Aye, sir."

The lieutenant turned away and Maegwin hurried after Rovann.

Rovann watched the lieutenant depart, making sure she didn't suddenly change direction and head to Hounsey's tent. When she was finally out of sight, Rovann let out the breath he'd been holding.

"Do you think she suspected?" Maegwin murmured.

"I don't know. But I don't like this."

The night was filled with a strange resonance. It

hummed on his senses like a note played out of key. It pulled him to the east, to the place where Hounsey had set up his headquarters.

He glanced at Maegwin. The skin between her eyebrows was pinched in a frown and her red-gold hair shone in the firelight. He itched to run his fingers through it and feel its silky texture against his skin. He remembered his shock as she'd kissed him and then the answering hunger that had welled up inside him. Why had she kissed him? And why had he kissed her back?

Another woman's face suddenly floated in his mind's eye. This face had dark hair, honey skin and tilted eyes the color of tilled earth. Istra. He staggered with the sudden pain that gripped his heart. How could he have forgotten her?

Maegwin reached his side in an instant. "Rovann? What is it?"

He shook his head. "Nothing. I'm fine."

He strode off. Maegwin moved silently by his side, eyes fixed on the road. Although they passed other soldiers on sentry duty, nobody challenged them. Perhaps they were fooled by the Hounsey uniform. Or perhaps not.

They entered the area of the camp reserved for the command. Larger tents, almost pavilions, filled the space. Squads of light infantry were stationed in a circle around this compound, standing in pairs and looking alert, despite the hour.

Spotting the guards, they ducked into the shadows behind a wagon and Rovann peeked out. His eyes came to rest on a tent much larger than the others. It was made of black fabric and had a pitched roof. A ring of guards surrounded it with torches burning at intervals. Hounsey's pavilion.

The entrance flap lay perhaps fifty paces away, no further. Fifty paces to the heart of this mystery. Fifty paces and Rovann might find answers to the questions of the prince's abduction and the plans of the Songmaker.

But instinct told him all was not as it appeared. There was a convergence here, a coming together of different futures. He felt a vibration within the fabric of the Realms.

Suddenly one of the guards, a tall man with a pale face beneath his helmet, looked directly at Rovann. His eyes met Rovann's. A smile quirked the corners of the man's mouth and he deliberately turned away.

And Rovann knew.

Hounsey was waiting for him.

Rovann's instincts screamed at him to flee. But he was King's Mage, First of the Council of Mages and that had to count for something. To his knowledge, there was no one living able to match his power in sorcery.

Then why is Hounsey so confident? he thought. *Why does he invite his enemy so close?*

If luck was on Rovann's side, the news of Maegwin's release may not have reached Lord Cedric Hounsey before he left the Highhold. Rovann needed every advantage possible and Maegwin's presence might just give him that.

Pulling in a breath, Rovann stepped out into the torchlight. He and Maegwin took two steps before the guards snapped to attention and drew their weapons in a ring of steel. But the guards made no move toward the trespassers as they strode through the perimeter and to the tent's entrance.

Maegwin sliced through the bindings on the flap and pulled it up. Ducking through the entry, they stepped into Lord Cedric Hounsey's headquarters.

Rovann found himself in a simple oblong room,

unadorned but for a large rug covering the floor and a camp chair at the far end. It was gloomy but Rovann made out a figure seated in the chair. Watching them.

Maegwin tensed and Rovann held out a hand to forestall her.

Not yet, he willed her. *Do nothing. All is not as it seems.*

Light flared and a brazier sparked into life, revealing a wiry man somewhere beyond his middle years with an iron-gray beard and hair to match. He wore black chainmail that bulged over his paunch.

"My Lord First," the man said. "So good of you to join me."

Rovann inclined his head. "Good evening, Lord Hounsey."

The warlord smiled although it didn't reach his eyes. "You will forgive me if I don't offer you refreshment. After all, we're not here for pleasantries are we?"

In the light of the brazier Rovann noticed the rug on the floor had a strange design, three interlocking serpents whose tangled bodies circled Hounsey's chair. The brazier sat on the head of one of the snakes so it appeared to be a red, glowing eye.

Rovann glanced around, looking for the tell-tale wards to indicate hidden observers. There were none. Rovann's unease deepened.

He straightened, looked Hounsey in the eye and said, "Cedric Hounsey, Lord of the Highhold, you are under arrest for high treason. I'm here to escort you to Tyrlindon where you will face trial for your crimes."

Hounsey raised a bushy eyebrow. "Is that it? I'm sure there's more you could add to the list. How about kidnap? Assault on the king's men?" His eyes suddenly snapped to

Maegwin. "Or murder perhaps? How many died in the temple fire, my dear? Sixteen? Seventeen?"

Maegwin cocked her head to one side and regarded him for a long moment. "You're older than I expected. And fatter. I thought you'd have black hair like your son. Not that it matters. I'm sure your insides are the same. I'll be sure to check when I open you up."

Hounsey grinned, his teeth startlingly white against his gray beard. "What charming friends you have, Rovann. But I think I'll have to decline your offer, my dear."

"Too bad for you," Maegwin said, taking a step onto the rug." I'm going to kill you, Hounsey. I'm going to cut you up and bleed you out into this carpet."

Hounsey narrowed his eyes at her. "You're the one who killed my son."

"You're the one who killed my sisters."

"Then that makes us even."

A humorless smile played across Maegwin's face. "Hardly. The price must be paid. A life for a life."

"So you've come to take mine in payment."

"Think of it as a mercy. I doubt many will mourn your passing."

For a second, Hounsey's composure slipped. A sneer twisted his features. "Worms! Both of you! You're already dead and you don't even know it."

"I do know it," Maegwin replied calmly. "I knew it from the moment you killed my sisters. The thing is, I don't care."

Hounsey clutched the arms of his chair. "Is that so? Nothing left to live for, eh? It's said those are the most dangerous ones. Not you though. My master has all sorts of plans for you. The twins will take you, and shape you."

Maegwin took another step on the rug. "What are you talking about?"

Hounsey slumped back and laughed.

Rovann stepped forward. "What have you done with Prince Owen?"

"Mind your own cursed business!" snapped Hounsey. "You mages think you're superior but you're blind, arrogant fools. I snatched the prince from the very heart of his own kingdom and none of you stupid bastards know where he's been taken or why. I like that. It makes me feel good."

Rovann struggled against a rising surge of anger. He suspected Hounsey was baiting them, trying to provoke a reaction. They had to make sure they didn't fall into the trap.

But Maegwin, he sensed, was on the verge of losing control. Her calm seemed to have become icy, ready to shatter at any moment. He must get what he needed from Hounsey before it did.

Maegwin stared at Hounsey. Could this really be the man responsible for all that had befallen her? He looked old and fat. Pitifully weak. Her lip curled in disdain. Inside, the Dark Goddess's power surged through her veins lighting her blood, making her skin tingle. All her rage and hatred had gathered behind a dam. When she killed Hounsey that dam would break and she'd finally be free. And yet she hesitated.

"This is quite a pair I have before me," Hounsey said. "My son's murderer side by side with the Slayer of Sandford Moor. Tell me, my dear, why shouldn't I tear your head off where you stand?"

"Try it," she growled.

He grinned. "Ah, there it is. That spirit my master likes

so much. The Songmaker has told me all about you, Maegwin of Sho-La. I know what you are."

Rovann cursed and Hounsey's eyes narrowed on him. "That's right, King's Mage. I've known about her from the beginning. You were a fool to think I didn't. Everything you've done, every step you've taken has been of the Songmaker's choosing."

"Stop talking," Maegwin growled. "I've had enough of your poison."

Hounsey threw his head back and cackled, a sound that set Maegwin's hair on end. "I begin to see why my master is so interested in you. All right. I give in. I forgive you for killing my son. There, isn't that better? No more bad blood between us, Maegwin." He leaned forward, hands gripping the arms of his chair. He reminded her of a vulture. "We're on the same side, you and I. We shouldn't be fighting one another. Join me and you'll have your vengeance."

Maegwin's hand tightened on her sword hilt. Hounsey was so close she could smell his sweat. "I will have vengeance when I kill you."

She stepped closer but halted as Hounsey threw out an arm and pointed at Rovann. "Your hatred is aimed at the wrong person, Maegwin. He is the one who should suffer your wrath. He is the monster here, not me. A river of blood lies at this man's feet. Isn't that right, my Lord First? How many have died at your hand? And you have the arrogance to judge me! Tell me, King's Mage, is there any difference between us?"

Maegwin glanced at Rovann and noticed the color had drained from his face. "Rovann? What's he talking about?"

"Why don't you tell her?" Hounsey crowed. "Why don't you tell her how thousands died at your hand?"

"Shut your mouth," Rovann hissed.

"Or what? You'll kill me? You see, Maegwin, that's how this man deals with anything he doesn't like." Hounsey's vulture eyes fixed on her once more. "Have you never stopped to consider why I fight against the king? To stop people like the King's Mage. To stop those with power destroying the lives of those without. The King's Mage paints me as a monster but he's no different to me. Have you never wondered why he's nicknamed the Slayer of Sandford Moor?"

Maegwin shook her head. Fog suddenly clouded her thoughts. She couldn't think straight. "You're a liar!"

"No," Hounsey whispered. "He deserves the name he's given, oh he most certainly does." He waved his hands and images enveloped Maegwin.

She waits in a crowd of people. The stink of unwashed bodies fills her nostrils. In her hand she grips a bloody spear she doesn't know how to use. She in on a moor, wind-blasted and barren. Around her the sea of people stretch in all directions. She glances at the person on her left, a fat, middle-aged woman wearing a cook's apron and wielding a carving knife. To her right stands a gaunt old man bearing nothing but a gnarled staff. What is going on here? These people stand in lines as if for battle, but they aren't soldiers.

She notices a man sitting astride his horse, watching them from the ridge above. He suddenly stands in his stirrups, his hand jabbing at the sky. Sorcery scythes into the lines of people. Bodies erupt in showers of blood. Limbs are torn off, people tossed into the air like leaves. Screaming fills the air. By her side, the old man pisses himself. Maegwin turns to flee but can't move. Unable to fight, unable to escape, she watches as the deadly sorcery stalks closer. She squints at the mounted man. He looks her way and she realizes he has icy blue eyes and wavy hair the color of straw.

Something grabbed her shoulders and she found herself back in the tent, staring into Rovann's fevered face. "It wasn't like that!" he panted. "I had no choice!"

Maegwin watched him, wondering if she was seeing him for the first time. She knew he could be ruthless. He'd killed the sappers on the riverbank without hesitation. Was Rovann any different to Hounsey? To her? They were all killers. The only difference was that Rovann tried to pretend otherwise.

"Yes!" shouted Hounsey. "You see it, don't you? You see the evil in him? Join me, Maegwin. Kill Rovann and have your vengeance!"

Maegwin felt the dark power clamoring inside her. *Yes, my child*, a voice said in her head. *A life for a life. You owe him nothing. His death will feel so sweet.*

She pushed Rovann away, raised her sword between them.

Rovann's golden hair lay in tangles on his shoulders. "It wasn't like that!" Hounsey, you bastard! You know it wasn't like that! The Songmaker put a glamor on them, forced them to fight. I didn't know they were camp followers!"

"Don't listen to his lies!" shouted Hounsey.

Maegwin glanced from Hounsey's triumphant expression to Rovann's horrified one. She'd never seen so much pain in someone's eyes.

Kill him, urged the voice inside.

No! she shouted silently. *I won't do it!*

She closed her eyes and brought memories to mind. Rovann's bright laugh as Leo sang one of his bawdy songs. His bravery as he went after the mage in Angard. His determination to see her healed by the Sentinel. Saving Leo from a crossbow bolt. Bearing the guilt of killing those sappers so others didn't have to. The tenderness with which he brushed a strand of hair from her face. The heat with which he kissed her.

She turned to the warlord, raising her sword. The fog lifted from her mind. "You twist the truth to justify your own crimes. I will never join you."

Hounsey shrugged. "Ah, well, it was worth a try." He stretched his arms overhead and yawned as if bored. His eyes snapped to Rovann instead. "She considered killing you for a moment there, King's Mage. Isn't she supposed to be your friend? Do you have any idea what lives within her? You profess to fight the Darkness and yet you bring one of its creatures with you!"

"Your sorcery won't work on me, Hounsey," Rovann answered in a voice hoarse with emotion. "Stop playing your games."

"Not a game. Only the truth. Has she told you who she really serves? I don't think you'd like the answer. Why don't you ask her, King's Mage?"

Rovann shook his head. "Where is Prince Owen?"

Hounsey cackled. "Safe. Along with that minstrel friend of yours. Leo, was it? The twins will deal with them. But you're changing the subject." He pointed at Macgwin. "How can you be so blind? You've even witnessed it, this rage that dwells in her soul. You suspect the truth. "

Rovann bared his teeth. "Where is Prince Owen? Where is Leo?"

"See the look in her eyes? She aches to kill me. She longs for revenge. It's the only thing left in her. She cares for nothing else!"

Rovann took a step closer, fists clenched. "Shut your mouth!"

Rage surged. Adrenaline pumped through her muscles. Hounsey was the man who'd murdered her sisters, destroyed her life. And now he was trying to turn Rovann against her.

Suddenly she was back in the clearing. She heard the hiss and roar of an inferno. The cruel laughter of Hounsey's men. The smell of burned wood and charred flesh. The screaming of her sisters.

Thought fled. Stillness flooded her. Black flames erupted along the length of her sword.

Realizing her intention Rovann shouted, "Maegwin, no! It's what he wants!"

But she didn't care. Hounsey was all that mattered. Revenge was all that mattered. She raised her sword. A satisfied smile spread across Hounsey's face. He opened his arms wide as if welcoming her blade.

With a howl, Maegwin plunged her sword into Hounsey's chest. She felt the blade graze his ribs, punch through the soft tissue of his heart, scrape along his spine, burst from his back and lodge itself in the wood of his chair.

Blood sprayed across Maegwin's face. A horrible gurgle escaped Hounsey's throat. His eyes rolled back in his head and his lifeless form slumped in his chair.

Maegwin ripped her sword out. She gasped for breath. Sweat slid down her back. And the dam of emotions inside her burst and she cried out.

As Rovann stared at Hounsey's lifeless form, he knew something had gone horribly, horribly wrong. Hounsey had wanted Maegwin to kill him. Somehow it was part of the Songmaker's plan.

Throwing his awareness wide, Rovann opened himself to the power of the Realms. And couldn't. His senses touched some kind of barrier and recoiled. In alarm, he tried again. His sorcery wouldn't respond. His eyes traveled down to the rug he stood on. He and Maegwin were encircled by two snakes.

Which glowed shiny black, like oil.

Not decoration at all, Rovann realized with a shiver, but a conduit. A conduit for a terrible power.

Wide-eyed, Maegwin gazed down at Hounsey, chest heaving, as the tip of her sword dipped.

Down which ran a rivulet of blood.

The red droplet hung on the end for a second. Then fell.

Onto the head of a snake.

Hounsey's body jerked. His head slowly lifted. And his eyes opened. "It's coming!" he laughed.

Rovann backed away. Everything suddenly made sense. How could the Songmaker use Chaos? Because his servants were not living. Not anymore.

"A revenant," Rovann breathed.

On the rug, the snakes moved, writhing around the edge of the carpet as if alive. Shadows rose from their sinuous bodies, forming an impenetrable barrier around Rovann, Maegwin and Hounsey. Rovann spun in a circle, looking for escape. There was none.

"What have you done?" Rovann cried at Hounsey.

But Hounsey only laughed.

There was a tearing sound and a ragged gash split the air. Tendrils of smoky darkness waved from it. Rovann staggered back as a wall of force hit him. He fell to his knees and looked up in time to observe a figure emerging from the rent. She had chestnut hair and skin the color of honey.

"Istra?" Rovann gasped. "Istra?"

His wife smiled. "Beloved."

Time stopped. Rovann stared into Istra's face and felt everything else float away. Her eyes were full of laughter, cheeks dimpling as she smiled. Just as he remembered.

Except her wrists bore two horizontal slashes that dripped blood onto the carpet.

"Why did you abandon me, beloved?" she said.

He struggled to shake his head, deny her words. "I never abandoned you, Istra. I had to lead the army at Sandford Moor. Can't you understand it was my duty?"

Her eyes hardened. "What about your duty to me? Did that not matter?"

"Of course it did," he whispered. "More than anything."

Images whirled through his head. Istra begging him to stay. The despair in her eyes as he left. The sick dread when he returned to find the house in darkness. The creak of floorboards as he'd gone upstairs.

And Istra lying on the bedroom floor with her wrists slashed.

"You drove me to it," she said. "I was so lonely. I had no choice."

"No," he gasped.

"Yes. It's your fault."

"Don't say that. Please."

She took a step. If she reached out she could have touched him. But she didn't. "I am damned, Rovann. For what I did. Damned to the Outer Darkness."

Rovann buried his face in his hands and moaned.

"There are terrible things in here with me. They frighten me. Will you help me, beloved?"

He raised his head, tears squeezing from the corners of his eyes. "How?"

"Tear the veil. Help me escape. I can't do it on my own."

Rovann looked at the swirling vortex. It stank of Chaos. From within, he heard whispering voices. Tear the veil? Was such a thing possible? Could he set Istra free? He staggered to his feet and took a step toward the rent. Then another. He reached his hand to the churning shadow.

Maegwin slammed into him, sending him crashing onto his back. She straddled his chest, pinning his shoulders.

"It's not her!" she shouted. "Rovann! It's not her!"

"Let me go!" he snarled. With a heave, he shoved her off him and staggered upright.

Maegwin wrapped an arm around him and dragged him back. "It's not her!"

Rovann fought Maegwin's grip. She tripped him and he crashed onto the carpet. With a cry, Maegwin whirled her sword and slashed the blade across Istra's throat. Istra's eyes went wide. Black blood fountained.

"No!" Rovann screamed.

Tendrils snaked from the wound, wrapping themselves around Istra's body. Her form rippled, dissolved into a shapeless, shadowy mass. With a hiss, it disappeared into the rent, which closed behind her with a sound like grinding rocks.

Rovann stared at the spot. *It wasn't her. It wasn't her.*

Hounsey howled in frustration. He surged from his seat, a red sword in his hand. Maegwin spun to meet him. Their blades met in a clash of red and black sparks.

"You will serve me!" Hounsey roared.

"I will kill you!" Maegwin screamed.

You can't kill him! Rovann tried to shout, but no words

would come. Emptiness filled him. It was hopeless. They were surrounded by a cocoon of Chaotic power. There was no way out.

Unbidden, a memory flared in his mind. An angel standing by his side.

Now you are two, the angel had said.

His eyes flicked to Maegwin and an idea formed. It might just be possible.

"Leave him!" he shouted. "We have to get out of here!"

Maegwin didn't seem to hear him. She circled Hounsey like a wolf intent on its prey.

He grabbed her wrist. "Listen to me!"

She spun, throwing off Rovann's grip. Her eyes blazed with fury. "Don't interfere! He's mine!"

He seized her shoulders. "You can't beat him! Listen to me, woman!"

With a snarl she smashed her fist into his cheek. His head snapped to the side. Blood sprayed from his mouth.

"I will have revenge!" she shrieked. "He's mine!"

Rovann tackled her from behind and sent them both sprawling onto the carpet. From the corner of his eye he saw Hounsey rushing them, red blade swinging. He gripped Maegwin's face in his hands.

"I'm sorry," he whispered.

Then, he relaxed his control, opening the floodgate of his power. Maegwin's eyes goggled as the will of the King's Mage rushed into her. Rovann delved into her mind, searching. There. Something bright blazed like a candle flame, deep within. The song of a Sentinel. Rovann grabbed it, stoked it to life. Power ripped through Maegwin. Her body bucked. Her lips parted and the Sentinel's song rippled out.

Rovann hugged her close as the Sentinel's power

enveloped them both. Around them the Eorthe blossomed. As the earth split and swallowed them, Rovann heard Hounsey's bellow of rage. Then there was the smell of mud and the crushing suffocation of rock.

With a thud he landed on something hard. Rovann opened his eyes and found himself staring into Syrie's startled face.

Chapter Twelve

Groaning, Rovann rolled over and climbed unsteadily to his feet. His head spun, his vision swinging in and out of focus. He staggered, fighting to stay on his feet. Syrie darted forward to help him but he waved her efforts away.

He swung around, looking for Maegwin. She sprawled on the cobbles a few feet away, unconscious. Kneeling by her side, Rovann pressed his finger against her neck and felt a strong, steady pulse.

"Maegwin," he said, shaking her shoulder.

Her eyes flew open and she scrambled to her feet, looking around wildly.

"Where is he? Where is he?"

"We're back in the citadel," Rovann answered, holding out a placating hand. "Hounsey isn't here."

"Take me back!" she hissed. "You had no right to bring me here! Take me back!" Her eyes were wild, her face contorted into a mask of fury.

"I can't do that."

She flew at him.

Her nails scored a gash across his cheek, bringing a grunt of surprise and pain. He threw up his arm to defend himself just as a punch came at him from the left. Rovann caught her wrist but she dealt him a stinging slap with her other hand, powerful enough to snap Rovann's head to the side and send a gout of blood spraying from his mouth.

"How could you do that to me?" she gasped hoarsely. She tapped the side of her head. "I felt you, in here. You just came in and took what you wanted. How could you?"

Snarling, Rovann jabbed his hand at her midriff, calling sorcery. A wave of force knocked Maegwin to her knees.

"He was going to kill us both!" Rovann growled. "Would you rather I'd left you to die?"

The fire in Maegwin's eyes died. "Yes," she said quietly, climbing to her feet. "I'd rather that. It was all I had left. My vengeance. And you took it from me."

Rovann was shocked by the despair in her voice. "Maegwin I—"

She cut him off with a sharp gesture. "Don't say you had no choice. I defended you. When Hounsey said those horrible things about you, I defended you. But you used me."

"Maegwin, I'm sorry." He took a step toward her but Maegwin held out a hand to stop him.

"Don't. I want no more of this. No more of you and your war. It's taken everything I had. I'll never forgive you for this." She whirled and stalked off into the night.

Rovann watched her go. *Maegwin, please! I'm sorry!*

Syrie stepped to his side, laying a hand on his arm. "Are you all right? Are you hurt?"

Rovann stared after Maegwin. *Hurt?* he thought. *You don't know the half of it.* He shook his head at the mage. "I'm fine."

"Did you find the prince?"

Rovann winced at the hope in her voice. Syrie's hair was disheveled and dark rings around her eyes betrayed her anxiety. "No. Hounsey doesn't hold the prince but he let something slip. He spoke of the twins."

"The twins?" Syrie's brows pulled down in a puzzled frown. "The twin cities? Beyond the Edge?"

Rovann nodded. "I think so. Right now we must concentrate on our defense. Hounsey's retribution will be brutal. Be prepared to face Chaotic sorcery."

To her credit, Syrie didn't flinch. "He won't take us easily." She clasped his hand and flashed one of her rare smiles. "Good luck, my Lord First."

"Everyone to your posts! We're under attack!" Captain Tyan shouted from the battlements. He held his sword aloft, glinting orange in the torchlight. "They're bringing up their siege engines."

"I'll take the battlements," Rovann said to Syrie, "you take the tower."

She nodded once then whirled away. Rovann pulled in a deep breath and ran up the steps to the battlements. He approached Captain Tyan. The man looked tired; hair messy and uniform rumpled. Rovann doubted that he'd taken any rest since they arrived at Carrow Crossing.

Tyan's eyes flicked to meet his. His gaze was full of questions but all he said was, "There was no movement until perhaps ten minutes ago. Now something seems to have stirred them up."

Looking out, Rovann realized the enemy camp was alive with activity. The soldiers were forming into tight ranks, each soldier carrying a torch. The citadel looked as though it was surrounded by a sea of fire.

"Hounsey's plans have been upset somewhat," Rovann

said, laying his palms flat against the cold stone of the parapet. "He'll be content to wait no longer. He's going to throw everything he has at us."

Tyan nodded. "An unprepared army is an inefficient one. Or so we have to hope."

"Perhaps," Rovann said, although he knew they were clinging to a false hope. Time. That was the only thing they might buy with their lives.

A silent command passed through the enemy ranks and the army shivered like a great beast. The next instant, a roar issuing from thousands of throats shattered the night.

The front ranks of the army raised their weapons and charged.

In response, Tyan barked commands and defenders scurried to their positions. The leading soldiers carried scaling ladders and were guarded by others bearing shields above their heads. Arrows and crossbow bolts rained down on the attackers. Cries rang out. Men fell.

But still the enemy pressed on.

A high keening sound came from the tower and Rovann sensed the sudden bloom of sorcery. The ground before the wall began exploding in great gouts of earth and roots. Soldiers were torn apart in showers of gore. Others fell screaming into craters.

Rovann glanced at the tower and saw Syrie's silhouette against one of the windows. He sent silent thanks for her command of the Eorthe.

Syrie's attack had blunted the front ranks of Hounsey's army but had not stopped them. Those who avoided the explosions swerved around the craters. Under a rain of arrows and crossbow bolts, they reached the walls, threw up scaling ladders and climbed like rats.

Tyan's defenders ran to meet them. The first attacker

poked his head above the parapet, only to have a sword take off the top of his head. The man fell without a sound and three defenders heaved the ladder from the wall. It toppled with attackers still clinging to it, slamming into the ground and flinging its occupants to their deaths.

"Protect the gates!" yelled Captain Tyan.

Rovann saw a company of soldiers approaching the gates carrying another battering ram. This one was sheathed in metal and, Rovann guessed, the wood beneath had probably been soaked in water. No doubt, they'd learned their lesson from the fate of the first battering ram.

A detachment of archers lined up along the parapet, taking aim at the approaching ram. But those carrying the ram were heavily armored, protected by interlocking shields held above their heads.

"Hold your fire!" Rovann yelled. "Don't waste your arrows."

Narrowing his eyes, Rovann opened himself to the Realm of Fire. A line of living flame erupted from the ground in front of the gate, burning almost as tall as the parapet and with a ferocity that no water could extinguish. Rovann bound the casting into the soil so the Fire would burn as long as the soil held energy to nourish it.

The battering ram juddered to halt ten paces from the flaming wall, the defenders cowering back from the searing heat. For the moment at least, the gates were safe.

Seeing their attack on the gates thwarted, the front ranks of the attackers shifted and rows of archers stepped forward. The front line knelt as they took aim whilst the line behind stood tall, firing over the heads of their comrades. The air shook with the *thwack* of hundreds of bowstrings and the hissing of arrows.

"Take cover!" Tyan bellowed, throwing himself behind a merlon.

Rovann followed the captain's example. Arrows clattered around him, bouncing off stone and zinging past his face. Rovann heard desperate cries of pain and the thump of falling bodies as arrows found their mark.

The rain of arrows abruptly ceased. Rovann climbed to his knees and peeked over the wall. Under cover of arrow fire, more ladders had been thrown against the walls. Attackers swarmed up in their hundreds.

With a strangled cry of defiance, the citadel's defenders rushed to hold their positions. But they were too few. Hounsey's soldiers poured over the battlements. Close-in battles erupted along the parapet, some fighting with knives, shortswords and flails, some with fists and whatever else lay to hand.

A ladder thumped into view directly in front of Rovann, a helmeted head appearing over the top. The soldier growled upon seeing Rovann and planted his feet on the wall, ready to spring down.

"Lord First!" shouted Captain Tyan.

He threw a knife, hilt first, at Rovann who caught it, spun and sliced the blade across the gap in the man's armor where his thigh met his hip. As the man stumbled, Rovann kicked him down into the courtyard where he landed with a sickening crunch.

Tyan grabbed the top of the ladder and strained but the weight of bodies climbing held it securely in place. Rovann lent his own strength, pushing one side whilst Tyan pushed the other and slowly the ladder began to inch out from the wall. It reached its tipping point and Rovann watched as the ladder fell back, back, back, and crashed into the ranks of milling soldiers below.

Rovann spun and confronted a Hounsey soldier rushing him from behind. The woman's eyes went wide as she came face-to-face with Rovann, but in the next instant he channeled sorcery, lifting her up and tossing her back over the wall.

Pitched battles raged everywhere. Blood slicked the walkway. Rovann gazed out at the black tent in the distance.

Where are you, Hounsey? he thought. *Why don't you show yourself?*

"Watch out!"

Maegwin spun in time to register an ax swinging at her face. She ducked then stabbed upward with her sword. The Hounsey man grunted as his entrails spilled onto the ground. Maegwin scrabbled up, nodded her thanks to Sergeant Hannel, and kicked the legs from beneath a man slashing at Corporal Hesha. Hesha darted in and slashed open the man's throat.

Blood and gore spattered Maegwin's tunic. The grip of her sword was slimy with it. She fought with Hannel and Hesha by the tower door, fighting to keep Hounsey soldiers from gaining access to Syrie and the archers stationed inside. Everywhere she looked Hounsey soldiers were pouring over the walls. It was no good. The citadel was lost.

But Maegwin didn't care.

Her muscles screamed in protest, her lungs burned with effort. And yet she felt *alive.* Fighting meant she didn't have to think. About Hounsey escaping her vengeance. About Rovann...

She grunted as an arrow grazed her temple and thudded into the tower door. Sergeant Hannel knelt, aimed his crossbow, and shot the Hounsey archer in the chest. Spinning in the other direction, he shot a man creeping up behind Hesha then swung the crossbow into another man's face with a crunch of shattering bone.

Maegwin picked up a spear from the blood-slicked stones and rammed it into the injured man's stomach. He doubled over, allowing Maegwin to push him from the wall.

"Hannel!" Hesha's scream cut through the din of battle.

Hannel's eyes widened in surprise as a sword erupted from his shoulder. His own sword clanged onto the stones.

The Hounsey soldier, a woman with blood-matted hair, ripped the sword out and swung it for a killing blow.

With a scream of fury, Hesha threw herself at her brother's attacker. The corporal's sword punched into the Hounsey woman's chest so hard it exited from her back in a shower of gore. As Hesha ripped the sword out, the woman sank slowly to her knees. Hesha turned to Hannel. With a grunt of pain, the Hounsey woman reached for her belt.

"No!" Maegwin screamed in warning.

Too late. The soldier yanked out a knife and, with the last of her strength, plunged it into Hesha's back.

Hesha went rigid then crashed to her knees. She crawled two steps toward Hannel before collapsing.

"*Hesha!*"

Hannel darted to his sister's side. One arm hung useless, blood pumping from the wound in his shoulder. With his free hand he pulled the knife from Hesha's back and dropped it onto the stones with a *clink*. Tearing off his tunic, he balled it and pressed it against Hesha's wound before gently rolling her over. He ripped off his cloak and laid it over her.

Maegwin watched in horror, unable to move. She opened the throat of a man creeping up behind her, kicked another from the battlements, and turned to watch Hesha once more.

The corporal's breath came in ragged gasps. Bubbles of blood escaped her mouth.

"Hannel?" she whispered.

"What?"

"I'm cold."

"Cold? You've got my cloak over you. How can you be cold?"

"That mangy thing. Don't want it."

"You're never grateful."

Hesha smiled, showing a row of bloody teeth. "Always said I'd die before you."

"No you didn't. You said I'd get myself killed doing something stupid, like saving your life. Seems you got it the wrong way round."

She lapsed into silence. Maegwin could hear the unsteady rhythm of her breathing. "Hannel? I'm cold."

"I know, Hesha. Shush now."

Hesha's eyes slid closed. Her hand, where it clasped her brother's, went slack.

Maegwin looked away. Her eyes came to rest on the women who'd stabbed Hesha. She'd fallen on her back, not two paces from where Maegwin stood. A jolt of recognition passed through her. She'd met this woman before.

The woman reached out toward Maegwin imploringly. "Don't," she whimpered, eyes wide with fear. "Mercy. Please." The woman had startling blue eyes and black hair that tumbled free of her bear's head helmet. A white scar ran across the bridge of her nose.

Maegwin gasped as she took in the same black hair and blue eyes. The same white scar running across the bridge of her nose. This was the woman Maegwin had spared on the Sarth Road.

Look what your mercy has wrought, a voice inside her whispered. *You let this woman live and Hesha is dead because of your weakness.*

Maegwin staggered, her sword clattering onto the stones. *No. Hesha. No.*

Her heart contracted as she stared at her friend's lifeless face. Bile rose in her throat. Everything had gone wrong. Hounsey lived. Rovann had betrayed her. Hesha had died because Maegwin had let this woman live. She doubled over and emptied her guts onto the parapet, sour vomit stinging her nose and throat.

You see! crowed the voice of the Dark Goddess. *What does mercy bring you in the end? Only misery!*

Maegwin wiped a hand across her face, leaving a smear of blood. With an anguished cry, she jumped down the steps and fled into the citadel.

There. At last, Rovann saw movement by the black tent. A small figure emerged and faced the citadel. Hounsey. Four people gathered behind him, forming an arrow formation with the warlord at the tip.

"Mages," Rovann breathed, gritting his teeth. A smoldering anger formed in his belly. Traitors, the lot of them.

Rovann's fingers, where they rested on the parapet, began to tingle. The ground was shaking, he realized, so minute as to be barely noticeable.

By Hounsey's feet, three stains erupted like bruises on the trampled mud of the enemy camp. As Rovann watched, the stains began to elongate, spreading along the ground like black snakes. Unease squirmed in Rovann's belly. What devilry was this? In just a few minutes the stains had traveled twenty paces toward the citadel.

Where the stains spread, the grass withered, the flowers died, the soil dried and cracked. A few minutes more and the stains reached the back lines of Hounsey's army. An archer bent to recover some arrows, groping around on the ground. The man's hand brushed one of the black stains and the affect was instantaneous. He howled, drawing terrified glances from those around him. His body rippled, his skin bubbling like melting wax then he collapsed to the ground where he twitched for a moment before dissipating into a congealing puddle of black oil. Cries of fear and dismay rose from Hounsey's soldiers. The rearmost line of the army buckled as the soldiers scrambled away.

The defenders on the citadel had seen it too. As the deadly black stains edged closer, the defender's lines wavered, faces going slack with fear.

"Stand your ground!" Captain Tyan bellowed. "Hold your positions!"

Rovann stared, struggling to believe what he saw.

Those stains were pure Chaotic power. His heart thundered against his ribs. If those lines reached the citadel, it was over. But how could he fight Chaotic power? He had no experience of this kind of sorcery. Nobody did.

Think, curse you! he shouted at himself. *You are the King's Mage. How do you fight death?*

Then he had it. You fight death with life.

He knelt behind the parapet and closed his eyes. Forcing himself to take slow breaths until his breathing deepened, he at last felt stillness spread through him. He shrugged off his body and rose into the air. Here on the astral plane he saw the life energies of everything around him: the shimmering auras of the soldiers, the volatile energies of the river behind him, the black penumbra that surrounded Hounsey and his mages.

And in the ground the Chaotic power shone a sickly green, snaking through the earth like a disease.

Rovann let the life forces of the Realm of Earth pulse through him, filling him with their power. He took that life energy and formed it into three spears that glowed with a golden light.

Glancing down, he realized the Chaotic power was now just inches from the citadel walls. Screams of terror rose all around him.

With all his strength, he threw the spears at the earth. They smashed into the sickly green lines of Chaos with an impact that shook the ground. Rovann threw all his life energy into them, pushing, pushing as the golden spears dug deep into the earth, grinding against the Chaotic power with enough force to shake the ground.

The two energies battled, fizzing and crackling on the astral plane. As the Chaotic power devoured the golden spears, Rovann threw more and more of his life force into them until they glowed white-hot like molten metal. Feeling his strength ebbing, he pulled energy from the land around: from the trees, the rocks, the ground, the river. He became a conduit channeling the powers of Earth against this terrible alien force.

Pressure started to build inside him. The forces tearing through him were too great. They threatened to rip him apart. But he held on, a scream escaping his lips as pieces of his essence began to shred. Then, with a boom that echoed through the astral, the lines of Chaos snapped and were devoured by the spears of light.

With a cry, Rovann's astral form staggered, buffeted by the sudden absence of power. Feeling weak and disorientated, he returned to his body and opened his eyes. Blood streamed from his nose and ears. Bruises covered his arms. But he was alive. He sucked in deep breaths and forced his tired body to its knees so he could look out over the parapet.

The smoky stains had vanished. Three steaming craters marked where they'd been. In the distance Rovann spotted Hounsey and his mages lying unconscious on the ground.

Around him, the citadel's defenders raised a ragged cheer. But the respite lasted for only a moment. With a roar of defiance, Hounsey's soldiers redoubled their assault on the walls.

Rovann pressed his head against the stone, feeling its grainy solidity against his skin. Fatigue flooded through his body, turning his limbs as heavy as lead. He wavered on the edge of unconsciousness and dug his nails into his palms to keep himself awake. Bracing his arms on the parapet, he climbed to his feet and stood swaying drunkenly.

"Fall back!" Captain Tyan cried. "Everyone to the bridge!"

The area below the walls had become a seething mass of humanity, all jostling to get onto the scaling ladders. The siege towers Hounsey had been building slowly rolled forward, crowded with enough soldiers to overrun the citadel completely. Before the gates, the Fire Rovann had called still burned ferociously but Syrie's attacks with the Eorthe had stopped and the ground was now quiet.

Tyan grabbed Rovann's elbow. The man's eyes were frantic. "We're being overrun. This will be a slaughter! Can you do anything to hold them off while we retreat?"

Rovann scrubbed a hand through his hair. He was so tired he could barely form words. But there was one last thing he could try. "Perhaps. A ward. But the price will be high." He looked into Tyan's steely eyes. "Are you willing to pay it, captain?"

Captain Tyan nodded, understanding what Rovann meant. "Do it."

"No," a voice suddenly cried.

The citadel's commander, Lord Charis, waddled toward them with his corporal, Tanner, a step behind.

"I'll do it. Fates take, I'm the commander of the citadel and all I've done is watch from my window while my people die. I may be fat and old but I'm still a king's man and I'll be damned if I'll stand by and let those bastards take my citadel!"

Rovann studied the man's face. "You have to understand, commander, there is no coming back. It will cost your life."

The commander straightened, a steely determination coming into his eyes. "And? I vowed to defend this post with my life, sir."

Rovann gripped the man's shoulder. "The king will hear of your bravery."

"Just save my people. Then I'll die happy."

"Wait!" Corporal Tanner stepped forward. "I will stand with my commander. I also swore a vow, sir." His jaw was set, lips pressed into a flat line.

Rovann didn't have the strength to argue. He nodded and quickly issued instructions to Commander Charis and Corporal Tanner then watched as they jogged off in opposite directions, one to each end of the curtain wall.

When they were in position, Rovann moved to the center of the battlements, directly above the gates. Here he was equidistant from the two men, but horribly exposed to attack. It was a risk he'd have to take.

Placing his hands flat on the cool stone, he closed his

eyes and tried to concentrate. Any second he might feel an arrow slam into his body but he tried to push all such concerns away.

There was only himself and the stone. Himself and the stone.

After a moment, the heat and noise of the battle receded until he felt as though he was alone in the world with only the silence and the warm breeze for company.

In his mind's eye, Rovann formed a gate, burning at each corner with strong sigils. He pushed the gate open, letting through a trickle of Aethyr. He opened his eyes, clenched his fists together in front of him and swung them down as though driving a stake into the ground. A sheet of light erupted from his hands and spread out to both sides, anchoring itself into Commander Charis on the eastern end of the battlements and Corporal Tanner on the west.

The men went rigid, teeth bared, eyes staring. Sadness twisted Rovann's stomach. The ward would burn for as long as the anchors had strength, using up their life energy, bit by gradual bit, until they became lifeless husks.

Slowly, Rovann stepped back a pace. The ward flickered then steadied. The Hounsey soldiers trapped on the citadel side were quickly dispatched by the defenders. Above Rovann's head, a rain of arrows clattered against the ward and fell uselessly to the ground.

"Fall back!" Rovann shouted. "We don't have long!"

The withdrawal from the battlements was orderly and professional. Even the civilians didn't panic. The portcullis that led onto the bridge had been raised and Syrie was overseeing the evacuation of the defenders. The injured had been loaded onto crude stretchers and were the first to be carried across the bridge by the others.

"You need to leave, Syrie," Rovann said, coming abreast of her. "I'll torch the bridge from this end."

Her eyes widened as the import of his words sank in. "You're not coming with us?"

He shook his head.

"You don't have to do this," Syrie said, guessing Rovann's intent. "Come back to Tyrlindon with me and we can find another way."

Rovann smiled awkwardly. "Not this time. You know I must go after the Songmaker. Prince Owen and Leo still live. I have to find them. And I have to confront the Songmaker. If I don't, Amaury will never be safe."

"But you can't go alone, Rovann! It's madness!"

"Who else is there? Everyone is needed to defend Tyrlindon. Besides, you've seen the power the Songmaker wields. You know I'm the only one with a chance against him. Travel as quickly as you can and spread the word through the countryside as you move. Hounsey will raze everything in his path so encourage people to take refuge in the city." He glanced at the citadel gates. His wall of Fire had died and Hounsey's soldiers now battered the gates.

Syrie swallowed thickly. "I guessed you'd do this. There's a boat tied to the landing stage beneath the bridge. I've strengthened it with the Eorthe so it should be strong enough to withstand the Carrow. But I don't like this, Rovann. It feels wrong. How will we defend Tyrlindon without you?"

He laid a hand on her arm. "You'll have Falwin and Tiria and the rest of the college behind you. You'll do fine."

"But—"

Syrie was cut short by a strangled cry from behind them. Rovann spun. On the parapet Corporal Tanner suddenly staggered, clutching his head. Blood pumped from his nostrils. He sank to his knees then toppled face-first and lay lifeless on the stone. A heartbeat later, Commander Charis screamed and collapsed, one arm dangling over the edge of the parapet.

The ward wavered and broke with an audible snap.

"Go!" Rovann yelled. "There isn't time!"

Syrie whirled and sprinted onto the bridge, her footsteps echoing on the hard wooden boards.

Already Rovann could see the tops of scaling ladders springing up along the top of the battlements. A moment later, soldiers came swarming over them.

Rovann took a few steps back into the courtyard and sent a wave of Air hurtling at the soldiers. The wave slammed into the first line, taking them off their feet and carrying a few back over the wall with blood-curdling screams. Rovann spun back toward to the bridge. Too late he heard the tell-tale zing behind him then an arrow exploded through his forearm.

He staggered to his knees as white-hot pain washed through him. Another arrow whizzed past, inches from his throat. With a snarl, he ripped the arrow from his arm in a shower of blood then staggered through the tunnel. He kicked the wheel that controlled the portcullis and the iron grille came crashing down, blocking the exit from the courtyard.

It wouldn't hold the soldiers for long but might give him a few extra minutes. Ahead of him, the bridge climbed over the river. The defenders had not yet reached the other side. Time. He needed time.

He turned left and sprinted down a set of stone steps cut into the cliff and vaulted onto the wooden landing stage that jutted into the heaving river. A rowing boat jumped and bucked against the platform, its mooring rope pulled tight as the river tried to snatch it away.

Rovann grabbed the rope and pulled. It didn't move. His right arm had gone numb and hung uselessly by his side, blood seeping from the arrow wound. With only one good hand he couldn't grip the rope properly.

Above, he heard the citadel gates burst open.

"Come on, curse you!" he howled.

He yanked on the rope but it wouldn't budge. Fighting a pain that threatened to make him black-out, he grabbed the rope with his injured arm. But his grip was slimy with blood and the rope just slipped through his fingers.

Rage and frustration made tears well from his eyes. He howled wordlessly.

Then hands appeared on the rope next to his, pulling in time with him. Rovann turned to see a familiar figure kneeling beside him.

Maegwin.

She was covered in grime and blood, as bedraggled as he was. She'd lost her sword and her clothes hung in shreds.

"Maegwin?" he gasped. "What are you doing here?"

"Saving your backside by the looks of it," she growled.

"But I thought you'd gone with the others."

She met his gaze. "I almost did. But I changed my mind. Hounsey said Leo is alive. I'm coming with you."

Dizziness raced through his head. *Coming with me?* A strange sensation flooded through him. It took a moment before he recognized it. Relief.

She took his silence for something else. "Don't try and stop me. I don't take orders from you, remember?"

Stop you? he thought. *How could I? You saved me from tearing the veil to the Outer Darkness. I owe you more than you could know.*

But all he said was, "I remember."

The knot came free and the mooring rope slid from its ring. Maegwin stepped aboard the boat and took up the oars as Rovann pushed hard against the landing stage. Maegwin pulled on the oars and the boat inched into the river. Rovann braced his legs in the pitching vessel and stood in the bow, trying to watch the citadel, the bridge, and the fleeing defenders all at once.

Syrie and Tyan were still struggling across. They'd covered perhaps half the distance when the first of Hounsey's men appeared from the tunnel mouth. They saw the escaping defenders and let out a howl of triumph, hurtling onto the bridge in pursuit.

Rovann steadied himself in the swaying boat. Around them the river surged and roared. If not for Syrie's sorcery the boat would have been ripped apart. They were in midstream now and perhaps two hundred paces upstream from the bridge. From here, Rovann had a perfect view. At the far end of the bridge the citadel's defenders were disappearing into the thick forest that flanked the road. On the nearside, Hounsey soldiers were pouring out of the citadel and onto the bridge after them.

And Syrie and Tyan still weren't across.

Come on! Rovann cried silently. *Come on!*

Hounsey soldiers were gaining on them. Arrows and throwing knives thunked into the wood behind the pair.

Then Syrie stumbled and fell.

Rovann's stomach lurched.

Captain Tyan skidded and spun back to the mage. He picked Syrie up, slung her over his shoulder and sprinted.

Above the roar of the river, Rovann heard the howling of the Hounsey soldiers. They sounded crazed with blood-lust, desperate to get their paws on their prey.

Rovann's hands curled into fists. His heart raced.

Tyan's feet touched the ground on the far side of the bridge.

Rovann threw his senses wide, forged a burning gate in his mind and opened himself to the Realm of Fire. It poured into him like a stream of magma. He didn't try to control it. Instead, he made himself into a conduit and channeled the blazing energy at his target.

The bridge erupted into flames.

From end to end, the structure was engulfed by hungry red tongues, and burned like a giant torch. The soldiers on the bridge were incinerated. Rovann turned the Fire on the citadel and the red tongues licked the riverside wall, turning the stone white-hot. With a groan, the wall toppled inward, burying Hounsey's access to the riverbank in tons of rubble.

Rovann slammed the gate closed in his mind and the stream of Fire ceased. He turned his head and saw Tyan and Syrie disappearing into the trees.

Pain flooded through his body. He ached all over. Blood streamed from the arrow wound and a hundred other minor cuts. A raging headache tore through his skull. But most of all he felt tired. So tired.

He sank to his knees, fighting to stay awake. Maegwin caught him as he fell onto the hard boards at the bottom of the boat.

As unconsciousness pulled him under, he saw her silhouette looming above him. Then her voice whispered by his ear, dark with hunger.

"It's just you and me now, Rovann. And you're all mine."

Next in The Songmaker Series

vinci-books.com/kingsmage

The battle has been won, but the real war is just beginning.

Rovann and Maegwin survived Carrow Crossing, but the Songmaker's army advances. To stop him, they must embark on a perilous quest, where danger, betrayal, and the dark secrets within themselves threaten everything they hold dear.

Turn the page for a free preview…

The King's Mage: Chapter One

Rovann woke with a start. Searing agony throbbed in his right arm, sending spears of fire vibrating through his body, threatening to tip him back into unconsciousness. For a moment, it consumed him. He couldn't think straight. He couldn't see. He couldn't hear.

But worse than all of this was a terrifying realization that he couldn't breathe. His lungs strained for air but it wouldn't come. Something warm pressed against his lips, blocking his airways. Then his sight cleared to reveal a woman's face close to his. Green eyes burned from a face covered in dirt and grime.

Maegwin.

And her hand was clamped tight over his mouth, suffocating him.

The day's events flashed through his mind. He and Maegwin confronting Lord Cedric Hounsey only to discover he was already dead, a revenant held in thrall to the Songmaker's will. The betrayal in Maegwin's eyes as he, Rovann, denied her revenge against Hounsey and then invaded her mind to seize her power to enable them to escape.

More images flickered. The storming of Carrow Crossing by Hounsey troops. His vain attempt to hold them off while Captain Tyan, Mage Syrie and the soldiers escaped. The enemy arrow that exploded through his right forearm.

Then finally the words Maegwin had whispered to him as he fell into unconsciousness.

It's just you and me now, Rovann. And you're all mine.

And here she was, a crazed look in her eyes, trying to smother him. A sliver of ice-cold fear stabbed through his abdomen. There was no recognition in Maegwin's eyes. Only a raw emotion that Rovann couldn't quite place. Covered in the blood and filth of battle, she looked like some wild she-devil dredged from an old saga.

She was going to kill him. After all they'd been through he was going to die at Maegwin's hands. His supposed ally. His friend.

No! I will not!

Summoning his ebbing strength, he reached for his sorcery only to find it gone. Where the burning core of his power should be, there was…nothing. Emptiness.

He'd spent too much of his strength in the citadel's defense. *Idiot*, he chided himself as his lungs burned and his consciousness began to fade. *Now your quest is over before it's begun.*

A small, traitorous part of him was relieved. It was over. Let someone else face the Songmaker. But another, stronger part shouted in outrage that it should end like this.

I won't allow it! he raged. *I will not!*

He thrashed in Maegwin's grip, determined to break her hold.

"How many more times?" she hissed. "Be quiet, curse you! Do you want to give us away? Hush!"

Comprehension dawned. He went as limp as a doll. She watched him warily as she slowly withdrew her hand and Rovann drew in a rasping breath.

"What are you—"

She pressed a finger to his lips. "Hush! They're close."

For the first time, Rovann noticed his surroundings. He was lying propped against a tree. A thick tangle of under-growth surrounded him through which he could hear the murmur of the river. Over the growl of the water came something else: movement in the bushes, the sound of stealthy footsteps and low voices. Close.

Rovann froze. He held his breath. Slowly Maegwin drew her dagger.

Not more than five paces to Rovann's left a cry went up. "There! What's that? Is it a boat? It is! After them, you fools! And get archers to the riverbank! Move!"

Crashing sounded, uncomfortably close. After a moment it moved away from them, gradually dwindling into the distance. All was still. Rovann's heart thundered in his ears.

Maegwin crouched like a beast ready for flight. After several tense minutes she closed her eyes and sighed in relief, her shoulders sagging with released tension. Then she climbed to her feet.

"I'm going to have a look around. Wait here. I won't be long." Before he could protest she melted into the trees.

Rovann was left alone. The summer sun was halfway to the horizon, sending slivers of light to cast a patchwork pattern on the ground by Rovann's outstretched feet. Bees droned in and out of a bunch of purple foxgloves to his right and birds chattered in the branches above.

Rovann breathed deeply, trying to clear his head and find his bearings. Judging by the position of the sun, he guessed it was late afternoon, several hours since he and Maegwin had escaped from Carrow Crossing. A few hours? It felt like a heartbeat. Rovann could still hear the roaring of fighting, smell the stench of fear and taste the iron tang of blood. He could still see Lord Cedric Hounsey's grinning face.

He raised his hand to wipe sweat from his forehead but gasped as stinging pain ran up his arm and into his shoulder, making him dizzy. Gritting his teeth, he looked down. His right wrist was a mangled, swollen mass of torn flesh and encrusted blood. Where the arrow had penetrated, Rovann saw the white of broken bones and his fingers looked like thick, useless sausages. Slowly he raised the arm, grimacing against the pain.

"Don't."

Maegwin stepped into the clearing and crouched in front of him.

"Don't touch it."

Rovann sank back, laying his head against the tree trunk and resting the injured arm in his lap.

"Did you find anything?"

Maegwin inspected his injury and frowned at what she saw. "A party of Hounsey soldiers. The woods are full of them. We are being tracked. I suppose it was too much to hope that we got away without being seen."

"How far from the citadel are we?"

"Not as far as I'd like," she growled, straightening. "But as far as the river will allow. There's a waterfall ahead so I had to put in and get you ashore. I set the boat adrift hoping they might spot it and follow."

"It won't take them long to realize it's a decoy,"

Rovann said, glancing around their hideout as if expecting soldiers to come crashing through the trees any moment. "Then they'll retrace their steps. We can't hope to stay hidden."

"Don't you think I realize that?" she snapped. "We can't even get across the river. The far bank is a cliff with nowhere to land the boat."

This was not what Rovann wanted to hear. He needed time. Time to recover his strength. Time to treat his wounds. Time to think of a way out of this and form a plan to find the Songmaker. But he didn't have any.

"What of Captain Tyan, Syrie and the rest?" he asked. "Did they escape?"

Maegwin shrugged. "I don't know. I think so. You collapsed after you fired the bridge and I rowed us away as fast as I could. Soldiers were firing at us from the bank. I had to get us out of there."

Rovann studied her face. Although she was caked in crusted blood, none of it seemed to be her own. She seemed unharmed but exhausted. His earlier distrust suddenly shamed him. She'd saved his life. Again. And in return he'd suspected her of trying to kill him.

On impulse he reached out and laid his uninjured hand over hers. She startled, lifting her eyes to meet his.

"I'm grateful for your help, Maegwin."

And I'm sorry for what I did to you at Carrow Crossing. Although he didn't speak the words aloud, he hoped she understood his unspoken apology.

She stared at him for a moment before suddenly snatching her hand away. "I gave you my word, didn't I? I'm doing this to save Leo. And to avenge my sisters."

Not for you. I owe you nothing.

Rovann heard the message behind her unspoken words.

He nodded. It was as much as he could hope for. "Then we'd better get moving."

"How do you propose to do that? The woods are crawling with Hounsey soldiers. And you are in no fit state for travel."

Rovann shifted his weight, testing his injuries. Lances of agony tore through his hand and arm. Maegwin was right. In this condition, he would be easy pickings for Hounsey.

Maegwin watched him impassively. There was a cold, remote expression on her face as Rovann struggled to his knees, cradling his injured arm against his chest. Every muscle in his body screamed in protest and little dots of light danced in front of his eyes.

Get up! he shouted at himself. *Get moving!*

But his battered body wouldn't obey. Waves of pain and dizziness threatened to make him black out.

Maegwin watched him for a moment then seemed to reach a decision. "Stay still. You need food, water and treatment before we go anywhere."

"There isn't time. We could be caught any moment."

"If we're discovered with you in this state we're finished no matter. Now sit there and stay quiet!"

She disappeared into the trees, returning a few moments later carrying a package under one arm and a bunch of dangling green plants in the other. Folding onto her knees, she laid her wares on the ground. "Syrie provisioned the boat," she said by way of explanation.

Opening the package she revealed a canteen of water, some tough strips of dried meat and hard bread. Handing over the water bottle she said, "Here; drink."

Rovann took the bottle with his good hand and set it to his cracked lips, drinking greedily. When he'd taken his fill he accepted some of the bread and dried meat from

Maegwin and began chewing mechanically. The movement tore his already damaged lips but his body reacted to the sustenance. The dizziness passed. Solidity returned to his muscles.

Maegwin ate in silence, watching him. When she was satisfied that he'd eaten enough she fetched two stones from the river's edge and began pounding the green plants into a sticky paste.

"What are you doing?"

"Making a salve," she replied without looking up. "These are rosewort. Good at keeping out infection and by the looks of your hand, you're going to need it. It's already festering. I think the arrow may have been poisoned."

Rovann didn't argue. From the sickly reek and yellow pus oozing from the wound, he knew infection was already starting to set in. Rovann had seen such wounds on the battlefield many times. As often as not they led to gangrene, amputation and death. He looked away, determined not to entertain such notions. He would be damned if he would fall to a stray Hounsey arrow.

As Maegwin worked, Rovann thought. They needed help. Shelter. Rest. Food. Horses. But where to find it? The countryside on this side of the river was in rebel hands. All the safe havens lay on the far side of the river. He knew of no settlements that might offer them what they required. Except...

He sat up straighter. "There is a place, perhaps a day's walk west of here. If we can reach it, I think the people there might help us."

She glanced at him but didn't stop working. "What place?"

"A small town, more of a village really. Stoneshowe."

"I've never heard of it."

No, not many have, he thought. *And only the desperate would willingly seek the place out. Yet, we have no choice.*

Maegwin straightened and held up the mashed rosewort to sniff it. "It will have to do. Normally I'd add comfrey or yarrow to the salve but I can't find any nearby and daren't go far into the woods to look. Hold out your hand."

Grimacing against the pain, Rovann slid his right hand down his thigh toward her. Maegwin leaned over, inspecting the wound and then shook her head.

"This is going to hurt."

"Yes, I thought it might."

Pursing her lips, Maegwin scraped the mashed weed onto the end of her finger and quickly smeared it over Rovann's injury.

Despite himself, Rovann yelped in pain and laid his head against the tree trunk as blinding white agony consumed his body. It lasted for perhaps three heartbeats before a cool, soothing sensation began tingling from his elbow to his fingers.

Maegwin ripped some strips from the hem of her tunic. "Hold still."

She lightly wrapped the material around Rovann's injured arm, immobilizing the fingers and thumb. When it was done, he found that the pain had lessened and he was able to stagger to his feet without the danger of passing out. He leaned his good hand on the tree and stood with his head hanging as the waves of scalding dizziness passed. Finally, he lifted his head.

"Here," Maegwin handed him a stout branch to use as a walking stick. He accepted it gratefully, acutely aware of how reliant he was on Maegwin. He didn't like it one little bit.

"Thanks."

She shrugged. "Lead the way."

Rovann turned in a slow circle, trying to get his bearings. After a moment, he fixed on what he hoped was the right direction. Shuffling like an old man, Rovann led them west.

Maegwin stared at Rovann's back as they marched. He hobbled along maybe five paces ahead of her. His pain was evident in the hitched and hesitant gait of his walk. Gone was the powerful King's Mage. Instead he was just an injured man who needed her help. Maegwin wasn't sure how she felt about that. In fact, she wasn't sure how she felt about anything.

She ought to feel angry. At Rovann, at Hounsey. But she didn't. She felt... nothing.

Thoughts whirled in her head, a never-ending cycle that brought her no relief. Rovann had betrayed her. He'd promised her revenge against Lord Cedric Hounsey, the man who had burned down her temple, murdered her sister priestesses and turned Maegwin into a friendless refugee. Killing him had become the burning goal of Maegwin's life, the thing she clung to. But when the time had come and she'd had Hounsey within her grasp, Rovann had let Hounsey go.

Her hands clenched into fists and her gaze fixed on Rovann's back as though she meant to burn holes into it. How could he do that to her? How could he? Hadn't she kept her word, done everything he asked of her? So why had he done it?

She ducked under a low branch and then halted as Rovann paused, looking from left to right. After a moment he set off once more and Maegwin followed, keeping a few steps behind him.

Perhaps she ought to be watching for Hounsey soldiers —Rovann was in no condition to do it—but she couldn't bring herself to make the effort. If they were attacked she would fight and do her best to kill her enemies. At the moment her plans went no further than that. She had no idea where this place was he was taking them or what they'd find there. If she asked she doubted he'd tell her. Another one of his damned secrets. Let him keep them. She didn't care.

They struggled on at a pace that made her grind her teeth in frustration. Finally, she pushed ahead of Rovann. "We're heading west, yes? I'll find a path for us. You just follow."

She didn't stop to check whether he had obeyed her command but strode ahead into the forest. The terrain was different from the forest that had surrounded her temple. There, the trees had been huge and old, with vast spaces beneath their trunks in which herds of deer would often be seen grazing. This forest was dense and tightly packed with tangled undergrowth that made it difficult to find her way. Evening would soon be upon them and they'd need a place to camp for the night. She intended to be well clear of the Hounsey soldiers by then.

She wove in and out of the trees, listening to any sounds that might indicate an ambush. All she heard was the chirping of birds and the moan of the breeze. Rovann was already out of sight behind her but she knew he would be able to follow her trail.

She reached a dry gully choked with last year's leaves and hesitated. The ditch was deep, with high sides that Rovann would struggle to climb with his injury so

Maegwin turned left and followed the channel's meandering course, looking for an easier place to cross. Her attention focused on her path, she didn't see the tripwire until it was too late.

Her ankles caught and she went sprawling to the ground, palms scraping painfully against sharp stones embedded in the mulch of the forest floor. She twisted in time to see armed men bursting from the undergrowth. They wore the greens and browns of woodsmen but Maegwin saw from their weapons that they were Hounsey soldiers.

Maegwin scrabbled at the dirt, trying to gain her feet but one of the men backhanded her across the face hard enough to send her sprawling onto her back. His hands tangled in her hair and a blade suddenly pressed itself against her throat.

"Move and I'll kill you," the man said. "Understand?"

"Yes," she murmured as the icy cold edge of the blade bit her flesh.

The man leaned close, peering at her with narrowed eyes. His stink reached her nostrils: stale sweat, damp leather, unwashed skin. She wrinkled her nose.

"I reckon this is the one," he said to his men. "She matches the description the captain gave us." Turning back to Maegwin, he demanded, "Where's your friend?"

Maegwin pressed her lips into a flat line.

The man raised an eyebrow. "Oh, defiance is it? I like that in a woman, makes them more of a challenge. Doesn't matter anyway, little lady. We'll find your companion soon enough." He turned and bellowed orders to his men. "Follow her trail and find the other one. Hanlon you go as well and be on your guard. By all accounts this man is dangerous."

"Yes, sarge." Two soldiers and a robed man who might have been a mage nodded and disappeared into the woods.

Maegwin watched her captor. His eyes were fixed on his departing men but as soon as she began moving her hand toward her dagger, his eyes snapped to her. He increased pressure on the blade and hot blood trickled down her neck.

"Oh no you don't, little lady," he said, pulling out her knife and tossing it away. "I'm going to let you up now but if you so much as breathe in a way I don't like I'll cut your throat. Understand?"

"Yes," she murmured.

He stared at her for a moment more before removing the blade and rising to his feet. Maegwin's hand flew to her throat where a small nick had opened. She swallowed a few times, steeling her courage, and then rose to her feet.

"What are you going to do with me?" she demanded.

The sergeant leered around at his men before answering. "That's the question, little lady, isn't it? You see, our orders were to capture your companion. He's the one our boss is interested in which means you are surplus to requirements." He gestured at her with his blade. "However, there could be other ways you might prove useful."

She narrowed her eyes. "What do you mean?"

He sauntered over and lifted her chin with his index finger. "Oh, I'm sure you can use your imagination." His hand went to her breast and squeezed, hard.

She slapped him across the face, snapping his head to one side, and then backed away. "Keep your filthy paws off me."

He slowly straightened. A line of blood dripped from his nostril. "Oh dear," he said. "A fighter. Still," he shrugged. "I've always enjoyed a challenge."

He moved like lightning. She barely had time to register

his approach before his fist caught her on the cheek and sent her sprawling into the dirt. He dropped his weight on top of her, pinning her to the ground. She punched and scratched at him but he grabbed her wrists with one hand and yanked her arms over her head. With his free hand he began untying his trousers.

Maegwin screamed in rage and frustration. She writhed, trying to bring her knees up but he was too heavy for her.

"My, my, you really are a fighter," he murmured. "Hold her down," he growled at his men.

Maegwin shrieked as the soldiers grabbed her ankles, pulling her legs wide and holding her there, spread-eagled on the ground.

"Try to enjoy it," the sergeant said in her ear. His hand traced a line up the inside of her thigh and then began fumbling at the lacings on her doe-skin leggings. "The more you struggle, the more it'll hurt."

But suddenly the pressure on her legs eased and Maegwin thrashed, trying to kick him away.

"What are you doing, curse you!" the sergeant bellowed at his men. "I told you to hold her down!" He glanced over his shoulder and his eyes widened. In the next instant he scrambled to his feet, quickly tying his trousers and yanking his sword from its scabbard.

Maegwin sat up and scooted backward, coming to rest against a broad tree trunk where she sat slightly dazed, trying to get her bearings. The soldiers had spread out and taken a ready stance with swords drawn, facing away from her. A figure emerged from the trees and halted ten paces from the line of soldiers.

Rovann.

"I believe this is yours."

He tossed something to the ground and Maegwin realized it was the robe the Hounsey mage had been wearing. On top of it Rovann dropped the two swords the Hounsey soldiers who'd gone looking for him had been carrying.

Rovann stood straight, feet shoulder-width apart and chin lifted defiantly. There was no trace of the injury he carried. The soldiers shifted uncomfortably. The sergeant motioned with one hand and his men moved out silently to surround Rovann.

"Don't be a fool now," the sergeant said. "You might have overcome Hanlon and the others but there are ten of us. Our orders are to take you back to Carrow Crossing. If you come quietly, you'll not be harmed."

Rovann cocked his head as if considering the sergeant's offer. "Very generous. And my friend?"

The sergeant glanced to where Maegwin sat against the tree. He shrugged. "Of course. We'll take her back as well."

"Is that before or after you rape her?"

Rovann's voice had gone deadly quiet and the threat in it made Maegwin's hair stand on end. She climbed to her feet and stood, warily trying to watch everyone at once. The sergeant seemed oblivious to the menace in Rovann's tone. Perhaps he still believed he held the upper hand. Fool.

"Spoils of war, my friend," he said, grinning. "Spoils of war."

The sergeant flicked his wrist and his men attacked in a flurry of bellowed curses and swinging swords. Rovann didn't stand a chance. They rushed him from all sides, giving him no time to respond.

Yet he seemed to melt away from their attack only to reappear behind them. In his hand he grasped a sword with a blade of silver light. The tiniest flick of the weapon and a man's head went flying from his shoulders. Turning in silence, Rovann opened another man from chest to abdomen. The man watched his entrails pour onto the floor before collapsing face-down on top of them. A third man swung in low, aiming for Rovann's calves but he merely threw out his hand, palm facing his attacker and the man was thrown through the air to collide with a tree trunk with a thump.

The rest of the soldiers backed away. Rovann went still, sword tip dangling into the soft mulch of the forest floor. He watched them in silence.

The sergeant ran a hand over his sweaty brow and then gestured at Rovann. "Now, we don't have to go letting this get ugly do we? How's about we let you go and tell our boss we never found you? How does that sound?"

Rovann said nothing. He dropped his sword by his feet where it hissed and disappeared. He raised his hands out to either side as though he would bestow a blessing on the soldiers. Around him, the wind whipped up in a churning whirlwind. Dead leaves and plant matter swirled around his feet. The pressure in the glade intensified, almost pushing Maegwin flat.

The sergeant and his men threw down their weapons and turned to flee but with a word, Rovann froze them to the spot. They turned wide fearful eyes on him.

"Wait!" cried the sergeant. "We was only following orders! We was only doing our job."

"I know," Rovann said and Maegwin thought she detected a hint of sadness in his voice. "And I'm only doing mine."

The pressure increased again and Maegwin clamped her hands to her ears at a sudden sharp pain. Rovann lowered his arms and a wave of power went rippling outwards. It ripped into the Hounsey soldiers. Maegwin gagged as they were torn into pulpy lumps of meat.

Silence fell. Rovann slowly collapsed onto his knees amid the carnage. Maegwin didn't move. Bile churned in her stomach and her pulse hammered in her ears.

Flee! A voice whispered inside. *Go now, while he's helpless!*

She took two steps away from him and then halted. He'd saved her from rape. He'd saved her from the noose in Mallyn. *So? You don't owe him anything! Flee now!*

But she didn't. She closed her eyes, pulled in a steadying breath. Counted her heartbeat: one, two, three, and then opened her eyes. Turning on her heel, she strode to Rovann and went to her knees in front of him.

He seemed barely conscious, eyes closed, breath shallow and rattling. She laid a hand on his shoulders and his eyelids fluttered open. His blue gaze found hers and she saw the barest recognition.

"Maegwin, are you all right? Did they hurt you?"

She shook her head. "No, I'm fine."

"Good. I'm glad." His eyes slid closed and he sank forward.

Maegwin caught him, supporting his weight on her shoulder. "Rovann, you have to wake up. We have to get moving."

No response.

She grabbed his shoulders and shook him. "King's Mage! On your feet! On your feet now!"

His head snapped up, eyes flicking open. She stuck her hands under his armpits and hauled him to his feet. He scrabbled, getting his feet under him and then stood leaning on her heavily.

"I have no strength left, Maegwin. I don't know if I can make it."

"You can and you will," she growled. She pulled one of his arms over her shoulder and slung her arm around his waist. "Stoneshowe isn't it? You guide me, and I'll get us there"

"West, head west."

"Right. Come on."

They limped off into the forest.

———

Several tense hours later they made camp between two huge boulders that had fallen from a granite cliff that bisected the woods. Maegwin dared not light a fire so she spent a restless and uncomfortable night staring out into the dark whilst Rovann shivered and moaned in his sleep, caught in fever dreams.

Maegwin roused him before first light, forced him to eat, redressed his wound and then helped him stagger into the west once more. The forest soon retreated and they began to climb to higher ground where heather replaced the trees and the wind moaned ceaselessly.

She didn't like this exposed terrain. If caught here they would be easy pickings for Hounsey's soldiers. But they labored on into the afternoon and saw no sign of pursuit. Toward evening they began to descend into a land of broken canyons and stunted trees. They passed from beneath the boughs of a gloomy copse and found themselves standing on a rutted track.

Maegwin motioned for them to cross it and take cover in the trees on the other side but Rovann halted.

"No, we turn south here and follow this trail."

She glanced around. "Are you out of your mind? We have no idea where Hounsey's soldiers might be. We should stay off the roads."

Rovann smiled thinly. His skin had taken on a sickly

gray pallor and dark rings circled his eyes. "It's unlikely we'll meet soldiers on this road. This is the way to Stoneshowe."

Maegwin frowned but didn't argue. Taking Rovann's weight once more they began hobbling up the trail.

Steep canyons soon grew to either side of the track, so high that the path was cast into almost perpetual twilight. The skin between Maegwin's shoulder blades itched. This was the perfect place for an ambush. In the darkness every sound seemed amplified: Rovann's ragged breathing, the trickle of water somewhere nearby, the rush of stones falling from the canyon wall. Maegwin's head whipped round at every noise until she was as tense as a bowstring.

"I don't like this," she murmured. "This place is dangerous."

"Yes," Rovann agreed. "We're being watched. No, don't turn around. Just keep walking."

Maegwin fixed her eyes on the bright spot that marked the end of the canyon. They reached it unmolested and Maegwin walked out gratefully into the evening sunshine. Beyond, a wide valley opened out and in this valley nestled a squalid town. Maegwin saw rows of huts, corrals full of skinny goats and slat-ribbed dogs nosing through the muddy streets.

Rovann raised his head and looked around. "Stoneshowe," he breathed. He didn't sound particularly glad to have reached their destination.

"What is this place?" Maegwin asked. "It doesn't strike me as the kind of place where we'll find help."

Rovann snorted. "No it doesn't. But appearances can be deceptive. Come on."

They made their way into the town proper and Rovann guided them to what appeared to be the center of the settlement: a wide cobbled square surrounded by long stone buildings that Maegwin guessed might be shops or other businesses. The square was crowded and the noise of arguing and haggling was almost deafening after the silence of the wilderness.

"Over there," Rovann said, pointing.

They crossed the square and settled onto a wide stone bench next to a cracked fountain.

"What now?" she asked impatiently.

Rovann shrugged. "Now we wait."

Maegwin looked around. To an untrained eye it might appear that they were being ignored but she noticed many furtive glances flick their way and knew their arrival had been marked. She tensed. Almost every person carried a weapon of some kind, be it a knife, a bow or a curled piece of wire hanging at the waist which Maegwin assumed to be a garrote.

"You still haven't told me what this place is," she said quietly. "Why won't Hounsey soldiers come here? Is Stoneshowe loyal to the king?"

Rovann snorted. "Hardly. Soldiers won't come here because I doubt they know of it. Stoneshowe appears on no map. Officially this place does not exist just as the people who live here do not exist."

"What do you mean?"

He turned to look at her. "Stoneshowe is a criminal settlement, peopled by those who've been banished by King William or have fled his justice."

"What? And you thought—" her words trailed off as she realized that someone had moved to stand in front of them.

Her eyes traveled up from the man's muddy boots, to his broad chest and scarred face. In one hand he carried a double-headed ax.

Maegwin began to rise from the bench but Rovann put out a hand to stop her.

"He'll see me?" he said to the man.

The man grunted. "Follow me."

Without waiting for an answer he turned and strode away. Rovann lurched to his feet and hobbled after. Maegwin paused for a moment, cursed under her breath, and threw up her hands in frustration. She hurried after Rovann and together they followed the man from the square and through a series of dark alleys to a nondescript door.

The man thumped on the door three times and then ushered them inside as it creaked open. They found themselves in a bare room with only two wooden chairs and a battered old table.

"Sit." The man said before disappearing through an inner door.

Maegwin slid into a seat beside Rovann and glanced around at their sparse surroundings. The room smelt of mildew and the only light came from a grimy window looking out into the alley.

After what seemed an age the inner door opened and another man strode through and stood looking down at them with his hands on his hips. The man wore knee-length leather boots, a black tunic and had two morningstars tucked into the belt at his waist. He was so tall his head almost brushed the ceiling and a wild mop of unruly dark hair curled to his shoulders.

The man scowled. "Singer burn my eyes!" he cursed in a deep, powerful voice. "I never thought to see your sorry face again, Rovann. You've got a nerve coming here you traitorous mage-born scum!"

Rovann looked up at the man. "Hello, Thaldan."

"Who's he?" Maegwin whispered.

The mage turned a wry smile on her. "He's my brother-in-law."

Rovann watched the expression on Thaldan's face twist into one of fury and a sinking feeling filled the pit of his stomach. What had he expected? A welcome? After all that had passed between them?

He shifted his weight, wincing at the sudden pain. It was becoming increasingly difficult to concentrate. "Thaldan, listen to me," he said, placing his good hand flat on the table. "I've come to you for help. I need medicine and supplies for a long journey."

Thaldan raised an eyebrow in a gesture so reminiscent of his sister. "Oh, is that all you need? Why didn't you say so? I'll have it ready in just one moment." The tall man leaned forward, placing his hands on the table. His dark eyes looked Rovann up and down, taking in his injured arm and bedraggled state. "Look at you," he said, shaking his head. "The vaunted King's Mage brought so low. You know, I spent years dreaming of this meeting, dreaming of how I'd take my revenge against you. And here you are, come crawling to my door like some beggar. Why would I help you, King's Mage? After everything you've done to me?"

"I did what I had to," Rovann replied. "You left me no choice." He glanced around at the small, dark room. "And it looks as if you haven't changed, Thaldan. This one of your secret meeting rooms? Still in the trade I see."

The tall man went still as if sensing a trap. "Is that why you're here? Have you brought the king's army to Stoneshowe? Have you broken your word yet again?"

No," Rovann replied. "You're safe, I promise. You have nothing to fear from me."

Thaldan crossed his arms over his chest. "That's what you told my sister."

"That's not fair."

"Isn't it? She'd still be alive if not for you. I lost count of the number of times I warned her against going south with you. Mages care nothing for others. It doesn't matter who gets caught in the crossfire. Istra was just another of your victims, wasn't she, Slayer?"

Rage surged through Rovann's veins, pumping energy into his tired limbs. He lurched to his feet, sending the table flying.

"Shut your mouth!"

In a flash, Thaldan pulled the morningstars from his belt and held them up threateningly. "Go on then, King's Mage," he said in a low dangerous voice. "Try me."

Rovann open his mouth to retort but Maegwin was suddenly pulling him back and interposing herself between him and Thaldan.

"Stop it!" she snapped at the two men. "Stop your stupid, boyish posturing." She turned to Thaldan. "Rovann is hurt and needs help. If you're not willing to offer that help just say so and we'll be on our way."

The tall man frowned at her. "And you are?"

She lifted her chin. "Maegwin de Romily."

"A mage?"

"No. I'm a priestess of Sho-La."

His eyes narrowed. "Why would a priestess be traveling with the King's Mage of Amaury?"

"That's my business."

"And now it's mine," Thaldan growled. "Answer my question or neither of you will leave this room alive."

Maegwin glanced briefly at Rovann before answering. "We are on a rescue mission. A friend was kidnapped by the Songmaker. We intend to free him."

Thaldan shifted, a strange expression flashing across his features. "If he's been taken by the Songmaker then he's already dead."

"How do you know that? Rovann asked. "What do you know of the Songmaker?"

Instead of answering Thaldan thumped on the inner door and three armed men filed into the room. One of them trained a crossbow on Maegwin.

"Try any of your trickery, King's Mage," Thaldan said, "and your friend will end up being a pincushion. I don't want to hurt anyone so don't force my hand."

"What are you going to do with us?" Rovann growled.

"For now? Nothing. I don't trust you. You say you've brought no other mages but I think I'll send my men to look around before I take your word for that. In the meantime you'll be our guests."

He gestured and two of his men moved forward to bind Rovann and Maegwin's hands. The third man kept his crossbow trained on Maegwin's chest. Rovann grunted in pain as the man wound rope around his injured wrist. For a second black dots danced in front of his eyes and he thought he might faint. After a moment it passed and he straightened to find Thaldan watching him with an appraising look in his eyes as though trying to gage the extent of Rovann's weakness.

Rovann stared right back.

The tall man waved his hand. "Take them away."

They were led through the inner door and into what Rovann realized was a warren of small rooms and tight, dark corridors. All the doors were shut but from behind some he heard muted conversation and from somewhere up ahead wafted the aroma of cooking. The three men ushered them unceremoniously into a small room that was more like a cell and then slammed the heavy door behind them. Keys rattled as the door was locked.

"What are you doing?" Maegwin yelled. "Let us out! We've done nothing wrong!"

"Save your breath," Rovann said sliding down the wall to sit with his knees hunched to his chest. "They won't come until Thaldan's ready."

She scowled but then seated herself in a corner. "Thaldan really doesn't like you, does he?"

"You noticed?"

"So what happened between you two? Why such venom?"

Rovann laid his head against the wall and closed his eyes. Seeing Thaldan again had triggered memories that he'd thought long buried. Memories of Clan Tamarand, of his brother-in-law's enmity, but most of all of Istra. He'd forgotten how much she resembled her brother. "Thaldan is a criminal, and a major one. For years he was the head of a smuggling network that brought illegal weaponry into Amaury across the western border. I had him arrested and put on trial."

"You arrested your own brother-in-law?" Her voice was incredulous.

He looked at her. "What was I to do? Turn a blind eye because he's family? I have a duty, Maegwin."

"I know," she said. "But banishing him? It seems a little...harsh."

"Harsh?" he grated. "He should have hanged! It's only because I pleaded with the king on his behalf that he still has his miserable life. I thought perhaps he might remember that and help us." He leaned his head back once more. "Seems I was wrong."

"What will he do?"

"I don't know."

She was silent for a time and Rovann could feel her eyes on him. She seemed to be working herself up to something. At last she said, "Rovann?"

"Yes?"

"Thank you. For saving me from those soldiers, I mean."

He raised his head to find her staring at him intently. "You're welcome."

She glanced away, began picking at the hem of her tunic. "What you did in the forest, could you do it again? Get us out of here?

He shook his head. "I've got nothing left, Maegwin. And besides, even if I could get us away from Thaldan's men, how would we get out of Stoneshowe alive? Thaldan will have alerted the town to our presence and if we tried to leave without the proper escort, we'd be hunted down."

"Great. Just great."

The door creaked open and two armed men entered. One covered Maegwin with the crossbow whilst the other placed two trays on the floor.

"Courtesy of the boss," the man said before they both turned and left, locking the door behind them once more.

Maegwin scooted over to the trays and whistled under her breath. "These men might be criminals but they eat fit for a king." She pushed one of the trays across the floor to Rovann and then pulled one to herself and began shoveling pieces of food into her mouth.

Rovann glanced down. In a large clay bowl thick slabs of meat sat in a dark sauce. Tender green vegetables were piled on the side. On a smaller plate sat a loaf of golden bread and a pot of what looked like honey. A pottery beaker was filled to the brim with wine.

Rovann's mouth watered at the scent of the food. With his good hand he picked up a fork and shoveled pieces of meat into his mouth, chewing greedily. After the weeks of soldier rations the juiciness of the meat threatened to make his taste buds explode. When the meat was finished he picked up the dish and slurped down the rest of the sauce. Then he ripped up the bread, smeared the slices with honey and wolfed them down. Finally he set the beaker to his lips and drank noisily. When he'd finished he wiped the back of his hand across his mouth and sat back as sustenance flowed into his battered body.

"If we're prisoners," Maegwin said with her mouth full. "Why are they feeding us like this?"

"It's a message I'd wager," Rovann replied. "Thaldan wants me to know how well he's doing despite my attempts to ruin him." He shrugged. "But if he wants to carry on proving his point, that's fine by me."

Maegwin snorted. "Agreed."

They sat in silence for a while and Rovann began to doze. Then suddenly Maegwin spoke. "Are you going to tell me what's going on?"

He opened his eyes, blinking to clear his thoughts. "What?"

She pulled her knees up to her chest and hugged them. "I brought you to Stoneshowe and asked no questions. But if I'm to help you on this quest I need to know the plan. Where are we going? Where do you think we will find the Songmaker?"

He didn't answer for a long time as though weighing up how much he could say. Finally, he sighed. "Do you remember what Hounsey kept saying in the tent? He kept mentioning 'the twins'. He claimed that's where Leo and Prince Owen had been taken."

Maegwin looked at him blankly. He wasn't surprised she didn't remember. She'd been so intent on killing Hounsey he doubted she'd heard a word that was said.

"Hounsey couldn't resist goading me but I think he may have inadvertently revealed the Songmaker's hideout."

"Go on," she prompted.

"There have always been rumors that the Songmaker's base is outside Amaury, somewhere in the lands beyond the western border. I think the rumors are true. There is a legend that says Tyrlindon once had a twin city, one that has long been lost. I think that's what Hounsey was alluding to, Tyrvanan, Tyrlindon's twin. I think that's where we'll find Prince Owen, Leo and the Songmaker."

Maegwin frowned. "So you're basing this whole mission on rumor, legend and a few hints dropped by a revenant? That's not much to go on, King's Mage."

"I know," he said, leaning his head against the wall. "But it's all we have. And it feels right. I can't explain it any more than that."

"So if there were rumors of this other city, why didn't you send someone to investigate? You could have captured the Songmaker a long time ago."

He looked at her and smiled wryly. "Ah. There we have it. It was a rumor only, Maegwin, one of many. We couldn't act on so slim a possibility when the dangers would be so high. You see, the legend says that Tyrvanan lies beyond Roamsford Edge."

Maegwin's eyes widened slowly as comprehension dawned. "You mean—? We have to cross it? Roamsford Edge?"

He nodded.

"Have you lost your mind? Even in the temple we knew of the Edge. It has a dark reputation, Rovann. Nobody enters it. The forest does not suffer people to pass."

"I know," he said. "But we will find a way. We must."

She stared at him for a long time. Then, shaking her head and muttering to herself, she lay down and turned her back on him.

Rovann settled down onto the hard stone floor and fell into an uneasy sleep. The throbbing pain in his arm woke him at regular intervals meaning his rest was fractured and not refreshing. He shivered uncontrollably even though his skin burned. The infection was spreading. He didn't have much time.

Sometime later he was awoken by someone kicking his leg. He jerked upright and squinted against the glare of a torch. Thaldan stood looking down at him with a troubled expression on his face.

Rovann ran his tongue around his cracked lips before speaking. "Your men found nothing I assume?"

"No," he replied.

"So you believe me?"

Thaldan waved his hand irritably. "Yes, I believe you. But that's not important now."

Rovann frowned, detecting an undercurrent in the man's words. "Then what is?"

The smuggler stared at him for a long moment. Rovann could almost see the thoughts turning behind his eyes. "You will see. Come."

Thaldan's men dragged him and Maegwin to their feet and led them from the cell and back through the maze of rooms and corridors. After only a moment, Rovann was totally lost and had no idea in which direction they were heading. They reached a set of stone steps that led down into darkness. Thaldan raised his torch and set it in a bracket on the wall then led the way down the stairs.

Rovann found himself in a low stone cellar. The floor was nothing but bare earth and the place stank of mold. A large white sheet covered what looked to Rovann to be three dead bodies. Thaldan turned to face him.

"My men didn't find any of your mages when they scouted around Stoneshowe. But they did find these."

He crouched and pulled back the sheet to reveal three dead men. Their skin was almost white, bloodless, as though they'd been drained. The men were naked and on their chests had been carved a broken circle with the letter S in the center.

Rovann crouched unsteadily next to Thaldan. "Who are these men?"

"Three of my own. They were on a job on the western border but they never made their rendezvous with my supplier. Seems like they ran into some trouble."

Rovann reached out his good hand and held it several inches above the chest of the nearest man. Lingering sorcery tickled against his palm. "You've seen this before, haven't you?"

Thaldan straightened and rubbed his chin. "Yes. For over a year now I've had a rival on the western border. It started with shipments going missing, suppliers missing their rendezvous, things like that. Then it got nasty. Instead of just shipments disappearing, my men started vanishing only to turn up days or weeks later with this carved into their chest."

Rovann slowly climbed to his feet and stood leaning against the wall. His head was pounding and his legs had gone weak. He really needed to lie down. "You recognize the symbol?"

Thaldan frowned. "I wish to the Singer that I didn't. The last thing I need is to get caught up in your cursed mage war. It's him, isn't it? The Songmaker."

"Yes, I'm afraid it is," Rovann said, eyes roving over the bloody symbols. "This is his mark. Your men aren't the first to turn up dead with it carved into them. And they won't be the last. It seems you've inadvertently solved a mystery, Thaldan. The Songmaker has been gathering an army in secret in the borderlands for months. We wondered how he'd supplied his troops without us finding out. Seems now we know. He's been smuggling weapons and materials over the western border. Looks like you've been getting in his way, Thaldan."

A snarl curled the man's lips. "Bastard. I'll have his cursed hide for this!"

"No you won't," Rovann replied. "If you tried he'd destroy you. You can't take him on, Thaldan. The only way to stop this is to help me."

Thaldan hooked his fingers into his belt and glared. "Every time I see you, King's Mage, I get dragged into your mess. You're like a carrion crow—never far from death and destruction."

"This isn't my 'mess', Thaldan. The Songmaker is a threat to the whole of Amaury. Whilst I'm sure your concerns extend no further than yourself, I'm trying to stop this man destroying the kingdom! Now are you going to help us or not?"

The dark-haired man rubbed his chin. "You think you can stop him?"

"I don't know. I'm going to try."

Thaldan watched him in silence. His eyes darted to the

three dead men then back to Rovann. At last he seemed to reach a decision. "Then you'll have my help."

This time he and Maegwin were led back into the complex but taken to different rooms. Rovann found himself being ushered into a large bedroom. Thick rugs covered the floor and a bed stood in one corner. A window overlooking the street filled the room with light.

Two middle-aged women entered and bade Rovann lie down on the bed. He did as they asked. One of the women set a hessian bag down on the floor, from which she pulled a host of medical supplies that she set out on a bedside table. She peeled back the dressings covering Rovann's wound and hissed through her teeth.

"Blind my eyes! This won't do, this won't do at all! You'll be lucky if you keep your hand, young man."

Rovann ground his teeth against the aching pain. It had grown so bad he no longer cared if he kept his hand as long as the pain stopped. "Do what you can."

The two women conferred in hushed tones. One of them stripped off his clothes and then washed him down as gently as she could. The other began mixing powders and liquids into a flask which sent an acrid odor stealing through the room. She carried the concoction over to Rovann.

"We'll need to clean the wound, set those broken bones and sear the infection from your blood. It will hurt. It's best if you're asleep when we do it. Here, drink this."

Rovann eyed the flask warily. "What is it?"

"Something that will send you into a deep sleep. Now drink it!"

Rovann took it in his good hand and set it to his lips. The concoction was so strong it made his eyes water. Steeling himself, he tipped the flask back and gulped the contents in one long swallow.

Almost immediately something seemed to grab his consciousness and drag him under. As he faded into sleep his last thought was, *I hope Thaldan hasn't decided to poison me.*

Rovann woke slowly. His bare toes brushed against smooth warm sheets and the comforting weight of a soft blanket covered his torso. The muted conversation of people passing on the street wafted to him and the scent of baking bread came from somewhere in the house. He opened his eyes. Dawn sunlight streamed through the window and dust motes danced in the shafts.

It took a moment for him to realize that the pain had receded. He felt... good. Rested. Whole. He turned his head slowly to the side and saw that Maegwin was dozing in a chair by his bedside. Experimentally, he pushed himself into a sitting position and was pleasantly surprised when the expected waves of dizziness and pain did not come.

His injured arm was bound tightly in clean white bandages and although it was tender when he poked it, it was the tenderness of healing rather than the agony of an infected wound.

Maegwin shifted in her chair. Her eyes snapped open. "Morning," she said, leaning forward to peer at him. "How do you feel?"

"Better. Much better. How long have I been asleep?"

"Almost two days."

"Two days!" he cried, throwing off the covers. "We have to go!"

"Get back into bed!" she commanded, flinging the blankets back over him. "Shilma will have my hide if I let you up before she's ready. She and Melnay worked on your wound for almost a whole day. You had gangrene and they thought you'd lose your hand for a while."

Just then the door creaked open and the women in question bustled into the room.

"I thought I heard voices in here," said the eldest of the two, coming to stand by Rovann's bedside. "It's good to see you awake. Are you having any pain? Dizziness? Nausea?"

Rovann shook his head. "You are Shilma? I owe you my thanks."

She waved his gratitude away, pulled back the covers and inspected the bandage on his hand. Taking a small sharp blade from the table beside Rovann's bed, she said, "Hold still while I take this off. Let's see how well the wound underneath is healing."

She deftly set the tiny blade to the bandages and began to slice it. Only then did he realize that rather than bandages it was some kind of hard cast designed to keep his hand immobile. When she'd sliced it down the middle Shilma carefully pried it away from Rovann's arm and then lifted it off.

He examined his injury with some trepidation. Bruising blackened his arm from his knuckles to his elbow but the skin was unbroken and the bruises were already starting to turn yellow in places. Where the arrow had pierced his arm was only a tiny white scar. Slowly Rovann clenched and unclenched his fingers, marveling at how they obeyed his command with only the slightest ache to show the bones had ever been broken.

Shilma nodded, a look of satisfaction on her face. "Good. It's better than I dared to hope."

"Better than any normal healer would expect," Rovann agreed. He caught the woman's gaze. "You're a mage, aren't you?"

She seemed about to deny it but then changed her mind and nodded. "I have some small skill with Fire. Enough to heal a few wounds but not much else."

"A most valuable gift, Shilma. Thank you."

She smiled. "I'll tell Thaldan that you're ready to travel."

She and her companion turned and left the room. Rovann swung his legs over the edge of the bed just as the door opened and Thaldan strode in.

"Good. About time," he said without preamble. "Get dressed. There will be a meal waiting for you downstairs. Then you can be on your way."

Rovann forced himself to meet the smuggler's hostile gaze. He bowed his head to his brother-in-law. "I know there may never be peace between us, Thaldan, but you have my thanks."

"Stop the Songmaker from killing my men, that's all the thanks I require." He rubbed his chin. "I'll have two horses saddled and provisioned. My people will make sure you're not followed from Stoneshowe. Now hurry up and get out of my house."

The King's Mage: Chapter Two

Rovann swung up onto the roan gelding and gathered the reins. Thaldan held his gaze for a long moment, his dark eyes probing. *Remember your promise.*

"This is Brye," the smuggler said, looking away. "A good horse. Take care of him."

Rovann nodded. "Thank you, Thaldan. I won't forget your generosity."

Then he kicked his mount into motion. As he rode away he did not look back.

He and Maegwin stole quickly through the waking town, thick cowls pulled up to hide their features. As they moved from shadow to shadow, Rovann felt like a fugitive, a wary denizen of the dark, eager to escape notice. But there were always eyes watching, he knew, and he found himself peering at the faces they passed, wondering if he was looking at a renegade spy.

Is this what we've come to? he wondered. *Convinced every friend is an enemy?*

They didn't speak and reached the outskirts of the town

as the sun was poking its head above the trees. Kicking their mounts into a trot, they followed the north road for several miles before finally pulling to a halt at a nondescript crossroads.

Twisting in his seat, Rovann gazed back the way they'd come. The road snaked like a silver ribbon behind them. Nothing moved upon it.

"What is it?" Maegwin asked.

"I'm not sure. But I feel…"

Swinging one leg over the saddle, Rovann dropped to the ground and placed his hand on the road's hard-packed surface. He opened his senses and sent them ranging outwards. The golden web of life engulfed him immediately but after a moment he began to detect the individual lives of the world. Somewhere on the road a farmer was pulling an unruly donkey to market, further north a chattering family was on its way to an early morning fishing trip.

"I don't think we've been followed."

"Then Thaldan has been true to his word." She looked around, gazing at the empty countryside. "What now?"

"We continue due west until we reach Roamsford Edge. Then we'll need to find a way through the forest. We should find Tyrvanan on the other side."

"And you're sure that's where we'll find Leo and Prince Owen?"

Rovann nodded and remounted his horse. Maegwin was a stony, glowering presence at Rovann's side. Her expression didn't invite conversation and Rovann could feel the annoyance radiating from her. He opened his mouth to speak but then thought better of it. He didn't have any words to say that would ease her mood.

They halted around midday and as Rovann cooked a meal, Maegwin watched him from across the fire.

"What are you running from?" she asked suddenly.

Startled, he looked up. "Running? Is that what you think I'm doing? Surely we're moving *toward* danger rather than away from it?"

"Not for you, I think. Seems to me you'd rather consort with criminals in Stoneshowe than stay in Tyrlindon. I heard what Thaldan said to you. You can't escape memories, Rovann. They'll follow you wherever you go."

He glanced at her sharply. She spoke as though from bitter experience and her gaze was unfocused, far away, as though images were playing through her head. "They change you. Make you into something new, whether you like it or not." Her voice was barely above a whisper.

"Maegwin?"

Her gaze snapped up. "Nothing. Never mind."

Rovann dished out a thin broth and handed Maegwin a bowl. They ate in silence, interrupted only by the raucous bickering of a pair of crows perched in a tree above. The day had become cool and blustery. The wind rattled the branches and kicked up streamers of dust along the path. To the north, a bank of dark clouds was gathering, promising rain later.

Rovann looked at the sky and sighed.

When they had eaten Maegwin gathered the dishes and took them to a stream. Rovann was relieved to be alone. He didn't like the feelings Maegwin's question had stirred up. Running away? Was that the truth? Was he shirking his responsibilities? Should he have returned to Tyrlindon?

Istra's voice echoed in his head. *Duty again, Rovann? Will you always worry about what you should do? Will you never be free of it?*

"I will never be free of it," he whispered.

The crows 'karked' loudly and flew off, their ponderous

wing beats slapping at the air. Rovann doused the fire then went to check on the horses. At Rovann's approach the roan swung up his head, snorted, then returned to ripping up tufts of grass. Rovann patted him on the neck.

"Time to go."

They took a route that cut across country and Rovann set a pace that would eat up the miles without exhausting their mounts. At first they stayed off the path, forging a way through undergrowth and using animal trails but late in the afternoon they swung slightly north and came out onto a little-used road.

Forest closed in on either side creating a gloomy, oppressive atmosphere with thick shadows beneath the trunks of the pines. The cloud-bank sealed the sky in a gray blanket but the rain held off.

Maegwin seemed lost in thought, staring as if seeing things that he couldn't. Rovann scanned the woods, alert for danger but the shadows between the boles were impenetrable as though they held secrets they refused to give up.

"I'm sorry," Maegwin said suddenly.

"What?" he replied, startled.

"I didn't mean to make you sound a coward. You're not that, Rovann. Never that."

Rovann stared at her for a long moment, unsure how to respond. He cleared his throat and looked away, desperately casting around for something to say. "It's a rare thing to be called into the service of a goddess," he blurted. "How did you become a priestess of Sho-La?

Maegwin pursed her lips in thought. "My earliest memories are of working in one of the tanneries of Mallyn with other street children. The master of the tannery was a cruel man. When I was seven he beat me so bad I ran away. I wandered the woods for days, slowly starving. But a woman came to me. She had silver skin and hair as blue as midnight. She led me through the forest until I found a temple. The sisters took me in. Sho-La had called me. It was my destiny to serve Her. What do you know of Sho-La, Rovann?"

"Not much," he admitted with a shrug.

"Ah, She is the light of the universe. She teaches compassion, kindness and a love that transcends all creation. With Her, I am never alone." She pulled her horse to a halt suddenly and stared into the shadows beneath the trees. Her voice became low and hesitant. "But there's another side to Her. Darkness, anger, retribution… sometimes I feel…" She shook her head. "It doesn't matter."

Rovann watched her, suddenly wary.

It's just you and me now, Rovann. And you're all mine.

"Your turn," she said, shaking off her sullen reverie. "How did you become a mage?"

Rovann clucked at his mount, urging him on. "Throughout my childhood I did strange things without knowing how: predicting the weather, sensing danger, that sort of thing. But when I was eleven I burned down my father's barn just by picturing a flame in my mind. After that I was packed off to the college in Tyrlindon."

Maegwin laughed, a sound like the tinkling of a stream. She flashed Rovann a brilliant smile and his stomach lurched. When Maegwin smiled her beauty was breathtaking. Suddenly uncomfortable, he nudged his horse ahead of hers and focused his attention on the road.

Throughout the day the landscape gradually changed. The brooding trees fell back to be replaced by stubby hills and rough gullies. Great moss-covered boulders stood out of the ground as though the bones of the earth were pushing through its skin. The road wound inexorably around these obstacles, up short slopes and then down again into shallow valleys. As a result, the going became tougher and Rovann was forced to ease the pace.

Rovann consulted the map Thaldan had given him. According to the faint, hand-written labels, they were passing into a region known as Turandor, a sparsely populated land of rocky soil. The few villages that existed in Turandor were spaced far apart and so as night approached, Rovann led them off the trail and into a grassy clearing.

Whilst Maegwin cooked supper, Rovann busied himself brushing down the horses. His roan suddenly raised his head, ears pricked forward, snorting and stamping. On Rovann's other side Maegwin's horse tossed her head nervously.

Maegwin came silently to her feet, dagger in hand. "Something's out there."

Rovann held out a hand to stall her, closed his eyes, and sent his senses questing out. He found it almost immediately: a presence moving toward them along the little-used path they had traveled most of the day. Biting back a curse, he crept through the scrub to the top of a rise that looked down on the road. Kneeling in the thick grass, he and Maegwin peered through a gorse bush.

Rovann cursed himself for a fool. He'd been so sure they'd not been followed. Damn Thaldan and his empty promises.

They waited for what seemed an age, silent, motionless. Faint sounds wafted to Rovann on the breeze.

Voices. Low, whispered.

Two figures emerged from the darkness, walking side by side. Then something large lumbered into view behind them and Rovann squinted, trying to make it out. The thing moved smoothly, making an odd creaking noise and the stomp and snuffle of horses carried on the night air. A caravan.

"Gypsies!" Rovann breathed.

Giddy relief washed through him. Thaldan had not betrayed him after all. Without thinking, he stood. The people on the road saw him silhouetted against the sky and broke into panic. Shouts rang through the night. Figures darted around. Horses whinnied in fear.

Rovann ran to the edge of the rise. "Wait! I'm sorry, I didn't mean to scare you!"

A deep voice called from the darkness, "Who are you?"

"I'm Rovann, my companion is Maegwin. We mean you no harm."

There was a whispered conversation and then the voice demanded, "Why were you watching us?"

"We heard noises. Travelers are seldom seen on this road."

Silence for a moment.

"Aye, that's true. If you're not bandits, you'll come down and make our acquaintance. But move slowly now, and bring no weapons."

"What are you doing?" Maegwin hissed, grabbing Rovann's arm as he made to walk away. "We're supposed to be traveling in secret!"

Rovann shook free of her grip. "We need information, Maegwin. They might be able to give us that."

"You have no idea if they can be trusted and you've just given them our names!" In the darkness Maegwin's eyes glinted with anger.

"Maegwin, gypsies travel all over the land and hear gossip. I need to know what is happening in Tyrlindon. I have to take the risk."

Without waiting for an answer he stalked off.

He approached the group of gypsies who eyed him warily. The two who had been walking in front of the wagon were tall young men carrying knives strapped to their waists. In the caravan a gaggle of children peeked shyly out of the opening, watched over by an elderly lady with her hair tied in a multitude of thin gray braids. At the head of the group waited a grizzled bear of a man with ruddy cheeks and a mop of brown hair, hands planted on hips and wearing a scowl. Beside him stood a slim, regal woman who regarded Rovann and Maegwin steadily.

"Aye, well you don't look like wights or bandits to me," said the man. "And you certainly ain't gypsies. What brings you out here?"

Rovann thought quickly, remembering what he'd seen on Thaldan's map. "We're traveling to Yatarn to visit my mother."

The man regarded them silently, as though trying to find the lie. Eventually he stuck out his hand which Rovann shook. "The name's Garn and this is my wife Etta." He nodded toward the caravan. "That there is Etta's ma, Reya, and the rest of those scallywags are our troupe. Acrobats and entertainers of the highest order, that's us! We're heading to Silverport."

Rovann sensed the opportunity for gathering information. "Silverport is a long way from here. Surely Tyrlindon would be easier to reach?"

Garn rubbed his chin and frowned. "Aye, it would. It's not safe round the capital right now though."

"Not safe?" Rovann asked, feigning ignorance. "Why not?"

Garn eyed him as though wondering how much to say. "You country folk ought to be safe enough I reckon, but if you want my advice you'll stay away from the capital. There's war brewing. A great big army marching on Tyrlindon is what I hear."

Rovann's stomach twisted. Had Hounsey found a way to cross the river after all? Maegwin stirred beside him, shooting him a worried look. "An army? Approaching Tyrlindon? Why?"

"Stone me, have you not heard the news? The land's at war, lad! The Songmaker's rebels are bent on ousting King William."

Rovann pursed his lips, putting on a thoughtful expression. "Well, news takes a long time to get out here. The rest of the land seems to forget we exist."

"Let's hope it stays that way and the war doesn't reach this far. If I had my way we wouldn't be traveling at all but earnings have turned pretty grim in this region ever since —" Etta gave him a sharp glance and he abruptly changed the subject. "Anyways, we won't be going any farther today."

"Maegwin and I have made camp over there. It's a good flat spot sheltered from the wind. Why don't you join us?" said Rovann.

Garn nodded. "Much obliged."

The troupe fell into the chore of making camp with practiced ease. The two older lads drove the wagon into the dell, unhitched the horses and began rubbing them down for the night. The children jumped from the cart and scurried to their tasks: collecting firewood, assembling tents, unpacking supplies, peeling vegetables, setting up a chair for the elderly Reya. Garn and Etta supervised the operation and soon there was a merry fire crackling in the glade with a pot gently heating over it.

They took seats around the fire and Garn passed around mugs of a hot, sweet liquid that smelled slightly of aniseed.

"Companions of the road," he proposed a toast.

Rovann raised his mug and took a swig. The sharp taste stung his throat and made his eyes water. It was all he could do not to cough it up.

Garn broke into a broad grin that showed all his enormous square teeth. "A bit robust for you is it?"

He chuckled and emptied his mug in one long draft just to show how it should be done. Following his example, Maegwin set her mug to her lips and drained it. She did not even flinch.

Garn stared for a moment than let out a bellowing laugh. "Well met! That'll teach me to brag eh?"

Maegwin raised her mug in salute.

Garn turned to Rovann. "You're traveling to Yatarn you say? Do you and your wife carry weapons?"

Maegwin looked up at Garn's assumption and met Rovann's eyes. Two spots of color formed on her cheeks. He shrugged slightly. Let the gypsies assume they were married. It hardly mattered.

"Weapons? Why would we need them?"

Garn glanced into the darkness then at Rovann. Firelight danced in his eyes. "The country up west is restless. Strange goings-on. Rumors of—"

"Monsters!" cried one of the children suddenly, a girl of five or six. "Monsters in the woods! They come at night and pull your eyes out!"

"Hush, Ryn," Etta breathed. Pulling the girl into her lap, she stroked her hair until she calmed.

Garn and Etta shared a troubled glance. The elderly Reya shook her head, making her braids clack and muttered something like a prayer under her breath.

Into the heavy silence Rovann said, "Garn? What is it?"

He rubbed at the side of his face. "Ah, I'd hoped the little uns hadn't heard the chatter. Does no good to go frightening children."

"Tell them," Etta said quietly, nodding toward Rovann and Maegwin.

Garn hunched forward and spoke in a low voice. "There are rumors that wights are abroad in the west country."

Rovann blinked. "Wights?"

"Aye, terrible things not from this world. Some say the barriers between the Realms are breaking and demons are coming through. If you are traveling west, be sure you can defend yourselves."

Rovann studied Garn's face. Fear rode behind his eyes. These people were fleeing something. But wights? He'd never heard of them encroaching so close to the haunts of people.

"We can defend ourselves," Maegwin declared suddenly.

Garn regarded her, nodded. "Aye, perhaps you can. But enough of such talk, it withers the soul. Saran, is that soup ready yet?" He pulled himself to his feet and lumbered over to the cooking pot.

But Etta and Reya's dark eyes regarded Rovann, suggesting they knew far more than they let on.

Garn ladled out the soup and two of the youngest girls brought a bowl over to Maegwin and Rovann, faces grave as though they undertook a solemn duty.

Rovann accepted his bowl and inclined his head, "Thank you, my lady."

The girl smiled shyly and then got embarrassed and ran away to hide behind her mother.

As they ate, Rovann did his best to steer the conversation to safer subjects. "So, what made you decide on Silverport?"

Garn gestured with his spoon. "Where better? We've spent the last few years touring the southern towns, mainly Mallyn and the areas around. But it's time we moved on. There's too many troupes in the south now and people aren't willing to pay as much. I've heard it told that in Silverport a troupe can earn a year's wages in a month!"

"Garn!" Etta scolded. "Don't go filling the children's heads with such fanciful ideas."

Garn shrugged. "Anyway, we left the south about a month ago and after hearing the rumors of war around Tyrlindon, thought it best if we took the north-west road and skirted Tyrlindon to the north. We hoped to ply our trade in the western provinces but...well things didn't quite work out that way."

When they had finished their meal Garn gathered the children around him for a bedtime story whilst Etta gathered up the dishes.

"Rovann will you help me with these?" she asked.

Rovann climbed to his feet and followed the dark-haired woman to the back of the caravan where a tub of soapy water waited.

Etta began scrubbing the crockery in silence. Rovann sensed there was something on her mind so he remained silent, giving her the space to collect her thoughts. She rinsed out a plate and passed it to him. Rovann dried it with a piece of cloth and placed it back in the tiny cupboard built into the back of the caravan.

"Your wife is very quiet tonight."

"Er, yes," Rovann floundered, "she's a little shy."

Etta's dark eyes flicked up to his and then back to the

wash tub. At last she said, "What do you know of my people?"

Rovann took a dish and wiped it dry. "That you are wanderers, going wherever the fancy takes you. Queen Sophia granted your people freedom of the roads."

Etta nodded. "It was not always so. Long ago, my people lived in the Vale of the Blackwood, which has now been swallowed by Roamsford Edge. We kept watch on Amaury's border and grew to know the wights of the Edge. As a result, we became learned in the ways of the Realms. When Roamsford Edge devoured our home, we decided to become nomads. Queen Sophia granted us freedom of the roads in payment for our long service."

She looked at Rovann and her gaze was intense, pinning him to the spot. "Be careful," she whispered, grabbing Rovann's arm in fingers like pincers. "My husband spoke the truth. Something roams the wilderness in the west. It is hunting something. Or someone. And it stinks of Chaos." She released his arm and Rovann realized she had placed something around his wrist: a bracelet of intertwined willow twigs with tiny feathers tied along its length.

"Wear this. It will help to keep you safe."

Rovann stared at the charm, sensing how it vibrated with Eorthic power.

"Thank you," he muttered.

Etta smiled. "I think we are done here."

Grab your copy...
vinci-books.com/kingsmage

About the Author

Elizabeth Baxter spent most of her childhood wandering the paths of the Shire, the trails of Narnia, and the sun-speckled glades of the Hundred Acre Wood. She wrote her first book when she was six years old and plans to continue until they nail shut her coffin. When she's not sipping a latte and dreaming up fantastical places for her readers to visit, she enjoys reading, hiking, watching cricket, and cramming as much world travel as she can into one lifetime.